SECOND THOUGHTS

Lizzie was sitting at her dressing table, brushing her hair. Matthew walked silently over to her and bent so that he could look at her in the mirror.

Lizzie, having heard nothing, almost fell off the bench, and then she rapped his hand with her brush when he tried to catch her.

"Matthew! What do you think you're doing? You have no business to be here!"

"I know that, Lizzie, Come dance with me!" he exclaimed, opening the music box so that the melody would begin.

"Dance with you? Have you quite lost your mind?" she demanded.

"No! I have found it!" he answered, sweeping her up from the bench and into the dance. "I have loved you all my life, Lizzie Lancaster—though I didn't know it until I thought it was too late to ever be able to do anything about it."

"And what do you think you're going to do about it now?" she demanded, clutching her dressing gown as they danced.

"I am going to marry you and take you home," he replied, folding her into his arms and kissing her firmly . . .

BOOKS BY MONA GEDNEY

A LADY OF FORTUNE

THE EASTER CHARADE

A VALENTINE'S DAY GAMBIT

A CHRISTMAS BETROTHAL

A SCANDALOUS CHARADE

A DANGEROUS AFFAIR

A LADY OF QUALITY

A DANGEROUS ARRANGEMENT

MERRY'S CHRISTMAS

LADY DIANA'S DARING DEED

LADY HILARY'S HALLOWEEN

AN ICY AFFAIR

FROST FAIR FIANCÉ

A LOVE AFFAIR FOR LIZZIE

Published by Zebra Books

A LOVE AFFAIR FOR LIZZIE

Mona Gedney

ZEBRA BOOKS
KENSINGTON PUBLISHING CORP.
http://www.kensington.com

ZEBRA BOOKS are published by

Kensington Publishing Corp.
850 Third Avenue
New York, NY 10022

All Kensington titles, imprints and distributed lines are available at special quantity discounts for bulk purchases for sales
promotion, premiums, fund-raising, educational or institutional
use.

Special book excerpts or customized printings can also be created to fit specific needs. For details, write or phone the office
of the Kensington Special Sales Manager: Kensington Publishing Corp., 850 Third Avenue, New York, NY 10022. Attn.
Special Sales Department. Phone: 1-800-221-2647.

Zebra and the Z logo Reg. U.S. Pat. & TM Off.

First Printing: February 2004
10 9 8 7 6 5 4 3 2

Printed in the United States of America

One

On the day that Matthew left for the war, the first daffodils starred the early golden-green of the garden. Even though Lizzie was only fifteen, her parents had permitted them a private farewell before the public one in the Lodge, for the couple's deep attachment was acknowledged and approved. As they strolled hand in hand through the spring garden, the world around them was awakening with a piercing tenderness, made more poignant to them because they soon would be hundreds of miles apart. For the first time, spring seemed a cruel time to Lizzie, mocking her with its promise of beginnings just as a part of her world was ending. She swallowed hard, determined to master the lump in her throat, and smiled at Matthew, who was looking down at her a little anxiously.

"Are you certain that you won't forget me once I've gone away, Lizzie? Perhaps you will find some dashing young fellow and not even be able to recall my name." Matthew's voice was teasing, but she could detect a hint of concern, too.

He had worn his Hussar uniform so that she could see him in his full military splendor. He looked magnificent, of course, in his blue jacket with the white facings and the white braid, the short fur-trimmed pelisse jauntily over one shoulder, but Lizzie could focus on nothing but the steady gaze of his gray eyes. That reassured her. He might look unfamiliar and rather stiff in his military regalia, but he was still her Matthew.

"Never," she replied firmly. "You know that I won't forget you, Matthew." She did her best to equal his teasing tone. "It is *I* who should be worried. You are the one going away into a new world, and I understand that the ladies of Portugal and Spain are lovely. Are you certain that you will remember *me* after a few weeks have passed and England is far behind you?"

"Absolutely certain," Matthew said, squeezing her hand and pulling her close to him. "And will you make time to write to me now and then?"

"Every day," she promised, "and I shall think of you every minute." She took from around her neck a chain bearing a golden medal of St. George slaying the dragon. She had ordered it months ago, and had worn it for a week herself before giving it to him, as though by doing so she could send something of herself with him.

"St. George is the patron saint of soldiers," Lizzie reminded him, standing on tiptoe so that she could slip the chain over his head. "He will bring you safely home to me."

"I will place my confidence in St. George, then—and in you." His voice shook slightly as he folded her close and kissed her.

The time had arrived for him to leave, and Lizzie knew that she mustn't cry. She had talked to herself firmly about that. Her duty was to send Matthew off cheerfully, to be a support to him rather than a source of sorrow and concern. She caressed his smooth cheek and then ruffled his dark hair, smiling up into his dear, familiar face.

"And now, dear heart, I fear that you must go in and

run the gauntlet of my family's farewells. I warn you now that Alice and Mama will cry, Papa will shake your hand gruffly and wish you Godspeed, Tussie will give you a book to improve your mind and keep your spirits up, and Cook will have sent out a basket of delicacies so that you may keep up your strength. She puts no faith in foreign food."

Cheered by her manner and forewarned by her words, Matthew went in with her to face the group awaiting him. All went just as Lizzie had told him it would. Mrs. Lancaster's handkerchief was already a damp ball of lace before he could hug her, and Alice, though only eleven, had already developed a fine theatrical sense and had to be borne away in hysterics by their governess, Miss Tussman. Tussie, also agitated by his leave-taking, slowed just long enough to press into Matthew's hand a slim volume of *Pilgrim's Progress* and to remind him that time would pass quickly and that soon he would be home again in the bosom of his family. Then she hurried from the room, pressing her handkerchief to her eyes and murmuring audibly, "So young, so young."

Mr. Lancaster cleared his throat several times, shook Matthew's hand firmly, clapped him on the shoulder, and finally said, "Godspeed, my boy. Come back to us safely." Then he turned and disappeared abruptly into the library.

Mrs. Clary, the cook, who had been awaiting her opportunity behind the door to the dining room, hurried out and thrust a large wicker basket into Matthew's arms, saying "God bless you, sir! Take care of yourself!" Then she too pressed a handkerchief to her eyes and bustled from the hall as Matthew called his thanks after her. Mrs. Lancaster retired tactfully, still sobbing, so that the pair could have their final good-bye in privacy.

Determined not to become a watering pot too, Lizzie hooked one arm through the handle of the basket. "I shall have to help you carry it, I know," she told him in a low voice so that she could not be overheard. "I watched Cook filling it. She began two nights ago and then kept thinking of things that you might need once you left British soil. If she had had another day, you would have enough here to sink the transport."

"It was very kind of Mrs. Clary to prepare this feast for me," said Matthew, smiling. "She always fed George and me in the most royal manner when we were young."

"And you know how she loved doing it. Nothing has ever pleased her more than feeding hungry boys who think that her kitchen is just one step down from heaven."

A small stable boy had brought Matthew's horse around and, casting an admiring eye at the glory of Matthew's uniform, handed him the reins and retired discreetly.

Lizzie inspected the basket and the horse in a businesslike manner. "Well, it is absolutely certain that you cannot carry this heavy basket on horseback, Matthew, even for the short distance back to Prestonwood." She removed the napkins covering it, opened the saddlebags, and began judiciously stowing the basket's contents within them. Touched, she saw that Mrs. Clary had even included a bottle of her famous blackberry wine—for medicinal purposes.

"I am afraid, Matthew, that you *shall* have to carry the steak and kidney pie back to Prestonwood with you. It simply will not survive a saddlebag, even for two miles."

He looked down at her gravely, but his eyes were merry. "You do realize, Lizzie, that carrying it will quite ruin my heroic exit. How can you possibly view me as the figure of romance I am attempting to be if I am riding away with my arms full of pie?"

"The pie will not interfere at all," Lizzie had assured him, laughing. "I shall be greatly struck by your heartrending exit—but be certain not to get it all over your uniform. That pie will not blend well with your colors."

Matthew kissed her lightly, then swung himself into the saddle, waiting as she handed him the pie.

"Do be careful with it, Matthew," she said anxiously. "After all her trouble, Cook would never forgive us if you dropped it right here."

"Tell Mrs. Clary not to fear," he assured her with becoming gravity. "I shall pack it up safely before I leave for the coast. This pie will accompany me to my ship and it will sustain me when England has slipped below the horizon and I can see her no more."

"I will tell her," Lizzie assured him with equal gravity. Then, to prevent matters taking a more serious turn, she dimpled and blew him a kiss. "A safe journey, love."

He returned the kiss, smiling, then turned and rode down the drive, stopping to wave—somewhat awkwardly, of course, because of the pie—before the road curved away into the grove of oaks.

"Good-bye, Matthew! Good-bye!" Alice was calling from the nursery windows on the third floor, where she and Tussie were frantically waving what appeared to be a white tablecloth in farewell.

Hearing them, Matthew stopped and waved once more, laughing, then rode on and disappeared among the trees.

Lizzie kept her pledge. She had indeed written Matthew every day, although the letters were posted only once each week. In return, he wrote to describe the new worlds he was encountering. His first letter told of the stormy seas on the voyage to Portugal. Virtually everyone on the transport had succumbed to seasickness, he wrote, but to his delight it had not affected him. Indeed, he had dined upon Mrs. Clary's pie with great gusto. Lizzie read and reread his account of his voyage and of the excitement of joining his regiment in the Peninsula. To his distress, he arrived in Spain too late to participate in the taking of Ciudad Rodrigo, but he was present for the dreadful battle at Badajoz and for the victory at Salamanca.

His letters were full of his admiration for Lord Wellington. "I would not say that the men love him," he wrote, "but they have confidence in him as a commander. They say that in battle they would rather see the Beau with his hooked nose and steely eyes among them than another commander who might later heap compliments upon them or supply them with extra gin. I only wish that I could be such a man. My chief comfort is that now that I have seen battle and held my own without turning tail, the others can no longer call me a Johnny Newcombe. I have at least proven myself to that extent."

Soon after this letter had come another, in which he wrote that he had had an unbelievable stroke of good fortune. At Salamanca, Wellington had seemed to be everywhere during the battle, with no regard for personal danger. At one point, his horse was shot from beneath him, and the telescope that he always carried to survey the progress of the battle had flown from his hand during the fall. Matthew had leaped from his own mount and called, "Take mine, sir!" and scrambled down a ravine to retrieve the telescope and restore it to him. Wellington, tall and spare in his plain gray frock coat, had sprung into the saddle, nodded at him, and galloped away.

Two days later, he had been surprised to be summoned to Lord Wellington's headquarters and thanked by him personally. Although he had not known Matthew's name, he had known at a glance his regiment, and had sent one of his aides-de-camp to make inquiries about the young officer who had lent him his horse. Matthew's mount was returned to him, and Lord Wellington had asked if there were any kindness that he might show him for the loan of an excellent mount at a critical time—and for retrieving the indispensable telescope. Gathering his courage, Matthew had taken his opportunity. He had asked to be taken as an aide-de-camp on Wellington's personal staff, knowing that such a favor was most unlikely to be granted. Although the commander had several very young men on his staff, Matthew knew that they had come from noble families. The famous cold gray eyes had appraised him narrowly—"I felt as though he could look right through me," he had written—but finally Wellington had nodded, saying shortly, "We shall try it."

And from that time, Matthew had served on his staff. Lizzie heard much about life at headquarters—of Wellington's days of hunting with his own pack of hounds, of the long days of work and the General's meticulous attention to detail, of the exciting reports of scouts and spies, of occasional theatrical evenings and supper parties. "We have excellent wine here, but the quality of the food is indifferent," he wrote. "Mrs. Clary would be horrified to hear that we often have cold meat for dinner when we are on the march, and at such times the General himself sometimes goes for an entire day with only bread and a boiled egg that he has carried in the pocket of his coat. On nights that we do sit down to dinner, it is the conversation and not the food that makes the meals memorable."

For two years Lizzie had looked forward eagerly to Matthew's letters, rich with the details of his days. When Alice demanded to know if she did not feel jealous, Lizzie had only been amused.

"Why should I be?" she had inquired, certain that Alice was going to tell her whether she asked or not.

"Why, it's as plain as a pikestaff, Lizzie! Because Matthew is having adventures—a perfectly wonderful time, in spite of the fighting—and you're still here in the same old place, doing the same old things!"

She scrutinized her older sister for a moment, then shook her head when she could see that her words had made no impression. "What do you do here?" she demanded. "The same boring thing every day—and you are satisfied with it!"

Lizzie had nodded with what Alice could only consider as the most irritating calmness. "You are right," she agreed. "I am indeed satisfied with my life here." And she had picked up the book she had been reading and moved closer to the fire.

Alice had given an exaggerated sigh of exasperation, thrown her hands into the air, and marched from the room. Once she was safely gone, Lizzie slipped Matthew's latest letter from her book and read it one more time.

She was grateful for each one that she received. For as long as she was reading a letter, she felt close to him once more. She could imagine him sitting here with her by the fire, recounting each of his adventures, just as he would when the war was over, and he came home once more. Then they would be married, and sit beside their own fire together, talking over all that he had experienced. Their children would grow up hearing the tales of their father's adventures with Wellington in the Peninsula as they worked to defeat the armies of Bonaparte.

When she was not reading one of his letters, the Peninsula and Matthew—and their marriage—seemed very far away indeed.

Two

On the morning that her world fell apart, Lizzie stood for a long time at the window, the letter still in her hand. She stared blindly at the familiar white sweep of gravel that appeared from the distant grove of oaks and curved gently to the front of their house. How many times had she stood in this same place, waiting anxiously for him to ride out of the shadows of the grove and into the sunlight? No matter what horse he had ridden, she had always been able to identify Matthew at a glance, by his dark hair and the easy manner in which he handled his mount.

Unbidden, recollections of him flooded her mind. One of her earliest memories was of him riding down the drive on a sturdy little pony. He had successfully evaded the company of the groom and, taking his first ride on his own, had come proudly over to see her brother George. George had saddled his own pony, and together the two of them had trotted away, off on one of their many escapades. A few years later, on one of the golden days of her life, she had been allowed to tag along with them. However, her mother had made short work of that, announcing firmly that no daughter of hers would be running gypsy-wild for all the countryside to see. Then George and Matthew had been sent away to school, and thereafter their larks—at least many of them—had been confined to holidays.

When she was fifteen, her parents had held a Christmas ball. Despite her age, she was allowed to attend because the guests were just the families of the neighborhood. Matthew, in the highest of spirits because his father had promised to purchase him a commission in the Hussars, had suddenly noticed her that night. He had been away for more than half a year, and when he saw her, his eyes had lighted with a sudden warmth, and she had known that the time she had been waiting for had come. He had walked directly across the room to her, ignoring pretty Bella Simmons, who had been attempting to flirt with him.

"Lizzie!" he had exclaimed, taking both her hands and smiling down at her. "How could it be? I go away for a little while, and when I come home, I find that you have grown up overnight!"

"Perhaps it is because I am putting my hair up now, Matthew," she had responded demurely, her heart beating so quickly that she had thought it might burst.

"Perhaps," he said, "but I see that I must keep a more watchful eye on you."

Hugh Simmons had come up just then to claim her for a quadrille, but Matthew had shooed him away, tucking Lizzie's arm through his own and announcing to the indignant Hugh that he had already engaged her for that dance.

"It could be, Lizzie," Matthew had added, looking down at her thoughtfully as he led her out to dance, "that we shouldn't have laughed at our fathers. Perhaps they were wiser than we knew." At his words, Lizzie had felt her cheeks grow warm.

Both their families, the Lancasters and the Websters,

had known for years—from the time Matthew was six and she was still in leading strings—that their fathers wished for the two of them to marry. The men shared a friendship as close as that of their sons, and it had appeared highly desirable to them that the families be officially united.

Like the others, Lizzie had always laughed at their old-fashioned notion, but she had been secretly delighted, even if everyone treated it as a joke. She had always loved Matthew Webster, but to him she had merely been George's little sister. Then, on the night of that Christmas ball, he had danced with her three times and had kissed her under the mistletoe.

From that time on, when Matthew came to call at Lancaster Lodge, he came to see Lizzie, his gray eyes lighting up whenever she walked into the room. By the time he left for Portugal, the talk of their eventual marriage was a serious matter rather than a family joke. She had been too young to become engaged at the time, of course, and Matthew had been going away to fight in the war, but it was understood that they would one day marry.

She had been able to think of nothing more deeply satisfying than marrying Matthew and settling at Prestonwood, here in the neighborhood where they had grown up together. For a brief time she had thought that their marriage might come more quickly than she had ever imagined. Poor Mr. Webster had died only two months after his son's departure for Portugal. As the heir and only son, Matthew could have sold out and returned home when he received the news, but he had chosen to remain with his regiment. Nevertheless, Lizzie knew that he would eventually return and that their children would grow up at Prestonwood.

After a year had gone by, her mother had suggested that

she have a formal coming-out in London during the Season, but Lizzie had refused. She had no great fondness either for London or for society life and, since she already knew that she was to marry Matthew, she told her mother that she had neither the desire nor the need to be a part of the Marriage Mart. Although Alice had criticized her decision passionately, her parents had accepted it, and she had remained peacefully at Lancaster Lodge, waiting for the war to be over and for Matthew to come home.

"But of course you should go to London!" Alice had insisted. "Don't be such a pea-goose, Lizzie! Matthew is off seeing the world. Why shouldn't you have a little fun instead of poking around here? What harm could having a Season possibly do? You can still marry Matthew!"

Lizzie had patted her sister's arm. "There's no need to worry about me, Alice. I'm perfectly happy as I am, and Matthew will be home once Bonaparte is defeated."

How confident she had been about her future.

As she stood looking out over the drive, a sudden sharp pain shot through her, scattering the memories and leaving her unable to draw a breath. The day was warm, but she was shivering uncontrollably. Turning from the window, she stared blankly about the room. Nothing in the cheerful drawing room, with its Turkey rugs and curtains of gold velvet, looked familiar.

She sat down abruptly, the letter fluttering from her hand to the floor. With a curious detachment, she reflected that she felt exactly as she had last winter when Red Rover had balked at a fence and pitched her headlong to the frozen ground. She had lain there for what had seemed like forever, unable to catch her breath as she watched the world spinning around her. Although she was now in a warm and comfortable room, she felt as cold and lost as she had then.

"Lizzie?" The door opened and her mother bustled in, the ribbons on her tidy lace cap streaming behind her. "Lizzie, Walton tells me that you've had a letter from Matthew. How *is* the dear boy? Does he say when he will be coming home?"

Here Mrs. Lancaster paused, taking in her daughter's blank expression and the letter on the floor.

"What is it, Lizzie?" Her mother's voice was filled with concern. "Is he ill? Has something happened to Matthew?"

Lizzie nodded stiffly, and Mrs. Lancaster's eyes filled with tears. Through all the months that Matthew had been away in the war, they had feared for his safety daily. Now it appeared that the proclamation of peace had given them a false sense of security about his well-being.

"Oh, my dear child," she said gently, sitting down next to her daughter and slipping her arm around Lizzie's shoulders.

To Lizzie's relief, there were no more questions, and they sat in silence until Alice hurried through the door with Tussie following in her wake.

"What does Matthew say, Lizzie? Is he still with Wellington in Paris or has he already gone to Vienna? Where is he now and why hasn't he come home to see us? Will he be here for Christmas?"

The barrage of questions stopped only because Alice had to pause for breath. Tall and slim now, she was quick in everything she said and did and impatient with those who could not keep pace with her.

Taking advantage of the interval, Mrs. Lancaster glanced gravely at her younger daughter and Tussie, then shook her head slightly. "I think we should talk about this a little later, my dear."

"Yes, of course," agreed Miss Tussman hurriedly,

putting her hand on Alice's shoulder. "We should finish your French lesson, Alice, so that you have time to practice on the pianoforte before we take our walk."

Hearing her sister's unladylike snort at this plan for her afternoon would usually have won a sympathetic smile from Lizzie, but today there was no response. Noting this, Alice shot a puzzled glance at her mother, but she reluctantly allowed Tussie to guide her from the room.

As the door closed behind them, a tear slid down Lizzie's cheek. Mrs. Lancaster saw it, and stroked her hair gently. This was the calm child that never gave way to tears, so her fears for her daughter's happiness sharpened. What could have happened to Matthew, she wondered. The war was over, with Napoleon safely tucked away on the island of Elba, but accidents occurred, of course, even to young men—especially, she feared, to young men living abroad. Everyone knew that life on the Continent was more dangerous than life in England. How dreadful it would be if Matthew had come unscathed through two years of battle and rough living only to be taken from them after the return of peace.

Whenever news had reached them of each of the Peninsular battles, they had waited anxiously for Matthew's letters, assuring them that he was well. Mrs. Lancaster now waited uneasily to hear the worst, wishing that she could protect her children from all the pain that she knew life held in store for them.

Finally Lizzie leaned over and retrieved the letter from the floor. To her mother's astonishment, she crushed it into a tight ball and flung it across the room. Mrs. Lancaster stared at her daughter, shocked. Not only did Lizzie treasure all of Matthew's letters, packing each away in a rosewood box, but she also never made an exhibition of her feelings. Lizzie never allowed her emotions to run away with her. Alice was the daughter who gave way to anger and tears, Lizzie, the one who kept the household steady.

"How could he do it, Mama?" she demanded, brushing away the traitorous tears with her hand. "How could Matthew dream of doing such a thing?"

Mrs. Lancaster, who had been preparing to comfort her for the injury or death of her fiancé, stared at her. "What do you mean, Lizzie? What has Matthew done? Is he not injured?"

"Injured?" Lizzie's pale face flushed and her fingers curled together to form two small fists. "I should say that he is not—although I promise that he would be if I could place my hands upon him! *I* am the one who has been injured! It is our family that has been injured!"

Lizzie stood and began to pace the floor, stooping to pick up the crumpled ball of paper so that she could crush it once more, then she threw it down and attempted to grind it into the carpet with the sole of her slipper. "Matthew, on the other hand, appears to be in fine fettle!" she said, her voice bitter.

"That's good news, is it not?" inquired her mother cautiously. "That he is in good health, I mean." Mrs. Lancaster was so taken aback by her daughter's unusual behavior that she was almost afraid to ask the question.

"I daresay that all of his friends are delighted for him!" snapped Lizzie. "Particularly Miss Teresa Blackwell!"

"I see," murmured Mrs. Lancaster and, unfortunately, she did. The introduction of the name of an unknown young lady into the midst of Lizzie's distraught diatribe had exposed the heart of the problem. More unwilling than ever to probe an open wound, she sat and waited for further information. It was not long in coming.

When Lizzie began to speak, her words fairly tumbled over one another.

"To think that I believed him, Mama! When he wrote that continuing to serve on the Duke's staff, even after the war, was too great an honor to refuse, I believed him! What a blind fool I was!"

"But it is indeed a great honor," ventured her mother. "There was nothing foolish in believing that."

"But that is clearly not why he accepted the position! I should have known something was amiss when he wrote to me so seldom these last months. Even when he didn't bother to come here to see me while he was back in England this summer, I was goose enough to think that he still loved me and still planned to marry me! I must have feathers for brains!"

The speed of her pacing had increased as her voice rose. To Mrs. Lancaster's dismay, her daughter's anger was rising to a fever pitch. So concerned was she about such uncharacteristic behavior that she could not spare a thought for the serious consequences that Matthew's defection would have for their family.

The failure of the last two harvests and of some of Mr. Lancaster's investments during the war years, coupled with the outrageous gaming debts that George had acquired, had placed a severe strain upon the family's finances. Only a week earlier, just before leaving to bail George out once again, Mr. Lancaster had observed to his wife that Lizzie's wedding could come none too soon. Matthew's father had provided a substantial settlement for Lizzie and her family in his will. It was, however, payable only upon her marriage to Matthew.

"But you know that the Duke kept Matthew busy during the short time he was in London," she reminded Lizzie consolingly. "There were all the celebrations and

Matthew doubtless had work to do to prepare for the Duke's removal to Paris."

The Duke of Wellington had been appointed British Ambassador to France, as well as Commander-in-Chief of the army of occupation in Belgium, and Matthew was serving on his staff. "And it is a two-day journey here from London," she added, playing her trump card. "Why, he didn't even plan to come home to see his own mother."

"No, he did not," agreed Lizzie grimly. "Mrs. Webster went to London hoping to see him—and now we know precisely why she hasn't yet returned home, even though Matthew has already gone back to the Continent. Undoubtedly the poor woman has been waiting for him to inform us that there will be no wedding so that she doesn't have to come home and do it herself."

Here she kicked the wad of paper across the carpet. "Since this letter comes from Vienna, I daresay he has also written to tell her that it is safe to come home again."

Mrs. Lancaster shook her head. It was true enough that Letitia Webster had been gone for over two months. She had traveled to London in June for the lavish entertainments celebrating the defeat of Napoleon. She had not been certain that she would even see Matthew, for as a junior member of the Duke of Wellington's staff, he had remained behind in Paris to prepare for the Duke's imminent return as ambassador. Still, his mother had hoped that he might be in London for at least a week or two, and had gone to stay in the home of Lord Bradbury, a distant cousin of her late husband.

She had invited Lizzie to accompany her, but she had declined. Although Lizzie was fond of Letitia Webster, she had had no desire to spend several weeks constantly in her company, nor had she wished to be a country miss in a great London household. What she had wanted was to see Matthew at home, where they might have at least a little time alone together. In London, she doubted that there would be such an opportunity, for Mrs. Webster was naturally anxious to be with her son, too, and there Matthew also had the responsibilities of his position to fulfill.

Alice, in a voice of great disgust, had announced once again that Lizzie had lost her mind. "I would have gone in an instant!" she had assured her sister. "Why, you might even have gotten to see the Iron Duke himself had you gone! Half the country is going on pilgrimage to London to see the man who defeated Napoleon, and you choose to stay at home like a stick!"

Even Mrs. Lancaster, who was well aware of the reasons for Lizzie's reluctance, had felt that she was making a strategic error, but Lizzie had remained firm. And Matthew had not come to her—even though she had learned later that he had been in London for at least two weeks, so that he could have made the journey had he truly wished to do so.

Now she knew why he had not.

"Perhaps this is all a tempest in a teapot," suggested Mrs. Lancaster hopefully. "After all, what do we know of this young woman? Young men often lose their hearts— or at least think that they have—to completely inappropriate females. Why, my brother Robert once fancied himself deeply in love with an opera dancer, and it cost our father a thousand pounds to show him that his ladylove could be bought and had no real affection for him. Matthew has probably already had time to reconsider his letter to you and to regret it."

Lizzie shook her head stiffly. "He is to marry Miss Blackwell," she replied, not meeting her mother's eye.

"Her father is a colonel, recently retired from the 18th Hussars. Matthew writes that they are to marry in Paris as soon as Matthew returns there from his assignment in Vienna."

Mrs. Lancaster shook her head in dismay. If that were true, the young lady was undoubtedly an acceptable partner for a young man of comfortable means and respectable family. If it had not been for the embarrassment of his earlier connection to Lizzie, she had no doubt that Matthew's mother would be delighted with the match. As it was, her situation would be awkward for the moment, since all of their local society knew that the pair had been informally engaged for years. Indeed, since the end of hostilities in Europe, many of the neighbors had begun to talk of Matthew's return and the long expected wedding.

Lizzie had now reached the more than marriageable age of eighteen, but Matthew, having been away for two years and busily engaged on Arthur Wellesley's staff for the majority of that time, had made no recent reference to a wedding in his letters. She had not set eyes upon him since her seventeenth birthday, when he had unexpectedly appeared at her party and danced with her. They had not even known that he was in the country, but he had been sent with a delegation to London to present the Prince Regent with the baton belonging to Marshal Jourdan and with King Joseph's sword, both seized after the triumph of Vitoria. Matthew was to return to Spain immediately, but he had ridden nonstop, rather than resting, so that he could see her and his mother.

That night he had presented her with an exquisite music box that played the haunting melody of "Greensleeves." He had danced with her to that same song at the long ago Christmas ball, when she had been wearing a gown of green silk, and he had whispered to her that the green of her eyes would put emeralds to shame. Since then, the small gold box had held the place of honor on her dressing table, solid, reassuring proof that he still loved her and had not forgotten her.

After that evening, she had half expected him to appear without warning once again, this time to announce their wedding, but he had not come. After a few months, she had received fewer letters, even after Napoleon's surrender and consignment to Elba. As a matter of fact, his letters had grown briefer and more impersonal with the end of the fighting, just at the time she thought he would have more time for her and would write of coming home to stay. She had begun to fear that Matthew found his work too exciting to leave and that, when they married, she would have to move with him to Paris. She had thought at the time—innocently enough—that he did not wish to upset her by telling her such a thing, knowing how she loved it here.

"Why do you think he has not come to see me, Mama?" she had asked just that morning.

"He will come to you soon enough," Mrs. Lancaster had replied calmly. "You have said that the Duke is sending him to Vienna, to report upon events happening there. After they have settled everything in Vienna, I am certain that he will be coming home, at least for a while."

Only this morning, her mother's explanation had seemed reasonable to Lizzie. She knew how excited Matthew was to be singled out by Wellington himself and sent to Vienna. The Iron Duke, held in awe by the members of his staff as well as by what seemed to her the vast majority of Europe, had assured Matthew that he needed all of the trustworthy intelligence possible. The meeting in Vienna was a most important affair, a congress of nations to determine the fate of Europe now that Napoleon had been removed from power.

The Duke would, of course, remain in Paris for most of the time, but he would be in close contact with England's representative to the congress, Lord Castlereagh, by means of their flying dispatch service. Moreover, Wellington had chosen those on his staff for their loyalty, and having a trusted junior officer present in Vienna would allow him to hear gossip that might not be repeated to more important and powerful men.

All of this, she knew, was heady stuff indeed to a young man like Matthew. The gathering in Vienna was the greatest assembly of statesmen and royalty that Europe had ever seen. And it was also to be the most glittering gathering, for many fashionable members of European society who were to play no active part in the negotiations also planned to be present. For the first time in decades, travel on the Continent was safe once more, and thousands were flocking to Paris and Vienna and Brussels. The whole world, Lizzie thought bitterly, seemed to be celebrating.

Exhausted by the revelation of Matthew's letter, Lizzie finally retired to her own chamber, refusing company and food. She would not light a candle as the sun went down, nor would she allow a maid to light a fire for her. Instead, she sat at her window, looking out into the darkness and waiting for the coldness to melt from her heart. Anger had comforted her briefly, but she could not sustain it. Misery had returned, and she knew that she faced the future alone.

Suddenly, however, an idea occurred to her, and for the first time since reading Matthew's letter, she felt a brief rush of hope. She did not go to bed but, wrapping herself in a blanket, waited for the dawn.

Three

Lady Thalia moaned and pulled the covers up over her head. The room was dark, although a thread of pale light shone at one window where the curtains had not been properly drawn together.

"Have you gone *mad*, Beavers?" she demanded of her maid in a muffled voice rigid with reproach. "You know *perfectly* well that I wasn't to be disturbed before noon today! I shall turn you out without a character! Go and pack your things immediately!"

Unruffled by the threats of her mistress, which she knew were made for the sake of drama rather than truth, Beavers regarded the lump in the bed patiently. "There seems to be a pressing problem downstairs, ma'am, so I thought that you would wish to be told."

Lady Thalia sat up abruptly amid the covers and stared at her, wide-eyed. "What has happened, Beavers?" she demanded. "Is the stable on fire?" She spoke her worst fear first but, to her relief, Beavers calmly shook her head.

"Then is it the house that is afire?" she asked, collapsing back against a sea of lacy pillows. "Should I be running for the stairs or the window? Are they bringing a ladder for me?"

Again Beavers shook her head, unmoved by any of

these dramatic possibilities. "It is Miss Lancaster, Lady Thalia," she replied. "She rode over from the Lodge and asked to see you immediately."

"Miss Lancaster?" repeated Lady Thalia blankly. "Here before *dawn?* Has someone died?"

Again Beavers shook her head comfortably. The peculiarities of those she served—save for cruelty—never troubled her. She was forty years old, and had begun her life in service when she was seven. Thus far she had waited on four women, and Lady Thalia had been her mistress for the past ten years. If Beavers had anything to say about it, she would stay with her until she died. The members of the *ton* might consider Lady Thalia Stanhope an eccentric, but, in Beavers' opinion, she was a good mistress. Her manner was theatrical, and her behavior was often unusual, but she had a generous heart. So far as Beavers could see, that made up for everything.

Lady Thalia groaned again, then demanded her dressing gown. "I suppose you must have her come up—but *do* bring us some chocolate, Beavers. *Something* must atone for getting me out of bed at this ungodly hour."

She stumbled to her dressing table and brushed her dark hair, already threaded with gray although she was only thirty. She had long ago chosen never to marry, having her own fortune and her own tastes and not wishing to subordinate herself to anyone else. Nonetheless, she was still a woman of distinctive appearance and took great pains to remain so. She was by now considered a spinster by the rest of society, but she was also considered an interesting paradox. She was fashionable but well-educated, frivolous but well-read—and, most important of all, she was well-funded. She spoke her mind with disarming—and sometimes alarming—candor, and she expected others to do the same. Her drawing rooms in

the country and in London attracted an unusually rich
and entertaining variety of guests, for Lady Thalia hated
to be bored.

She had become a local fixture since moving to Hayworth Manor five years ago. It was a small property
belonging to her family, one that had become her pos-
session at the age of twenty-five. The manor, although
well kept by her family's staff, had seldom been visited
until Lady Thalia had taken up residence there. The
Stanhope family was highly respected, and it was not long
until she herself had made her own reputation in the
district. Her house parties were elegant, if somewhat
irregular in nature. Most of the guests came from a considerable distance and were clearly people of fashion, but
she always had a healthy mixture of poets and politicians
and artists. To be invited to one of her parties, the guests
had to be intelligent, entertaining, or discerning—
discerning because they recognized the worth of others.
She preferred, naturally, that they possess all three char-
acteristics. Guests at her parties could speak their minds
with little fear that they would hear their words repeated
elsewhere. She herself had often been the subject of
gossip, but that bothered her not at all.

Lady Thalia had met Lizzie Lancaster shortly after setting up housekeeping at the Manor. She had encountered
the young girl, just turned thirteen, at a lending library in
town, and had been immediately attracted by her choice
of reading. Aside from More's *The Shepherd of Salisbury
Plain* and Godwin's *The Life of Lady Jane Grey*, and several
gothic novels, Lizzie had a small book entitled *A Vindica-
tion of the Rights of Woman* by Mary Wollstonecraft. Lady
Thalia had looked at Lizzie curiously.

"Do you mean to read all of these?" she had asked.
After all, the girl looked more likely to spend her time

selecting fabrics for gowns than selecting thought-filled reading materials.

Lizzie had regarded the newcomer closely, clearly surprised by the question. "Of course," she replied. "I wouldn't take them with me if I didn't mean to read them." Then, feeling that she been somewhat abrupt, she added in an interested tone, "Will you read all of yours?" And she had indicated with a nod the books Lady Thalia had stacked on a nearby table.

Far from being affronted, Lady Thalia had been pleased with Lizzie's response. "A very fair question," she said approvingly. "I shall indeed read them all—unless, of course, I find that I do not care for some of them."

"Even if I don't like one, I feel that I should read it straight through so that I can think about why I don't like it," Lizzie had responded seriously. "That is a good thing, don't you agree?"

"Why, yes, I do," Lady Thalia had answered, more surprised than ever. "And after you finish reading your books, I would very much like it if you would come to call upon me at Hayworth Manor and tell me what you think of them."

Lizzie, unaccustomed to having adults—or children, for that matter—interested in her opinions, had flushed with pleasure and promised gravely that she would do so. Accordingly, a few days later she had ridden over to Hayworth Manor and spent a delightful afternoon with Lady Thalia, enjoying the gothics, discussing the oppressively good and contented shepherd, the impressive scholarly accomplishments of Lady Jane Grey, and the unheard of matter of the rights of women.

Both ladies found it such a wholly satisfactory experience that they had repeated it many times during the next five years. Lizzie's grave manner contrasted sharply

with Lady Thalia's lively one, but they enjoyed one another's company tremendously. The girl promised to
be a lovely young woman, but, to Lady Thalia's pleasure,
she was anything save self-absorbed.

After Lizzie's seventeenth birthday, she had been allowed to attend a number of parties at Hayworth and
had met there a host of interesting people. Lizzie had
enjoyed them far more than she had expected, and Mrs.
Lancaster, although doubtful at first about the wisdom
of allowing such visits, had decided that the outings
might help to take the place of a Season.

Lady Thalia was determined to broaden Lizzie's experience as much as possible, and she had enjoyed
watching her protégée grow into a promising young
lady. Although she had regretted Lizzie's deep attachment to Matthew Webster, she had been forced to admit
that it was only to be expected, and that he was, at least,
a likable and reasonably intelligent young man.

"I am so sorry to disturb you at such an hour, Lady
Thalia," Lizzie said earnestly as Beavers shepherded her
into the room and directed her to a chair by the fire.
"But I simply had to talk to you as soon as it was possible
to do so. I could not wait."

Her hostess could see that her guest was not overstat-
ing the matter. Lizzie leaned toward her, her gaze intent.
She looked not at all like herself, Lady Thalia thought
uneasily.

"What do you need to talk about, Lizzie? What has
happened?"

"I've had a letter from Matthew," she replied. "He will
be marrying someone else very soon."

Although Lady Thalia's first reaction was that Lizzie
had received a merciful deliverance from marriage, she
did not allow herself to say so or to show it by so much as

the flicker of an eyelash. Instead, placing her hand on Lizzie's, she said with all sincerity, "I know how this must hurt you, my dear. I am so *very* sorry."

Lizzie shook her head. "That isn't why I've come, Lady Thalia—not for sympathy. Mama can give me that—although I truly don't want it."

Lady Thalia sipped her chocolate thoughtfully and waited. After a few moments, Lizzie took a deep breath and continued.

"I know that I am presuming greatly upon our friendship, Lady Thalia, and upon the kindness that you have shown me—but I *must* ask you. When you leave for the Continent on Friday, may I accompany you as your companion?"

Lizzie's gaze was still fixed on her friend, who carefully put down her cup and cleared her throat. "Go with me as my companion?" Lady Thalia repeated.

Lizzie nodded eagerly. "I could do whatever you or Beavers tell me to, and I could read to you when you're tired, or bring you your tea. I have listened to your stories about your travels to Italy and Portugal and Spain and Greece—and even to Paris during the Peace of Amiens. I should love to see those places for myself."

"And yet, Lizzie, you did not think to mention your longing to see them until just *this* very morning," observed Lady Thalia.

Lizzie colored and looked away. It was true enough that she loved the stories about foreign places, but she preferred hearing or reading about them to traveling to see them herself. She had frequently announced that she was a homebody, content to have her adventures vicariously.

"I know that you also plan to go to Vienna, and I

should like to see Matthew again—preferably before he marries," she admitted in a low voice.

"My dear child, what will you do if you *do* see him?" Lady Thalia's voice was kind, but one eyebrow was lifted quizzically. "After all, Lizzie, you can *not* force a gentleman to love you if he has given his heart elsewhere. And indeed I should not think you would *wish* to have him under those circumstances."

"Oh, I know I must sound ridiculous, but—but, you see, Matthew did not say in his letter that he had stopped loving me. He said that—"

Here she broke off and took a very wrinkled piece of paper from her pocket and tried to smooth it. Then she read from it carefully.

"Here is what he said."

Had I been content to remain at home and ruralize, then I might not have outgrown our relationship and been satisfied to settle at Prestonwood and raise a family. Now, however, I realize how much more the world has to offer, and I know that I should only make you unhappy by forcing you to live a life in which you would be uncomfortable, or make myself unhappy by coming home and trying to pretend to be satisfied with such a life. We have, I fear, grown too far apart to be comfortable together.

At this point she paused and folded it back up again, then continued in a low voice. "Matthew goes on to say that the lady he has fallen in love with is quite my opposite and that it is with her that he desires to live the rest of his life."

Lady Thalia, thinking that she could have cheerfully

throttled Matthew Webster for such a pompous, patronizing letter, held her silence so that she would not say something that they would both regret.

Misinterpreting her silence, Lizzie sighed and shook her head. "I do apologize for burdening you with my problems, Lady Thalia. It is just that I do not think myself such a dowdy little dab of a thing as Matthew seems to, capable only of living in the country. Even though I have always preferred life here, I daresay that I could be just as polished and sophisticated as Miss Blackwell, were I given the opportunity."

"I am quite *certain* that you could," Lady Thalia agreed firmly. "After all, during the past year your parents have permitted you to attend several of my evening parties, and you have become quite comfortable moving amid a *very* distinguished company. Why, I have watched you discuss art with Thomas Lawrence and poetry with Lord Byron and everything under the sun with Henry Brougham."

She did not add that she had been delighted to see that Lizzie, always rather quiet and self-effacing, had grown more and more self-assured. She felt that Matthew Webster would be quite shocked were he to encounter his Lizzie now. She smiled to herself at the thought.

Lizzie's face brightened perceptibly at Lady Thalia's words. "That is so," she agreed. "Perhaps I would not be at a complete loss in an assembly such as those Matthew attends."

"Of *course* you would not!" said Lady Thalia encouragingly. "Or at least not so long as you had anyone *intelligent* with whom to talk. Assemblies are not necessarily rife with such people."

She studied her guest with a speculative eye. "Of course, we shall have to provide you with a more suitable wardrobe. After all, we shall be keeping *very* fashionable company on the Continent."

"I'm afraid that I cannot afford to be extremely fashionable," Lizzie replied hesitantly. Then her eyes lit up as the full import of Lady Thalia's statement burst upon her. "May I indeed go with you, then?" she demanded, throwing her arms around the neck of her benefactress.

"*Indeed* you may," Lady Thalia replied, wondering if she would soon regret this hasty decision. "We must first get your parents' permission, however."

"Only Mama's," replied Lizzie. "Papa and George will not arrive home for a sennight." She found herself unreasonably grateful for this, for she knew that she could persuade her mother far more easily than her father.

"Then by all means take yourself home, my dear," said Lady Thalia. "I shall call upon your good mother as *soon* as propriety will allow. At least *I* will wait until the sun has fully risen."

Lizzie sprang from her chair, hugged Lady Thalia once more, then hurried from the room, transported by her good fortune.

Lady Thalia eyed her bed longingly for a moment, then shook her head briskly and rang for Beavers. There was much to be done before Friday.

Four

Daniel Thoreau studied his fellow passengers with interest as the old French diligence lumbered along the road from Calais to Paris. He was keenly aware that the ladies had wished to have the coach to themselves, but unfortunately it had been the last Paris-bound vehicle available. He had been to Calais to see off a friend of his on a packet bound for Boston—if it could thread through the British blockade—and so he had already noted the general squalor of Calais. He had had no intention of being forced to wander about its streets the rest of the day and put up at some filthy inn for the night, so he had cheerfully made himself one of the party in the diligence, ignoring their protests. The French postilion had silently accepted the money that he offered, and had ordered Thoreau's luggage loaded onto the coach.

The ladies had been assisted into its vast interior, eyeing its cracked leather seats with disfavor and pressing perfumed handkerchiefs to their noses to ward off its musty smell. Thoreau had climbed in behind them and seated himself next to an older woman attired in a plain dark pelisse, who appeared to be a servant.

"*Really*, sir, if you must *insist* upon forcing your presence upon us for the journey, you might at least ride on top of the coach. My footman is riding there in order that we may have our privacy," observed the sharp-eyed lady seated across from him. Self-assured and elegantly dressed, she appeared to be in charge of the other two.

"Surely you would not be so cruel as to deny me such charming company," he replied pleasantly, ignoring the fact that he had been placed in a category with her footman and quite certain that she would deny him anything that was within her power—particularly their company. "And, quite apart from that, it appears to me that it might well rain soon. I would prefer not to arrive in Paris soaked to the skin."

When there was no immediate reply other than a chilly glance, he added, "Since we are to be traveling together, allow me to introduce myself. My name is Daniel Thoreau, and I am originally from New York, most recently from Ghent."

"An American," said the sharp-eyed lady, nodding. "Yes, that *would* explain it, of course."

In Thoreau's experience with the British, which this lady clearly was, such an observation was not a complimentary one, so he was surprised to see her look amused and offer her hand.

"I am Lady Thalia Stanhope and this is Miss Lancaster." The dark-haired young lady seated next to her nodded and smiled. Miss Lancaster was, Thoreau thought, quite charming in appearance, even though she was not as modishly dressed as her companion.

When no other introductions were forthcoming, Thoreau raised his eyebrows and glanced briefly at the lady seated next to him.

"And this is Miss Beavers," added Lady Thalia, who did not usually introduce her maid, even one as highly valued as Beavers. But then, she reminded herself, the Americans that she had met had most unusual ideas.

They were, she had found, often amusingly refreshing—
if undeniably provincial—in their thoughts. Beavers
nodded comfortably and almost immediately lapsed into
a gentle doze.

"For the sake of polite conversation, I would ask you
ladies where you are bound, but since you are obviously
on your way to Paris, I suppose I must think of something
else."

They rode in silence for a few miles, while the gentleman studied the toe of his polished boot reflectively,
apparently devoting himself to the consideration of
other conversational gambits. Eventually, he glanced up
and grinned at Lady Thalia. "It must be a great relief to
your countrymen to be fighting only one war now."

Lady Thalia was surprised by his choice of subject, but
she was certainly equal to commenting upon it. "It was,
of *course*, a relief to see Bonaparte defeated," she conceded. "Naturally, little attention could be paid to such
a *minor* fray as the one with your country while we faced
such a serious threat."

He nodded in appreciation at this home-thrust. "I noticed, however, that as soon as the French were taken
care of, thousands of Wellington's troops were shipped
off to North America to assist with that fray."

"That could well be," she replied, with the air of one
who had paid no attention to such unnoteworthy devel-
opments. "On the whole, I find war a *tiresome* subject. The
Jacobin threat and Bonaparte belong to the past, and *soon*
the problem with your country will be resolved as well."

"I quite agree," he said amiably, not committing himself
to any observation as to what that resolution would be.
Judging by the newspapers, no one in Britain appeared to
be aware that the government there was presently negoti-
ating a peace with American representatives at Ghent.

Lizzie, who had been paying little attention to this exchange, drew their attention to the passing countryside.
"The dwellings do not look nearly so—" She paused a
moment as she searched for the word. "They are not
nearly so tidy-looking as they are in England."

Lady Thalia laughed. "Very true, my dear. In *fact*,
when so many of the French came to London this summer to celebrate the end of the war, some of them
believed that we had cleaned up the villages and farms
along the Dover Road ex*press*ly for the purpose of im-
pressing our visitors. They could not imagine that such
places *always* looked so well-kept and orderly."

Gazing at the crumbling chateaux and down-at-the-
heels farms and remembering the dirt and beggars of
Calais, Lizzie could understand why the visitors would
have thought such a thing. The English farms and villages looked clean and well cared for, but the countryside
in this part of France was quite the opposite. She was beginning to wonder if she had made a serious mistake in
coming on this journey. They would be gone for months,
she knew, and suddenly home seemed even more attractive than it always had. Aside from grieving for Matthew,
she was now assailed with a painful longing for home.

Seeing her forlorn expression and guessing a part of
the reason for it, Thoreau remarked, "This certainly
doesn't remind me of the country around New York either. I have been away from home for well over a year
now, and I confess I look forward to seeing it again."

"I should imagine that you *do* long for it, Mr. Thoreau.
I know I should after so long a time," said Lizzie. She
paused for a moment, then added, "How do you keep
yourself from always thinking of it?"

He had hoped that she would ask, so his reply was ready.
"I look more closely at everything about me—at the peo-

ple and what they are saying and doing and probably feeling, at the details of the place and its appearance and sounds and smells. Once I have focused my attention outside of myself, the longing passes because my mind is fully occupied. Then there is no space left for unhappiness."

"What a *very* sensible idea," said Lizzie, her eyes bright for the first time since they had met. As though he had prescribed a medicine, she turned her gaze once more to the passing landscape and firmly forced herself to take it all in. Wallowing in despair would certainly do her no good, and Lizzie was always practical.

Lady Thalia gave him an approving glance, took up her book, and began to read. They had suddenly become, Thoreau thought, a very domestic party. Miss Beavers was still sleeping, Lady Thalia reading, and Miss Lancaster was watching the world go by, occasionally remarking upon a particularly fine apple orchard or an interesting ruin. Comfortable now, he took out a newspaper he had brought with him from Ghent and began to read.

They traveled in such a manner for a number of miles before it began to rain. At first there was a spattering of large drops like gunfire, then a blinding downpour. The team slowed to a walk and the diligence rolled painfully onward. After a mile or two more, it creaked to a halt. The rain was still lashing down, so they could see nothing and hadn't the least notion what was happening outside. Finally, the wheels turned once more, and Lady Thalia sighed in relief.

"I feared for a moment that we could go no further, and I can think of *nothing* more dreadful than being stranded in this abominable coach."

"We are in complete agreement on that point," said Thoreau, and Lizzie nodded fervently. Beavers was snoring gently, the feather in her bonnet keeping time with the rise and fall of her breathing.

All too soon they again came to a stop, and the three of them waited anxiously for the coach to move forward once more. This time, however, the door opened and a gust of rain blew in over them.

"I'm afraid we can go no further, my lady." At the door stood Henry, Lady Thalia's footman, holding his great-coat. "We have stopped at an inn and the coach is as close to the entrance as possible."

With Henry's assistance, Lady Thalia stepped down under the protection of the greatcoat. One by one he shepherded each of the ladies inside, and Thoreau splashed in behind them. The inn was a tiny one, no more than a single serving room and a kitchen, but it was moderately clean and there was a fire. The travelers gathered in front of it, grateful for its warmth against the damp chill of the autumn afternoon.

One other gentleman had arrived before them, a slender young man with dark hair curling from the damp, who emerged from the kitchen with a bottle of brandy.

"It's the very devil out there, is it not?" he demanded cheerfully, shaking hands with Thoreau and bowing to the ladies. "I very nearly drowned getting here after my chaise got stuck just down the road. My poor driver led the horses in, and he is out there now, prying the rig out of the mud." He glanced down at the bottle in his hand. "Since the landlord is the entire staff and he is putting up the cattle, I decided that I would assist him within. Gregory Mansfield, at your service."

As the introductions were being made, Beavers and Henry disappeared into the kitchen to inspect the possibilities. The gentlemen pulled the settles closer to the fire to block the drafts and placed a table between them. Mr.

Mansfield poured brandy for them all to keep out the cold, and in very short order Beavers and Henry appeared with hot coffee and a crusty loaf of bread.

"That is all that we could find, my lady," Beavers told her mistress apologetically, "but there are fresh eggs, so there must be chickens, too. We shall do better for dinner."

"Don't forget, Beavers, that Mrs. Clary sent a basket with me from the Lodge," said Lizzie. "It is still in the diligence."

The company made very short work of the bread and the coffee, laughing and talking with the genial Mr. Mansfield as they were revived by food and drink and warmth. Soon, however, Thoreau saw that Miss Lancaster's eyes were closing and that she was beginning to sway slightly. He caught Lady Thalia's eye and nodded toward the young lady.

To Lizzie's surprise, she awakened some three hours later, stretched out on one of the settles. Henry had brought in one of Lady Thalia's trunks, so Lizzie now had a pillow in a silken case under her head and a soft woolen blanket tucked around her. Lady Thalia was seated beside her, and she and the gentlemen were still talking.

Lizzie lay there, listening drowsily and trying to follow Mr. Thoreau's advice. She concentrated intently on the scene before her. The wooden settles, high-backed and unyielding, had been polished to a glossy sheen by the countless people who had sat there over the years. The flickering of the wood fire—apple wood, she noted appreciatively—and the two guttering candles cast shifting shadows on the walls and on the faces of the people across from her—Mr. Mansfield, well-bred and lively, giving the impression of movement even when he was seated; Mr. Thoreau, solidly reassuring, talking with the ease of an educated man—but in an American accent, of course. The wood smoke from the fire and the savory scent of roasting chicken, the faint cold dampness from the stone floor and the smell of melting tallow from the candles, all mingled with the rose-petal sweetness of Lady Thalia's perfume.

Mr. Thoreau was correct, she mused dreamily. She had been grief-stricken and homesick earlier in the day, and the inn where she found herself now was strange and uncomfortable—so much so that awakening there had again filled her with unhappiness. Nevertheless, giving her determined attention to the details of the scene that was her world for the moment *did* fill her mind and crowd out thoughts of the Lodge and her family.

"I believe that Miss Lancaster is rejoining us," observed Mr. Thoreau. "She appears to have been drifting in and out of sleep for some minutes now. Perhaps dinner will restore her to us completely."

"I know that it will do so for me," agreed Mr. Mansfield. "Only the fear that I might slow the cook's work has kept me out of the kitchen. The smell of that chicken roasting has been driving me to distraction."

As though on cue, the door to the kitchen swung open and Henry emerged, carrying a platter bearing three roasted chickens. Beavers followed on his heels with a hot steak and kidney pie, made with Mrs. Clary's own hands and firmly sent with Lizzie to sustain her on her journey to foreign places. Their meal was rounded out with toast made from Mrs. Clary's bread, a tart made from apples that Beavers had discovered in the kitchen, slices of cheese, and more hot coffee.

"I could not be happier if I had just eaten a meal prepared by the great Carême himself," announced Mr. Mansfield, leaning back as comfortably as the settle would allow.

"I don't believe that he would trouble himself with such simple fare, however," observed Mr. Thoreau. "Perhaps if we had been served larks encased in pastry lined with chicken livers or turbot in a lobster sauce—or, more likely, a dessert of cake and spun sugar, shaped like the Parthenon—*then* we might think of Carême."

"I am impressed that an American would even *know* of such a famous chef," said Lady Thalia. "I thought that in *your* country people confine themselves to eating whatever they can shoot."

"Oh, that is true, of course," he replied easily. "We are much like the English in that respect, you see." He glanced at her briefly and was pleased to see that she acknowledged the hit with a smile. "As to my knowing about Carême, I pride myself upon being well-informed, and I took note of him when Talleyrand first employed him some years ago."

Talleyrand had then been the French Foreign Minister. As the Bishop of Autun, he had participated in the opening of the Revolution, but he had left France just before the execution of the king, seeking safety first in France and then in America. After a few years, his friends at home had managed to remove his name from the list of *émigrés* so that he could safely return to his country. Aside from being a most astute politician, managing to survive and prosper during most of the changes in government, Talleyrand was also a noted gourmet.

"An extremely interesting man, Talleyrand," mused Mr. Mansfield.

"As crafty as they make them," agreed Thoreau. "His mind moves like quicksilver. It will be fascinating to see how the fox manages in Vienna. No doubt he will find a way for France, the nation defeated, to do more than hold her own during the negotiations."

Lizzie's attention was completely captured by the mention of Vienna, and she leaned forward attentively, eager for what crumbs of information she could gather.

Gregory Mansfield nodded. "He will be facing a master of manipulation in Metternich, however. And then Tsar Alexander will, of course, provide an erratic element to the mix. One can never be certain what he will do. And the Prussians are the very devil to work with."

Mansfield again shook his head. "I don't envy Lord Castlereagh the weeks of meeting with them. Even though he believes the Congress will last only a few weeks at the most, I am glad that I am merely a lowly member of the staff, fit only to fetch and carry."

"You are on Castlereagh's staff?" demanded Thoreau, clearly impressed. "That *is* good news! I have been reading about the Congress and there are some matters I'd like to discuss with you."

"And will you merely be *reading* about Vienna, Mr. Thoreau?" inquired Lady Thalia, before Mr. Mansfield could respond. "Or, like *us*, do you plan to travel there as well?"

Thoreau ignored the thorn in her question. "Both," he replied. "But I didn't realize that you and Miss Lancaster were traveling beyond Paris."

"We stop in Paris for only a few days," she said, not adding that a little time was needed to outfit Lizzie more appropriately.

"I had already been looking forward to my Viennese experience," said Mr. Mansfield, with a flattering sincerity, "but now I shall expect my pleasure to be tripled."

The gentlemen's discussion lasted far into the night as they talked of the difficulty of Castlereagh's position as he tried to achieve a balance of power among the nations of Europe that would be acceptable to the English.

"No doubt he would like to unite Austria and Prussia so that they provide a barrier for Russia," Lizzie heard Mr. Thoreau observe.

"That would be sensible," agreed Mr. Mansfield. "Of course, Talleyrand would like that as well, since it would provide a buffer between France and Russia."

That was her last recollection of the evening's conversation. Beavers and Henry had made makeshift beds on the settles for the two ladies. The servants were sleeping in the kitchen, and, when the gentlemen retired, they planned to roll themselves in their greatcoats and sleep close to the fire.

"It is unorthodox, of course," Lady Thalia had said matter-of-factly to Lizzie, "but in *these* circumstances, it will answer very well."

Lizzie had been unperturbed by the arrangement, which seemed both sensible and as comfortable as possible. Hearing the murmur of now familiar voices as she drifted off to sleep was reassuring.

And tomorrow she would see Paris. She had heard Mr. Thoreau and Mr. Mansfield talking over the arrival of the Duke of Wellington in Paris a few weeks earlier. Lady Thalia had told her that they would both be attending a reception at the British Embassy and that she would actually get to meet the famous Peer. Lizzie smiled sleepily to herself, thinking of what Alice would have to say when she wrote to her that at last she had met the Iron Duke.

Then she sighed. She knew that she would not see Matthew there, of course, for he had written that he would be in Vienna, but she would at least see the place where he worked and the people with whom he spent his time.

As sleep washed over her, she imagined Matthew— unexpectedly called back to the Embassy just in time for the reception, of course—walking toward her with outstretched arms. "Lizzie," he said to her, folding her close, "Lizzie, I've been the most awful fool! Can you ever forgive me?"

Finally, the last candle burned out, its flame drowning in a puddle of melted tallow, and the fire burned low. Even the gentlemen gave up their conversation and their brandy, wrapped themselves warmly in their coats, and fell asleep.

And Lizzie dreamed happily—for tomorrow she would be in Paris, and that much closer to Matthew.

Five

They did not make an early start the next morning, for the examination of the two vehicles by their postilions took some time, and then the gentlemen in question strolled out to inspect the road in order to be certain that it could be safely traveled and the vehicles not become too deeply mired in mud. A lengthy discussion followed, and the postilions required fortification, so they retired to the kitchen and drank deeply. Mr. Thoreau, finally becoming thoroughly annoyed, told them bluntly—in his best French—that *he* could see no problem with the road.

The two postilions were deeply offended by his lack of confidence in their expertise, and it required the more tactful approach of Mr. Mansfield to move them. He assured them that he could appreciate the difficulties that they faced in making their decision, knowing that they must consider both the well-being of their passengers and that of the equipages by which they earned their livelihood. Their expressions lightened noticeably as he soothed them and beckoned to the innkeeper to refill their glasses.

Finally, under the guidance of Mr. Mansfield and after the exchange of several folded notes, it was decided that only the diligence, as the heavier and more trustworthy vehicle, should brave the rest of the perilous journey, and

Mr. Mansfield's rented chaise should return to Calais. The postilions, pleased both by the extra money that they had received and by the appreciation of a gentleman for their delicate position, were then eager to depart.

"But there is no danger connected with this journey!" protested Thoreau, as Mansfield climbed into the diligence after him. "There is only inconvenience—and mud!"

"Naturally," said Mansfield agreeably, settling himself next to Thoreau and smiling at the ladies. "But there is no honor or excitement in inconvenience, my friend. It is necessary that they invest their lives with some drama, you see."

"Well, I do see, but I don't approve!" grumbled Thoreau. "We would never tolerate such an attitude at home."

"But you are not in America," Mansfield pointed out to him. "This is France, and there must be honor—and danger, of course."

Finally, to everyone's relief, they were under way. Lizzie watched the passing scene carefully, listening to the gentlemen only now and then. They seemed to find much to talk about, which pleased her, both because she liked to see others happy and because she had no wish to be engaged in conversation herself.

It seemed to her that the oddest thing about their journey, as they grew closer and closer to Paris, the very heart of France, was that she saw so few other vehicles. She had been to London several times, and one of the things that had overwhelmed her was the traffic, which was thick even before they reached the city. Paris seemed to be a different matter—or at least it was now, so soon after the war.

She was pleased with the windmills and vineyards of

Montmartre, and at last, just at dusk, they could see Paris in the distance. Finally they reached the *barrières* that fenced in the city and made their way slowly along behind a wagon of hay. Despite the oil lanterns swinging in the wind, the scene seemed very dark to Lizzie as the diligence wound through narrow streets toward the hotel in the Saint-Germain quarter where Lady Thalia had reserved rooms for them. Very soon after entering the city, both ladies were forced to take perfumed handkerchiefs from their reticules and press them to their noses once more. They had grown accustomed to the staleness of the air in the diligence, but the present stench almost overcame them.

"I fear that the Grand Canal is an unpleasant aspect of the city," conceded Mr. Mansfield apologetically. "However, Paris has other charms that will atone for it."

"The Grand Canal?" said Lizzie weakly from behind her handkerchief.

Lady Thalia nodded. "A sewer that circles the city. Unfortunately, much of it is open—not at all like what we are accustomed to in England."

Seeing Lizzie's eyes, horror-stricken above the handkerchief, she patted the girl's hand reassuringly. "We shall *not* be troubled by it at our hotel—unless, of course, they gave away our rooms when we did not arrive yesterday."

To Lizzie's great relief, their rooms had been held for them—and there was no trace in the air of the malodorous Grand Canal. The gentlemen engaged to meet them for dinner the next evening and bade them good night, climbing back in the diligence to be borne away to their respective destinations. Soon Beavers was making up the beds with Lady Thalia's own linens and pillows. Lizzie was too weary even to eat dinner and fell gratefully into a deep and dreamless sleep.

The next morning their first call was upon a dress-maker. "Although I haven't been here in a decade," said Lady Thalia, "I understand that Madame Delacroix still maintains her establishment. She does *wonderful* work and she is very quick, which is important since we do not have much time here. If we are fortunate, she will have time to make up half a dozen gowns for you before we leave Paris."

"For me? But, Lady Thalia, I cannot afford a new wardrobe!" She had managed to push the family's financial problems, aggravated by Matthew's defection, to the back of her mind.

"There is *no* difficulty," Lady Thalia assured her. "Wonderful fabrics may be had for a pittance in Paris, and you must remember, Lizzie, that, as my companion, you will be more in company than you have been accustomed to at home. I must *insist* that you allow me to gown you appropriately so that you are a credit to me."

Lizzie had not considered this aspect of the matter, so she reluctantly gave way to Lady Thalia. However, any lingering guilt that assailed her was swept away by the delights of the next three hours. Surrounded by a battery of tall mirrors, she was measured, then draped with fabrics of all hues and textures so that Madame Delacroix and Lady Thalia could determine those that were most becoming. By the time they left, two new morning gowns, two handsome walking dresses, and three evening gowns had been ordered. She was overwhelmed, both by the number of gowns and by the diaphanous fabric Lady Thalia and Madame Delacroix had chosen for one of the evening dresses. When she expressed some doubt about the suitability of the gauze-like gown, Lady Thalia had overridden her objection, reminding Lizzie that she was better acquainted with the society in which they would be moving.

Then, feeling that she had perhaps been a little too overbearing, Lady Thalia shepherded Lizzie to a *pâtisserie* for cakes and cheerful gossip about the people that she would soon be meeting. They would, she told her charge, take some time to look about the city before doing any more shopping for other necessities of her wardrobe.

Paris was a revelation to Lizzie. Accustomed to the gentle pace of a life in the country, the constant movement of Paris overwhelmed her. She had been to London, of course, but even there her senses had not been assaulted as they were in Paris. The crowds of people that swirled by them in the streets were by no means all French in nationality. They were of a variety of origins; she could hear them speaking many languages other than French or English, and their varied complexions and dress composed a rich human tapestry that seemed to surround her. Also, she noticed to her surprise that even when they were in the elegant Place Vendôme, the people on the pavement were not just the fashionables that she would have expected to find in such a place. Ragged porters and women in threadbare gowns also made their way through the front entryways of the tall stone houses.

"Do you suppose he really lives there?" she whispered to Lady Thalia, nodding in the direction of a man in a ragged frock coat far too large for him and boots that were caked with dried mud.

"It is possible."

"But how could that be? Would it not be too expensive for him? One would never find such a thing happening in Mayfair!"

Lady Thalia smiled. "That is very true. Here, however, living accommodations are arranged differently. In a house such as the one he entered, the poorest rooms with the lowest rent are to be found on the highest floors, the best ones with the highest rent are nearest the ground."

"But there is only one door! Do they all enter the same way?"

Lady Thalia nodded. "And they very likely share the same stairway as well. Sometimes the common area in such a place is a *fearful* mess, but then a door opens and you step into a set of rooms as well appointed as any you would find in Grosvenor Square."

"I don't believe I would care to live in such a way, no matter how well-appointed the rooms were," said Lizzie. "I greatly prefer the way we live at home."

"I've no doubt of it. I like England very well myself. However, you must remind yourself, my dear, that you are learning about the way *others* live their lives. After all, if you wish to make Matthew sorry that he is not marrying you, will you not have to show him that you are no longer a mere country miss?"

Satisfied by Lizzie's sigh and her despondent expression that she had made a home-thrust, she patted the girl's hand briskly. "Never mind that, my dear—but *do* promise me that you will try to enjoy yourself."

Remembering how much she owed to Lady Thalia's generosity, Lizzie had the grace to blush. "Forgive me," she said penitently. "I am *indeed* enjoying myself. I promise that I shall be better company."

Again she concentrated on taking Mr. Thoreau's advice, and turned her attention outward. With great determination she studied the faces of those passing by them, wondering why the old man with the white beard and the stiff gait was smiling to himself and why the pretty little flower girl, with a face as delicate as the lilies she was selling, looked so despondent. Strolling along one of the leafy boulevards in the September sunlight, they saw a small knot of people and paused with them to watch a nimble little terrier perform a battery of tricks, all at the command of his young master. Stalls filled with books and prints also slowed their progress, and it was with some surprise that she realized that it was time to return to the hotel and dress for dinner so that they would be ready when Mr. Thoreau and Mr. Mansfield came to call for them.

"And, my dear, you will be *amazed* by the place where we are going to dine!" Lady Thalia told her gleefully. "Just wait until you see the Palais-Royal! I do promise you that you have seen *nothing* like it in your life!"

Later that evening, as they strolled down the covered walks of the brightly lighted Palais-Royal, past busy cafés and *pâtisseries*, elegant shops and infamous gambling hells, Lizzie could see that Lady Thalia had not exaggerated. It was a little, she thought, like seeing Paris condensed. Once she had surrendered herself to it, she had been delighted by the sensual onslaught of daytime Paris, but evening at the Palais-Royal did indeed amaze her. She was grateful that Mr. Thoreau was at her side, for the bold glances of some of the gentlemen told her clearly that she and Lady Thalia would have been approached if they had not been escorted.

"Don't let them distress you," said Mr. Thoreau in a low voice, after he had caught her anxious glance at two swaggering young blades who had stopped to gaze at her with unabashed interest. "They won't trouble you at all."

She clung a little more tightly to his arm, careful not to look the young men in the eye. She was extremely uncomfortable and once again wished herself safely home at the Lodge.

Mr. Thoreau, determined to help her overcome her

homesickness and her natural timidity, began a disserta-
tion to divert her thoughts from her unhappiness.
"During the Revolution, they called this place the Mai-
son Egalité, you know. It was a center for public debate."

He felt her shudder at the mention of the Revolution.
"That is too awful to think about," she replied. "So many
people dying needlessly."

"That is true," he conceded. "There was a terrible
waste of life. It is unfortunate that their revolution could
not, in the end, have been as successful as our own in
America. They have a constitution now, but they also
once again have a monarch."

She looked at him with wide eyes. "Are you a Jacobin,
then?" she asked. "You do not think that the king should
have had his throne restored after Bonaparte's defeat?"

Thoreau shrugged lightly. "You must remember, Miss
Lancaster, that I am an American. We do not think so
highly of kings as the English do."

He paused to chuckle a moment over what he had just
said. "Naturally, with your old king incapacitated by his
madness at the moment, and the Prince Regent making such a spectacle of himself in so many ways, I daresay
a good many of the English feel that they could also do
without kings."

Lizzie was a little indignant at this jab at her country,
but she was forced to acknowledge the truth of it. "At
least King George has no control over his problem," she
responded. "He cannot help his fits of madness."

"Very true," he acknowledged. "At any rate, some of
the French, like the Americans, have felt that men
should have no king at all. It is a great shame that Bonaparte seized power and made himself emperor. Now the
poor French are just exchanging one supreme power for
another."

She pondered his comments and glanced about her a little more. "And so they met here to talk about their government?"

He nodded. "And the talk was not all of bloodshed. Understandably, the people wanted a better life for themselves, and they wanted a voice in the government so that they could achieve it. That has not been a priority for their kings or for most of their nobility—or even for their clergy."

With the arrival of their group at the café where they were to dine, the conversation moved to other topics, and Lizzie found herself drawn into it, feeling comfortable with the easy give-and-take among the four of them. During a momentary lull, she leaned back in her chair and surveyed the other three and the busy café in which they sat.

"A penny for your thoughts, Miss Lancaster," said Mr. Thoreau, smiling at her abstracted expression. "You suddenly look very far away."

"Forgive me," she said smiling. "It simply occurred to me that a week ago I could not have imagined myself in such a place as this, enjoying myself completely with Lady Thalia and two gentlemen who were so recently total strangers to me."

"I am glad, of course, that you are enjoying yourself," returned Mr. Mansfield, "and, as for myself, a week ago I could not have imagined that I would be spending my first evening back in Paris with two such lovely ladies."

"Very gallant," said Lady Thalia approvingly.

He inclined his head to her slightly, smiling. Then, turning back to Lizzie, he added, "and I am gladder still that you no longer consider Mr. Thoreau and myself strangers. I trust that all three of you now count me among your friends."

There was a murmur of agreement from the other three, and the evening had ended on a very satisfactory note, with all of them, even Mr. Thoreau, agreeing that they would see one another at the reception at the British Embassy the next evening.

"Even though our countries are at war?" Lizzie had asked him, a little surprised.

"I shall be inconspicuous," he assured her. "I am attending as one of La Fayette's party. I am a guest in his home, and he has insisted that I attend with him."

After they had said good-night to the gentlemen at the hotel, it suddenly occurred to Lizzie that she had spent very little of the day thinking of Matthew and home. And that, she decided, was not such a bad thing at all.

Six

The next day Lady Thalia and Lizzie returned to the Palais-Royal, this time to investigate the shops. Lizzie protested when she realized that Lady Thalia was again engaged in making purchases for her, but she held up a warning finger to Lizzie and reminded her lightly that her companion was to be a credit to her. Giving way once more, Lizzie entered into the shopping expedition with pleasure. To her delight, she was soon the proud possessor of three pairs of slippers, two of kid leather and one of Denmark satin; several pairs of silk stockings; two fetching bonnets; a cashmere shawl; an embroidered silk reticule; a seal muff; and a pair of pearl combs for her hair.

When she prepared for their evening at the British Embassy, she donned a simple white crêpe evening gown, for none of the confections being created by Madame Delacroix would be ready until the following day. She clasped a string of pearls round her neck and, with the help of Beavers, arranged the new pearl combs in her dark curls. Lady Thalia had lent her a handsome sash of red satin that matched her new red slippers, and she slipped on a pair of new white evening gloves. Well satisfied with the effect, she added the final touch, a dark blue shawl trimmed with the red of the sash.

The reception that evening was a crowded affair, held

in the house on the Rue de Faubourg Saint-Honoré that the Duke of Wellington had selected as the site for the British Embassy, purchasing it and its contents. The Hôtel de Charost had belonged to Bonaparte's young sister, the lovely Princess Pauline Borghese, whose portrait, rumor said, still hung in the Duke's chamber.

"How awkward it must be for him," Lizzie murmured in a low voice to Mr. Thoreau, watching the Duke in the center of a crowd of people. Lady Thalia had already been led out to dance, and Lizzie and Mr. Thoreau were engaged in inspecting the crowd.

Immaculate in the white breeches, white stock, and scarlet coat of his field-marshal's uniform, complete with ribbons and orders, the impressive Peer welcomed his guests. The salon in which they stood was filled with a throng in evening dress, studded generously with other jewel-like military uniforms.

"You know that some of these people were his enemies just months ago, and now he must stand and make polite conversation with them," she continued.

"And undoubtedly some still are his enemies," he murmured in return, "but I understand that the Duke has little trouble dealing with them. I imagine that he will do very well as ambassador. And I am certain that he keeps in mind the fact that all of the French army still keep their tricolors safely at hand, even though they now wear the Bourbon white cockade on their shakos."

"Do you mean they are still loyal to Napoleon?" Lizzie asked, her eyes wide. "But he has been exiled to Elba."

"Very true. And we must hope that he decides to remain there."

"Is there any doubt?" she inquired anxiously. The specter of a Bonaparte returning to France conjured a nightmare for all who had feared him.

"He promised his friends that he would return with the violets—and it is said that his supporters refer to him now as Caporal Violet and use the violet as their emblem."

"So he promised that he would return next spring?" Lizzie asked, her eyes wide as she considered this possibility. "Do you think it could be so?"

Mr. Thoreau shrugged and smiled. "Napoleon promised many things—and he has always seen himself as larger than life—so I doubt that you should let the thought of springtime and violets keep you awake nights, Miss Lancaster. After all, the Duke is here to stop him should he decide to put in an appearance."

Mr. Mansfield joined them just then, and pointed out some of the more famous figures in the room—among them the Duchesse d'Angoulême, the beautiful wife of the King's younger brother; the formidable and very intelligent Madame de Staël; Charles Talleyrand-Périgord, that master of duplicity; the wicked Duke of Cumberland, fresh from England; and the Comte de Chateaubriand, an egotistical, dangerous writer and politician.

"How fascinating this all is," remarked Lizzie. "It seems amazing, sir, that you should know so many important people in this foreign capital."

"You must not give me too much credit, Miss Lancaster. All of Paris knows those that I have pointed out to you. They would scarcely recognize me."

"You are modest, sir," she said, smiling up at him. Then, hoping that her tone was suitably disinterested, she added, "I suppose, Mr. Mansfield, that you know all of the Duke's staff here in Paris as well?"

Mr. Mansfield looked mildly surprised. "Why, yes—at least I believe that I do unless he has had occasion to take on someone new in the past few weeks."

Lizzie colored slightly. "Then I suppose you must be acquainted with Matthew Webster."

"Webster? Why, yes—indeed I am. A capital fellow! Is he a friend of yours, Miss Lancaster?"

She nodded, choosing her words carefully and keeping her tone light. "Indeed he is! I have known him all my life. He and my brother George were companions from the time they were in leading-strings."

"I am afraid that you will have to wait until you reach Vienna to renew your friendship with Webster, Miss Lancaster," he said regretfully. "I learned today that the Duke has ordered him there for the duration of the Congress—to be his eyes, so to speak."

"Well, at least I shall see him there," she managed to say with credible carelessness. "You have given me something else to look forward to, Mr. Mansfield."

He appeared to be struck by a sudden thought and turned to look about the crowded room once more. "Webster may not be here, but there *is* someone that I can make known to you immediately. He is recently affianced to Miss Blackwell, and I am certain that she is present tonight."

"Oh, that is not necessary, Mr. Mansfield!" she protested with convincing earnestness. "I don't wish to inconvenience you."

"Nonsense! No inconvenience at all! I shall be most happy to do it, ma'am. Allow me just a moment to search her out."

Before Lizzie could stop him, he had hurried away in search of his quarry. She could feel her heart sinking to the soles of her slippers at the thought of meeting the young woman whom Matthew found so irresistible. Mr. Thoreau was studying her with a quizzical expression.

"Do you not wish to meet Miss Blackwell?"

When she did not answer directly, he added gently, "There is no need to do so if you do not wish it, Miss Lancaster."

Lizzie made no pretense of hiding her feelings. "But how can I avoid it? If he finds her, then I must meet her."

"Not if you are no longer here. I can make my excuses to La Fayette and escort you back to your hotel. If Lady Thalia is not ready to depart, I am certain she would not mind your leaving. I could hide you behind a potted palm while I make the arrangements, and we could disappear in an instant."

"You are very kind, sir," she said gratefully, managing a shaky smile for his plan, "but indeed I cannot be so rag-mannered as that. But I do thank you for offering to rescue me."

In a few minutes, Mr. Mansfield reappeared at her side. "I am afraid that I must disappoint you again, Miss Lancaster. It appears that Miss Blackwell has already departed."

Lizzie found that she could breathe again, and did her best to look disappointed. "That is unfortunate, but I thank you for your effort, Mr. Mansfield. I am certain that I will have the pleasure of meeting her at another time."

"Yes," he agreed, brightening. "Since you and Webster are old friends, it must be so—and you will be delighted with her, I assure you. She is a charming young woman, much admired by everyone. Her father is an officer in the 18th Hussars, and I believe that I have heard some refer to her as the sweetheart of the regiment."

"Yes, I am certain that she must be delightful. I shall look forward to meeting her." Lizzie was able to speak with greater conviction now that she knew that she did not have to face Miss Blackwell.

After a few minutes, Mr. Mansfield was called away once more, and she turned to Mr. Thoreau a little self-consciously.

"You must think me very odd," she said, not looking up to catch his eye. "I feel that I owe you an explanation."

"I do not think you odd at all—and you assuredly owe me no explanation. In fact, I forbid you to offer me one." Offering her his arm, he deftly steered her toward a table placed in a palm-filled alcove and pulled out a chair for her. "I am going for refreshments so that you may recover your strength, Miss Lancaster. I shall return immediately."

Relieved to be tucked away in this private place so that she could regain her composure, she leaned back in the chair and surveyed the glittering group before her. How very comfortable Mr. Thoreau was, she thought—and how very perceptive. Knowing that he truly expected no explanation made her feel that she would unquestionably give him one. Even though she had known him for so short a time, she was certain that she could safely confide in him.

So lost in her own thoughts was she that she did not realize she was no longer alone until she heard a deep voice, and saw a tall figure bend over her, taking her gloved hand and pressing it to his lips. A dark man, attired in white breeches and a military coat of green and yellow, bristling with medals and ribbons, was speaking to her very attentively.

"Ah, mademoiselle, one so lovely as you should never be left alone. Allow me to present myself—Capitaine François LaSalle at your service, lovely lady. I implore you to allow me to join you here."

"And we would be delighted to have you join us, Capitaine. We shall only have to find another chair." Mr.

Thoreau had arrived, carefully balancing a plate of fruit for Lizzie and two glasses of champagne.

Chagrined, Captain LaSalle bowed to the newcomer. "Forgive me. I did not realize that I was intruding upon a *tête-à-tête.* I shall, of course, remove myself immediately—but most regretfully."

He turned to Lizzie, again taking her hand and pressing it to his lips. "Allow me to express my deep gratitude, mademoiselle, for wearing the colors that honor the flag for which I fought."

He bowed deeply once more to Lizzie, his dark eyes lingering upon her, and then turned back to the crowded salon.

"Well, well, Miss Lancaster," murmured Mr. Thoreau appreciatively. "A conquest! I turn my back for only a few moments and you have snared a prize from the French Dragoons."

"What nonsense!" said Lizzie, flushing, but mildly gratified. She had been grateful for Thoreau's appearance, for the French officer had been so imposing in appearance and so intense in manner that she had been quite overcome. "You could see that he is a practiced flirt, and I merely happened to fall into his path."

"I do not believe that for a moment," he said, smiling. "You are quite out of the way over here. I believe the captain was merely biding his time until you were alone."

"But what did he mean about my wearing the colors for which he fought?" she asked, eager to change the subject. As soon as she had said this, however, the truth dawned upon her and she clapped her hand over her mouth. "But he is correct! I *am* wearing the colors of the flag of the Revolution! The French flag is once more the fleur-de-lis."

Thoreau nodded. "Of course, I choose to think that you

are wearing the colors to honor *my* country, but I understand that the captain might not see it in that light."

"Splendid! One country we have been at war with, and the other we are at war with still! I was not thinking of that at all when I dressed for the evening! I wonder that Lady Thalia did not think of it."

"I doubt that it would occur to anyone other than those obsessed by such patriotic notions. As I told you, the French soldiers may wear the white cockade now, but they have saved their tricolors."

"What a goose I was! I shall be careful not to wear this color combination again."

"Nonsense! You look charming, Miss Lancaster. Merely pass off such remarks with a smile and a pretty shrug of your shoulders, and everyone will be satisfied. No one will charge you with disloyalty."

He watched her for a moment, the laugh lines around his eyes deepening. "Of course, there is one other option I have not mentioned—and this would not be nearly so gratifying to either the captain or me—you *could* be wearing the colors of your own country."

Lizzie stared at him for a moment, then started to laugh. "You must think me the most complete goose! I did not even think of my own flag."

"Miss Lancaster, I think you the most completely charming young woman I have met in some time."

"At least the most nonsensical one," she amended, still laughing.

They sipped their champagne in companionable silence for a few moments, watching the shifting kaleidoscope of the crowd.

"He was a member of the Dragoons, you said," she ventured at last. "It is possible, I suppose, that he fought in the Peninsula."

Thoreau nodded. "It is very likely." He watched her for a moment. "Have you a particular interest in that portion of the war?"

Lizzie was silent for a moment, then nodded without meeting his eyes. "A most—a most particular friend of mine fought there."

"Mr. Matthew Webster?"

Another minute or two passed as they watched the crowd, then she nodded, still looking straight ahead as she spoke.

"Matthew and I were not formally affianced, but we had an understanding that when he returned, we would be married. He has been gone now for well over two years. Just a fortnight ago, I received a letter from him that told me of his engagement to Miss Blackwell."

Mr. Thoreau remained silent, but he continued to regard her with a steady gaze. She could feel his eyes upon her and finally felt pressed to say something more.

"I know that I am foolish to think that seeing him again will make any difference. I daresay I shall only feel worse and appear ridiculous to everyone."

Mr. Thoreau seemed to be thinking the matter over, and she waited for his response. It should not be so, she knew, but she felt somewhat lighter in spirit after telling him about Matthew, and the lightness was not due to the champagne she was sipping.

"No, I don't think that you are being foolish. As a matter of fact, I think that you are quite courageous in going to face your fear."

She shook her head ruefully. "You notice that I did not wish to meet Miss Blackwell. I don't think that is an example of my being able to face my fear."

"Ah, but she is not the one you must face. It is Matthew Webster."

She straightened her shoulders and sat a little taller as she thought about his words. It was quite possible that he was right. She had been focusing her fears upon the young lady, but it was not, in truth, Miss Blackwell who was the source of the problem. It was Matthew. Had he truly loved her, he would not have put her by for some other woman, no matter how lovely. The decision had been Matthew's.

It was well that she had had the opportunity to think the matter through, for the crowd in front of them parted, and Mr. Mansfield appeared once more.

"Ah, Miss Lancaster! I knew that I should find you if I kept searching." With a theatrical flourish, he added, "And I would like to present to you Miss Blackwell, the fiancée of your good friend Matthew Webster."

And he stepped aside to reveal a dainty young woman in a filmy blue gown, its fabric too gauze-like to conceal any of the charms of her figure. Her pale curls shone in the candlelight, framing a perfectly heart-shaped face.

Both Lizzie and Mr. Thoreau rose automatically from their chairs, and the ladies dropped a curtsey to one another, then Mr. Thoreau was duly introduced and made his bow.

"But how delightful to meet a friend of Matthew's from home," said Miss Blackwell, two deep dimples showing in her creamy cheeks. She spoke to Lizzie, but her eyes were fixed upon Mr. Thoreau.

Lizzie's heart sank. Her nemesis was undeniably alluring. The Sirens of Ulysses could not have been more inviting. She could see that Mr. Mansfield was hanging on her every word, and she had no doubt that Mr. Thoreau would respond in much the same manner. There were some women, she knew, who appeared to have a fatal attraction for men. Matthew would have been helpless before her, and Lizzie wanted to do nothing so much as to turn and run from the room. Nonetheless, she caught herself in time and stemmed the rising tide of desperation. It was all over in a moment. She steeled herself, then gently returned the smile.

"You are very kind, Miss Blackwell. I understand that I am to wish you happy."

Miss Blackwell inclined her head demurely, dark lashes sweeping her cheek as she glanced up sidewise at Mr. Mansfield, who responded quickly.

"I must tell you that Webster has broken half the hearts in Paris with this engagement." He did not seem to be able to remove his gaze from Miss Blackwell, who smiled at him sweetly, then tapped his shoulder with her fan.

"Only half the hearts?" she quizzed him.

"Allow me to correct myself," he amended quickly. "Webster has broken the hearts of *all* the men in Paris."

"Ah, much better," she said, turning a roguish gaze upon Mr. Thoreau. "I believe that I see one gentleman whose heart has not broken, however."

Mr. Thoreau bowed. "You must forgive me, Miss Blackwell. I have been told upon the best authority that I have a heart that is impervious to romance, so you must not let the matter trouble you."

"Indeed?" she murmured. "Perhaps, Mr. Thoreau, you simply have not been in Paris long enough."

"Nor will I be. Soon I shall be safely in Vienna, with no need to guard my heart."

Miss Blackwell's lower lip protruded in a pretty pout that clearly enchanted Mr. Mansfield. "Everyone seems to be leaving for Vienna, and Paris will become deadly dull. Perhaps I shall have to go to Vienna as well."

"How wonderful that would be! Do you really plan to do so?" Mr. Mansfield's face was alight at the notion.

Miss Blackwell glanced up at Mr. Thoreau through her lashes. "If everyone felt as you do, I would feel that I *must* go. I could not bring myself to disappoint so many."

"I am certain that Mr. Webster would be delighted to see you there, ma'am," observed Mr. Thoreau, "and that must be all in all to you."

Her pretty mouth drooped slightly at this reminder of her fiancé, but she caught herself and, once again displaying her enchanting dimples, tapped his wrist with her fan. "How very good you are, dear sir, to remind me of my obligations. Perhaps I shall come to Vienna so that you may counsel me."

If she had hoped for a flirtatious rejoinder, she was disappointed, and Mr. Thoreau was saved from further attack by the arrival of several of Miss Blackwell's admirers. Under cover of the ensuing confusion, Lizzie and Mr. Thoreau made their escape.

He looked down at her, the trace of a smile in his eyes. "Miss Lancaster, I may well have been incorrect in saying that you must face only Matthew Webster. Miss Blackwell is more formidable than I had imagined. Nonetheless, now you have at least faced one of your dragons."

"Yes," Lizzie sighed, "but not slain her, I fear— although the notion holds a certain appeal."

He laughed and patted her hand. "Never mind, Miss Lancaster. Tomorrow is another day. Promise me a little time in the afternoon, and I shall show you something to take your mind from your troubles."

"Gladly," she responded gratefully. "What will you show me?"

"It will be a surprise—a most agreeable one," he assured her.

Before she and Lady Thalia departed that evening, Mr. Thoreau had received permission to call for Lizzie the next afternoon for a Parisian expedition. He had taken Lady Thalia by surprise with his invitation, but she had, after a moment of thought, agreed.

"I cannot spare Beavers, but my footman can accompany you," she had replied, nodding in Henry's direction.

"What will you do in the morning, Miss Lancaster?" he asked, as Henry was closing the door of their carriage after the ladies.

"I believe that I shall purchase a fan," said Lizzie, looking at him thoughtfully.

Her sally was rewarded by his sudden shout of laughter, which followed them as the carriage pulled away. Lizzie leaned back against the leather squabs of the carriage, pleased with herself.

Mr. Thoreau, still laughing, strolled away from the line of carriages. He was looking forward with considerable pleasure to spending the afternoon with Miss Lancaster. What a fool that young Webster must be, he thought, turning his steps toward the salon once more.

Seven

Lizzie did not allow herself to linger over thoughts of Miss Blackwell and Matthew when they returned to the hotel. Grateful that the day had tired her, she fell swiftly to sleep. The next day dawned bright and, to her surprise, she was in far better spirits than she had expected to be. Despite the lingering memory of Miss Blackwell enslaving virtually all the males that came within her range, she recalled with pleasure the fact that Mr. Thoreau had not fallen prey to her charm. Instead, he had appeared amused by the charade.

She was looking forward to trying on the gowns that Madame Delacroix had completed, and Lady Thalia had decreed that more shopping was in order after that, followed by a carriage ride to Notre-Dame. In the evening they were to attend a ball given by the Marquis of Belgrave at the Hôtel de Crillon on the Place de la Concorde. Most of all, however, she found that she was looking forward to her late afternoon outing with Mr. Thoreau. Lady Thalia seemed to be reading her mind.

"Mr. Thoreau is being *most* attentive to you, Lizzie," that lady observed idly, as they rode to the Delacroix salon. "If I did not know better, I would think that he is forming an attachment for you."

Lizzie experienced a slight sinking feeling at Lady

Thalia's words, but she spoke lightly. "And why should he not?" she inquired.

Lady Thalia looked at her with raised brows. "In part, because you are in love with Matthew and don't care a fig for Mr. Thoreau."

"You say that is in part. What are your other reasons for thinking that he will not form an attachment to me?" Lizzie was careful to speak casually, as though the whole matter was of no consequence to her—which, of course, it was not, she assured herself.

"Unlike us," Lady Thalia replied, "Americans are very direct in their manner. Although that lends them—or lends at least *some* of them—a certain charm, it does mean that they often say more personal things than we might say under similar conditions—but they mean very little by such intimacy. It is simply their manner."

Lizzie thought this over. "So you mean that I might misinterpret what Mr. Thoreau says to me because his manner is informal?"

Lady Thalia nodded, pleased that she had made herself clear. "Exactly so."

Lizzie shook her head. "I don't think that is the case, Lady Thalia, but I will think about it and be on my guard."

Lady Thalia was forced to be satisfied with that. She was pleased that Lizzie had not sunk into a deep melancholy over Matthew's defection, but she was not anxious to see her charge's affections quickly transferred to an unknown young American, no matter how charming.

Hoping to divert Lizzie's thoughts, she said, "Now *do* tell me what you meant by wanting to purchase a fan, my dear. Whatever made you wish for one?"

To her surprise, Lizzie began to laugh. "I had not realized until last night that fans could be used as tools of conquest."

"How *very* intriguing, Lizzie!" Lady Thalia's eyes brightened at this promise of entertainment. "Who did you see using one so effectively? Recount the scene for me precisely. Do not omit a single detail."

Lizzie gave her a vivid account of Miss Blackwell's performance, not missing the flutter of one eyelash, one sidelong glance, or one arch tap with a fan.

"You are quite in the right of it," Lady Thalia agreed, laughing when Lizzie had finished her tale. "You must by *all* means have a fan and learn to use it to advantage. We shall see to it directly."

Although fans were still used by ladies of the *ton*, their use was by no means as prevalent as it had been before the arrival of the simple, columnar gowns on the fashion scene. The old fashioned-gowns with voluminous skirts very effectively hid numerous pockets so that a lady could keep her hands free, while still carrying everything she needed upon her person. Modern gowns, however, offered few prospects for pockets, so ladies had begun carrying reticules to hold their personal effects. Thus fans had become one more item to carry and were not so likely to be included.

When they arrived at the Delacroix Salon, Lizzie tried on the gowns that were ready, Lady Thalia approved them, and Madame Delacroix boxed the dresses and sent them to the hotel. With that business taken care of, she and Lady Thalia set about their shopping. Aside from some ostrich plumes dyed a lovely shade of gold that would match one of her evening gowns, Lizzie's most delightful purchase was a trio of fans—a gauze fan ornamented with spangles and two brisé fans, one of tortoise shell and one of ivory, pierced so delicately that it looked like lacework.

"*Very* nice," said Lady Thalia approvingly. "Now you must practice using them."

"Practice? Do you think that is necessary?" asked Lizzie, surprised. Using a fan seemed simple enough to her.

"Of course! You must be graceful in your movements. Lead with your wrist." Picking up the tortoise shell fan, she demonstrated. "*Always* with the wrist. Your gestures must be artful so that you do not look as though you are about to jab the gentleman with the fan."

"Which in some cases might be a very good idea," Lizzie replied—but she took up the ivory fan and began to practice.

"And you must remember, Lizzie, not to behave coyly with your fan. Flirting—capturing a man's attention—with one is fine, but do not be too coquettish or you will lose the fan's effect."

Lizzie looked doubtful. "It seemed to me that Miss Blackwell was certainly being coquettish, but Mr. Mansfield seemed to find it most appealing." And that, she thought, was a case of understatement. Mr. Mansfield had been enchanted by Miss Blackwell and her annoying fan.

"You may count upon it that he was already infatuated *before* he encountered the fan," Lady Thalia said in a very positive tone. "Gentlemen do not care for young ladies who act too precious."

Remembering Miss Blackwell, Lizzie was far less certain, but she did not argue. Instead, she enjoyed practicing during the whole of their carriage ride to Notre-Dame, although she did relinquish it when they left the chaise. She decided that she would not carry a fan on her afternoon expedition with Mr. Thoreau. It would be more enjoyable showing him her new acquisition in the proper setting, where she felt certain he would appreciate its effect—and enjoy the reason she was carrying it. Since he was a guest in the home of La

Fayette, who had also been invited to the ball, she knew that she could count on seeing him that night.

When she and Lady Thalia arrived back at the hotel, Mr. Thoreau was waiting for her. Lizzie apologized hastily for her tardiness and hurried to her chamber to set herself to rights before going out with him. On her dressing table was a handsome bouquet of red and white roses, wrapped with a broad blue ribbon. The card was lying beside it, and it was, as she immediately suspected it would be, signed in the bold, black scrawl of Captain LaSalle, pledging his undying faithfulness and promising to call upon her the next day.

Lady Thalia opened the door between their chambers and gasped at the roses. "But they're *wonderful*, Lizzie! Who sent them to you?"

Lizzie told her about her encounter with LaSalle at the reception, and she was both amused and pleased. Her charge might have been jilted, but it was satisfying to know that she was not likely to waste away and die of a broken heart.

"A captain in the Dragoons! I must say, Lizzie, that you are doing *very* well! I am *most* impressed!"

"I wish you would not joke so about it, Lady Thalia. His attentions make me very uncomfortable."

"But why should they? *Every* young woman should have admirers, Matthew or no Matthew. You must remember that *he* has Miss Blackwell, so you must enjoy yourself, just as he is doing."

Lizzie nodded slowly. "That does sound fair," she agreed, "but it does not seem natural to me."

"It will," Lady Thalia assured her. "After all, why should Matthew be the only one to enjoy himself? *You* deserve to have some pleasure, too. Besides," she added sagely, "a young man, even Matthew, is *much* more likely to regret the loss of a young woman who is admired and full of life than he is one who is dying of love for him."

Having hastily splashed water on her face, straightened her bonnet and her sash, and applied a little of Lady Thalia's devastating perfume, Lizzie went down to join Mr. Thoreau. As they strolled out together, with Henry following at a discreet distance as chaperon, he looked down at her and smiled.

"You are looking very well today, Miss Lancaster," he informed her.

"Thank you, Mr. Thoreau. You are kind to say so," she replied demurely, tripping lightly along beside him. She paused a moment, thinking, then went on. "I realize that it is not discreet nor ladylike of me to tell you this, sir, but I know you will appreciate it."

"I am fully prepared to appreciate whatever it may be," he returned, straightening his shoulders, as though in preparation.

"I received a bouquet of roses—red and white—tied with a dark blue ribbon!" She looked up at him and waited expectantly.

"The captain of the Dragoons!" he exclaimed. "I told you that you had made a conquest, Miss Lancaster, but you would not believe me!"

She colored. "It was kind of him to send such lovely flowers, but I knew that you would appreciate the joke. I hope that you do not think it immodest of me to tell you." She would, she thought, have preferred that he not be quite so enthusiastic about her acquisition of an admirer.

"Not at all," he said comfortably. "I am delighted that he brightened your day. I daresay that I should have sent you a nosegay myself, but I am afraid that I do not usually think to do such gallant things. While your captain was ordering your roses, I was in the gardens at the Palais-Royal."

At her look of surprise, he added, "You can rent a morning chair there and read the newspaper."

"Ah, the newspaper." Lizzie nodded. "I have noticed how eager you are to keep abreast of the latest news."

His pleasant expression grew grim, and she looked at him curiously. "Was there something in the newspaper that upset you?"

"It appears that the British set fire to Washington," he said grimly.

"Your capital?" she gasped. "How terrible! Did the fire do great damage?"

"The capitol building and The White House—that is great damage." He looked down at her and made a visible attempt to lighten his expression. "However, in all fairness, I must say that the British are not the only ones to resort to burning. Both armies have done their share."

It seemed very peculiar, Lizzie thought, that they were talking together like this when their countries were at war. They walked on in silence, leaving the unhappy topic alone. Eventually, she became quite confused by the tangle of narrow medieval streets down which they had wandered.

"Where are we going?" she inquired, looking about her curiously.

"You will see in just a moment," he said, "and I believe you will think it well worth the walk."

They walked on silently for a few minutes more, and then they suddenly emerged from the warren of narrow dark streets into a space filled with the golden light of the late afternoon sun. It was the Place du Carrousel. Before them lay the Tuileries and the Arch of Napoleon, crowned by the bronze horses taken from St. Mark's in Venice. Everything they saw had been turned to gold by the light of the setting sun.

Finally Lizzie spoke. "I could say that it is lovely, but that simply does not do justice to this. I do not have the words."

They stood there gazing at the scene before them for a few minutes more, and then Mr. Thoreau led her to a small café on the sidewalk, where they ordered coffee and continued to look about them.

"This is the oddest city," said Lizzie finally. "Parts of it are so old and dark and dirty, and then there are the boulevards and parks—and now this."

Mr. Thoreau nodded. "Voltaire said that Paris—like the statue of Nebuchadnezzar—was built of mud and of gold."

"Well, I know nothing about Nebuchadnezzar's statue," she replied, "but I can quite see his point about Paris."

As twilight began to fall, the pair roused themselves from the reverie into which they had fallen.

"I must get you back to your hotel. After all, Miss Lancaster," her companion observed, tactfully avoiding any reference to Miss Blackwell, "you must array yourself in all your splendor tonight. It is always possible that your captain might appear."

"You overwhelm me. Perhaps I should wear one of his roses." She watched from the corner of her eye to see how he received this sally, but to her disappointment, he merely smiled.

When they said good-bye at the hotel, Lizzie held out her hand to him. "Thank you, Mr. Thoreau. This afternoon was a gift I shall treasure always—quite the nicest that I have ever received." Until recent days, the music box that Matthew had given her, now packed away in her trunk, would have held the place of honor.

"It has been entirely my pleasure, Miss Lancaster," he told her, holding her hand a little longer than necessary. "I can think of no one else with whom I would have cared to share it."

Lizzie was humming as she prepared for the ball. The gown was one of the confections prepared by Madame Delacroix, a sea-green silk edged thickly in white lace. Once again Beavers helped her put up her dark hair with the pearl combs, and before she left, she slipped the ivory fan into her reticule. She would practice upon the gentlemen tonight, and she looked forward to the laughter she expected to see in the blue eyes of Mr. Thoreau when she delicately tapped him with her fan.

She saw Mr. Mansfield first, and, to her pleasure, he led her out for Weber's "Invitation to the Waltz," the number which began the ball. Lady Thalia had insisted that she learn how to waltz, and Lizzie had been delighted with the graceful movements of the dance. When Mr. Mansfield escorted her back to Lady Thalia's side, Lizzie was gratified to find that her dance card filled almost at once. A handsome young lieutenant in the British Lancers was her partner for a quadrille, and the evening seemed to slip by so easily that she scarcely noticed it. The ivory fan frequently came into play, sometimes as a fan and sometimes—as she had seen Miss Blackwell use it—as a flirtatious device so that she could lean closer to a gentleman. She was amazed to discover how much she was enjoying herself, and how completely self-possessed she felt—not at all nervous or shy.

Mr. Thoreau had engaged her for a waltz and for supper, and as he led her onto the floor, he said, eyes crinkling in amusement, "I believe, Miss Lancaster, that you indeed have a fan."

Lizzie whipped it to attention. "Very true, Mr. Thoreau. And, if you will notice, dear sir, the management of the fan is all in the wrist." Here she demonstrated, first fluttering the fan before her face and then tapping him winsomely with it.

"I am overcome by your expertise," he confessed, sweeping her into the dance. "And I fear for the many hearts you will break with that fan."

"Do you think I could do so?" she demanded, cheered by the thought.

"Assuredly. Your conquests will be many."

"But you will not be one of them?" she inquired, eyes bright.

"Not because of the fan," he said, holding her securely as they moved lightly around the floor.

When the dance was over, he led her to a table where they would be having supper together. Settling her comfortably, he excused himself to retrieve their refreshments. All too soon, Captain LaSalle appeared at her side.

"Dear mademoiselle, did you receive my tribute?" he asked, bending low over her hand once more.

She smiled up at him. "They were beautiful, Captain. You were very kind to send them to me."

"They could not come close to your beauty, Mademoiselle Lancaster, but they were the best that my poor efforts could manage today."

"Why, Captain LaSalle, you have come to join us once more," said Mr. Thoreau, drawing close. "We seem to meet like this with somewhat painful regularity."

LaSalle bowed to him. "And once again I must proffer my apology for intruding upon a private supper." Turning back to Lizzie, he said, "I shall do myself the honor of calling upon you tomorrow at your hotel, mademoiselle. I hope that I shall find you in."

"I hope that I am there when you call, Captain," she said. "However, since tomorrow will be our last day in Paris, I am not certain what Lady Thalia's plans are for the day."

"You are leaving Paris so soon? I am devastated, Miss

Lancaster! Can I not persuade you to stay longer? Paris has so many delights that I am certain you have not yet enjoyed."

"I am certain that Paris has much to offer that I haven't yet seen, sir, but Lady Thalia and I have plans to travel to Vienna. I must not slow her."

He bent his head as though in acceptance. "Very well, Mademoiselle Lancaster. If it must be so, then it must. However, should you return to Paris, I beg that you will allow me to show you my city."

"I shall look forward to that," said Lizzie, plying her fan gently and looking up at him over its lacy edge.

After Captain LaSalle had bowed himself away, Mr. Thoreau turned to Lizzie, his eyebrows high.

"And what were you doing with that fan, Miss Lancaster?" he asked. "Were you flirting with our Captain of the Dragoons?"

"Only slightly, Mr. Thoreau," she responded. "I needed to practice, you see."

Before he could comment, Miss Blackwell and Mr. Mansfield appeared beside their table.

"Miss Lancaster, how delightful you look," said Mansfield, bowing low. "I am looking forward to our dance together."

Lizzie smiled at him automatically, but she could not respond to him because her attention was focused on Miss Blackwell. Around that lady's throat was a gold chain with the medal of St. George that she had given to Matthew.

"Miss Blackwell," she said, her voice sounding strained even to herself. "What a charming medallion."

"Is it not attractive?" she agreed. "It was Matthew's, but he *insisted* upon giving it to me." She lifted the medal with one finger so that she could see it and admire it. "It is not suitable with this gown, I know, but the dear boy was so anxious that I wear it. He begged me to think of him whenever I have it on." She looked at Lizzie and smiled. "But then, that isn't really necessary because I think of him all of the time."

"How commendable," replied Lizzie stiffly. "I am certain that he is grateful."

Miss Blackwell smiled at her again, then turned the full warmth of her charm upon Mr. Thoreau. "Perhaps, Mr. Thoreau, you might be able to call upon me tomorrow and tell me a little about America. I have always been so fascinated by your country."

"Delightful though that sounds, Miss Blackwell, I will be leaving Paris early tomorrow, so I fear your curiosity about America will have to wait for another time to be satisfied."

Miss Blackwell leaned closer to him and tapped his hand with her fan. "I shall look forward to that time, sir," she said, looking up at him through her lashes before Mr. Mansfield led her away.

Mr. Thoreau glanced at Lizzie, his eyes bright, to enjoy with her the matter of Miss Blackwell's fan, but he could not draw an answering smile from her. Lizzie found that she was so upset that she could not even enjoy Miss Blackwell's byplay with the fan. Instead, she focused on Mr. Thoreau's departure.

"You leave tomorrow?" she asked, her voice flat. "You had not mentioned it to me."

"No, although I was planning to do so," he assured her. "I shall see you very soon in Vienna. I will be going first back to Ghent, then I will be traveling to Vienna."

"But that will take quite a long time!" she protested.

"It will go quickly," he assured her. "You will have many new things to see there—and you will, of course, see Matthew."

When she did not answer, he looked at her gravely, then patted her hand comfortingly. "You will be able to face him, Miss Lancaster," he said in a reassuring voice.

Lizzie was not comforted, however, and the days ahead suddenly looked bleaker than they had. She said a sad good-bye to Mr. Thoreau that night, and when she returned to the hotel, she discovered that she could not sleep.

All she could see was the gold medal of St. George that she had given Matthew as protection, her parting gift to him, around Teresa Blackwell's neck. He had given it away.

And she would not be able to laugh with Mr. Thoreau for an unknown number of days.

Eight

Lady Thalia groaned with pleasure as she sank into the warm bath that Beavers had prepared for her. A hip bath had also been filled for Lizzie in her chamber.

"Every bone in my body has been jarred loose by that infamous journey, Beavers! How could Timothy Holywell *dare* to tell me that coming to Vienna would be no different from a journey from the Scottish highlands to Brighton? I thought that sounded grim enough, but it doesn't even bear comparison! Not only did this trip take *eons* longer, but I *can* not believe that the lowest wayside inn found anywhere in Britain could be as bugridden and noisome as the one where we stopped in Württemberg! The first two stops were dreadful, but that one was *unspeakable*!"

At that inn, the innkeeper and his wife, as well as the chambers themselves, were clearly unwashed. Bedbugs had crawled freely among the dingy bedcovers, and the entire place had smelled of boiled cabbage and unemptied chamber pots. Lady Thalia had taken one look at the place and marched her entire party back to the carriage despite the fact that the hour was late and no other accommodation was available.

"I prefer that we starve and go sleepless," she had told the others firmly. Although Lizzie, Beavers, and Henry

were not inclined to argue, being quite as disgusted as
Lady Thalia, the driver and postilions, being hungry and
less nice in their tastes, had grumbled. She had allowed
them to purchase their own dinner there before driving
on, but Lady Thalia's party went hungry that night, except for some fruit and a handful of Mrs. Clary's cookies
still kept fresh in a tin. Lizzie had divided those equally
among the four of them.

After that horrifying experience, Lady Thalia had decided that for the duration of the journey they would
sleep in the carriage and stop only to eat, to change
horses, or to stretch their legs. Beavers and Henry were
dispatched to the best-kept farmhouses they passed to
purchase food so that they would not have to depend
upon finding an inn or café with a decent kitchen.

Munich, at least, had been respectable—which was
just as well, for they had broken an axle there and been
forced to leave the carriage while it underwent three
days of repairs. She had been forced to admit that
Bavaria was really quite charming and she had discovered that she had a regrettable fondness for *strudel.*

After a fortnight of travel, they were all heartily weary
of picnic meals and the confines of the carriage. Fortunately, though, the weather had been fine and they had
encountered only one storm. Poor Henry, riding outside
with the coachman and postilions, had borne the brunt
of the bad weather. It had been with the deepest of gratitude that they had at last seen Vienna in the distance.

"I wouldn't be too put out with Mr. Holywell, ma'am,"
observed Beavers pacifically, handing her mistress a bar
of the scented soap that she preferred and that Beavers
had carefully packed in quantity. "After all, it has been
a good many years since he last made this journey. I
daresay he has forgotten just how hard a trip it can be."

Lady Thalia was unmoved. Timothy Holywell, some twenty years her senior and possessed of a wicked humor, was also one of her dearest friends. She was more than certain that he had willfully misled her.

"I should imagine that he is sitting at his comfortable fireside, chuckling to himself every time he thinks about us trundling along that miserable road! If I had the wretch here, he would pay *dearly* for that lapse in memory! As it is, I shall have to wait for months to avenge myself and must be content to playact the scene in my mind! I had *never* imagined traveling through such a dark, depressing countryside! Even the villages put me in mind of witches, and no doubt they were there, lurking inside those dim little houses, stirring their evil brew!"

She smiled suddenly as she lathered the soap across her shoulders, her mood brightening as she remembered that their situation was now quite different. "At least this hotel appears to be well run, and Vienna seems a pretty enough place. Don't you agree, Beavers?"

"Indeed I do, ma'am." Pleased with the shift in mood, Beavers was determined to encourage it. "There was so much green as we rode into town that I wasn't certain that we had really arrived in a city. It seemed more like we were driving through a great park."

Lady Thalia nodded in agreement, her irritation fading completely as she soaked in the warm, perfumed water and thought about the final part of their journey.

Seeing Vienna in the distance had been an agreeable experience for all of them, not just because they had almost reached their destination, but also because it presented such a pleasant prospect. They had driven up to the tollgate at the Linienwall, an outer wall of the city that once protected the suburbs of Vienna from the Turks more than one hundred years ago. Then they had made their way through the suburbs and across the Glacis, through vast green meadows with tree-lined alleys, to the Bastei, the old wall that surrounded the city itself and upon which the sociable Viennese strolled to look out upon nature. Inside the Bastei they had found a cheerful, bustling city, a highly ornamented tribute to the baroque era.

Lady Thalia had been most fortunate in her living arrangements, for Lord Danvers, a good friend of hers, had reserved three floors of a hotel close to the Hofburg, the vast home of Emperor Francis and the center of activity for the Congress. When Lord Danvers had heard that she too planned to travel to Vienna, he had insisted that she take one of the floors that he had reserved.

"For, my dear Thalia," he had told her, "you will find no other place at this late date, and you must not be left to the mercy of innkeepers."

Remembering his words now—and her experience with the dark little inn along the way—she shuddered, then opened her eyes and looked about her gratefully. A fire crackled below the marble mantelpiece, red velvet curtains heavily crusted with gold lace were closed against the autumn night, a gilt mirror upon her dressing table reflected the glow of firelight and candlelight, thick rugs covered the floor, and the bedcovers were turned back to reveal fresh, crisp linen. Their rooms were delightfully luxurious, and she felt that this augured well for their stay in Vienna.

"How was Lizzie when you left her, Beavers?" she asked. "She had gotten so *very* quiet as we grew near to the city that I thought she might have had the headache."

"I daresay she was just bone-weary, ma'am," replied Beavers. "She was about to take her bath, too, and when

I told her that you had ordered supper, she said that she would eat it if she were still awake."

"Once she smells the food, she will be able to eat. I should imagine that we have all lost weight during the past fourteen days, in spite of all the *strudel* I consumed. Lizzie ate very little, even in Munich. I shall go in to be certain that she dines with me tonight, for I don't want her gowns to hang upon her."

After wrapping herself in a warm red dressing gown, Lady Thalia sent Beavers off to her own chamber to bathe and prepare for supper. Henry had gone downstairs to order their meal and to supervise its delivery to their drawing room, where a table had been set by the fire. Lord Danvers had provided for them very well indeed, she thought, setting forth to shepherd Lizzie to the drawing room for supper.

Lizzie looked freshly scrubbed, but Lady Thalia noticed at once that her expression was nonetheless unhappy.

"What is wrong, my dear? I *told* Beavers that you did not look well, and she said that you were doubtless just bone-weary."

"Oh, indeed I am," she replied, grateful for Beavers. She had no desire to tell Lady Thalia about the medal of St. George nor to admit to her that she found herself missing the security that Mr. Thoreau's presence had offered her. "All that I care to do is to go to bed immediately."

"And so you shall—just as soon as you have had something to eat," said Lady Thalia firmly. "I can *not* allow you to go to bed when you have had so little real nourishment in the last three days. I have not seen you eat more than an apple and a few bites of bread in that time."

Lizzie shrugged. "I had no appetite."

"Well, you will in just a moment. Henry is setting out

our food in the drawing room now, so come along with me. As soon as you have dined, you may retire to bed and sleep for *just* as long as you wish."

Seeing that she had no choice, Lizzie allowed herself to be led down the passage, which was thickly carpeted like the rest of the rooms. However, as they neared the entry to the drawing room, the fragrance of well-cooked food greeted them. To her own surprise, Lizzie worked her way briskly through a bowl of nourishing beef soup, thick with vegetables in a dark brown broth, and then moved on to *Wiener schnitzel*—veal scallops breaded and fried to a golden brown—mashed potatoes, and beet salad. The meal was rounded out with cups of strong black coffee and *Bublanina*, a sponge cake topped with sweet dark cherries.

"That was delicious," sighed Lizzie. "I did not think that I wanted a bite to eat, but I have left nothing at all on my plate."

"Of course you haven't," said Lady Thalia, surveying her charge with satisfaction. "You have been *starving* for days without even noticing it."

Reaching to a silver salver placed on the table behind her, she picked up three letters, two addressed to her and one to Lizzie. "And now that we have fortified ourselves, we may read the messages that have been left for us." And she handed Lizzie her letter.

Lizzie turned it over and stared at it, puzzled. "Who would be sending me a letter? It is not from my parents, and no one else knows where to find me."

"Well, open it and find out, my dear."

Lady Thalia opened her first letter. "How *very* considerate! It is from Mr. Mansfield. He says that he is looking forward to our arrival. Such *pretty* manners in a young man!"

"Yes, he is very pleasant," agreed Lizzie absently, her letter still in her lap.

Lady Thalia smiled as she broke the wafer on her second letter and read the few lines scribbled on the heavy paper. "Danvers says that he is *delighted* that we have arrived at last, and that we should plan to attend a ball tomorrow night at the Redoutensaal. Everyone will be there and he has invitations for us." She folded the note. "Such a *dear* man! We will have a splendid time, Lizzie."

Lizzie was staring at her. "Everyone will be at the ball?" She hesitated a moment, then added, "Do you suppose, then, that Matthew will be there?"

"He might well be," said Lady Thalia briskly. "And if he is, that is a *good* thing, is it not? You want to see him, and what better place than a ball?"

"Yes, I suppose so," replied Lizzie slowly. "I just hadn't thought that I would see him quite so soon."

"Soon? You have waited *weeks* for this, and we have been preparing you for *just* this moment, Lizzie. You will look splendid, and Matthew will regret that he ever considered *glancing* at Miss Blackwell!"

Lizzie smiled. "I wish that it would be so simple."

"Who knows how it will be? There is no way of telling until you see him again." Lady Thalia looked at the letter lying in Lizzie's lap. "Aren't you going to open *your* note?"

Lizzie broke the seal and, as she saw the signature on the note, her expression grew bright. "It is from Mr. Thoreau!" she exclaimed. "I had thought that he would not be here for at least another week, but he writes that he was able to take care of his business much more quickly than he had planned and that he made excellent time on his journey to Vienna. He arrived here last night."

"Did he indeed?" remarked Lady Thalia dryly. "How *fortunate* he was not to have been traveling with us."

She studied Lizzie's face for a moment, then added, "*You* seem very happy to hear from our American friend."

"Of course I am! He has been a good friend to me, and he writes here that he will call at the hotel each morning until we arrive. He would like to be present to support me when I meet Matthew. How very kind he is!"

"Yes, quite extraordinarily kind," remarked Lady Thalia more dryly still. "I did not realize that *he* knew about Matthew—*nor* that the two of you had grown so close."

Lizzie flushed at her tone and the implication of her words. "As I said, Lady Thalia, he has been a good friend to me, and it would indeed be reassuring to have him present when I meet Matthew for the first time."

When Lady Thalia remained silent, Lizzie went on. "It seemed very natural to confide in Mr. Thoreau. He has been kind to me, and he appeared genuinely interested in my situation. After all," she added, seeing that her friend's expression had not lightened, "we know that he is not interested in me because of my fortune. He cannot have some hidden agenda."

Lady Thalia smiled at her remark. "We really know *very* little about Mr. Thoreau, however," she said slowly. "I can see that I shall have to remedy that."

"Well, I am certain that everything you discover will be to his credit," replied Lizzie.

"We shall see" was the answer that she had to be content with, and the two ladies took themselves off to bed, Lizzie to fall gratefully into a deep and dreamless slumber, Lady Thalia to lie awake for a little longer, considering the troublesome matter of Mr. Daniel Thoreau.

Nine

It was as well that Lady Thalia had reflected upon the matter of Mr. Thoreau before sleeping because that gentleman appeared the next day just as she was finishing her chocolate. She had slept later than usual, enjoying the luxury of a good bed and clean linen.

When Beavers announced his arrival to her, her first reaction was to have Henry send him about his business, saying that the ladies were unavailable. However, recollecting that she needed to have a private conversation with him, she decided that this would be the perfect moment. Lizzie was still asleep, and she would have the opportunity to speak with him before they took up their new life in Vienna.

She was satisfied that Mr. Thoreau had at least acted the part of the gentleman thus far and that he apparently had an adequate income to support him. She did not know much more than that about him, however, and his marked attentiveness to Lizzie was beginning to trouble her. She had not minded his attentions to the girl in Paris because it had seemed such a brief interlude—a period when all of them were more or less "between lives." However, she had not expected him to seek her out so pointedly once they reached Vienna.

As Lizzie had said, he could scarcely be a fortune

hunter since Lizzie had no fortune, but it was not unknown for gentlemen to prey upon innocent young women, particularly in unusual circumstances such as those their travels had imposed upon them. Too, since Lizzie was so distressed about Matthew, she might well be more vulnerable to developing a *tendre* for an attractive, attentive man—and Lady Thalia was forced to admit to herself that Mr. Thoreau possessed both of those qualities.

"Have Henry tell Mr. Thoreau that I will join him in the drawing room in a few minutes, Beavers," she said decisively. "And then see if you can find a morning gown less wrinkled than the others." Beavers had been unpacking her trunks, and she had a formidable amount of work to do if her mistress and Miss Lancaster were to be presentable at the ball that night.

In very short order, Lady Thalia entered the drawing room, where Mr. Thoreau was passing the time by staring out the window at the passers-by, three stories below him. Upon advice from Viennese friends, Lord Danvers had been careful to reserve his apartments well above the level of the street, where the bustle of the crowd in the narrow medieval streets would not trouble him and where his windows would catch what sunlight there was to be had.

"Mr. Thoreau, how *very* good of you to call upon us," she said brightly, entering the room and dropping a brief curtsey.

Mr. Thoreau bowed. "I had assured Miss Lancaster that I would see her as soon as she arrived in Vienna. I left a letter for her here at the hotel." He looked over her shoulder toward the door as though in search of Lizzie. "I trust that she is in good health after such a difficult journey."

"She is indeed," Lady Thalia assured him, seating herself and inviting him with a wave of her hand to do the same. She noted with a touch of annoyance that he had not inquired after her own health, which he apparently felt appeared satisfactory. "She is exhausted by so many days on the road, however, and will doubtless sleep the clock around. She will be sorry to have missed you."

"I am glad to hear that she is resting," replied Mr. Thoreau, crossing his legs and leaning back easily in his chair. "She will need to recruit her strength if she is to dance at the ball tonight."

His hostess looked at him in a mixture of surprise at his mention of the ball and irritation at his habit of making himself at home wherever he was. "*You* will be attending the ball at the Redoutensaal, Mr. Thoreau?"

He nodded, amused at her irritation. "No doubt you are wondering how I managed an invitation, being a mere American awash in a sea of Continental peers."

She decided to dispense with politeness for the sake of information, and her reply was brisk. "As a matter of fact, sir, I *am* surprised. I understood, of course, the connection between the Marquis de La Fayette and America, but here things are quite a different matter. I admit that I *have* wondered just what has brought you to the Continent at such a time—and why you have chosen to mix with, as you put it, 'a sea of Continental peers.' It *does* seem curious to me."

"I am flattered that I have been so much in your thoughts, Lady Thalia. And you have put your finger very astutely upon one of the reasons for my travels," he replied.

When she looked at him blankly, he prompted her. "Curiosity, Lady Thalia. With Napoleon defeated, what better time to travel to the places that war has made difficult to visit? And why not come to Vienna for the most illustrious gathering in history?"

"And so you are merely an interested observer, Mr. Thoreau?"

"Like yourself, Lady Thalia—but without the title, of course."

"You said that curiosity is *one* of the reasons for your travels," she remarked when he did not continue. "May I ask the others?"

"I fear, ma'am, that you would not find them of great interest—nor are all of them mine to reveal."

"How very *mysterious* you make it all sound, Mr. Thoreau! I have heard that Vienna is *thick* with spies. Are you perhaps one of them?" Possibly, she hoped, making outrageous speculations might serve to draw him out.

He chuckled, the lines around his eyes deepening in amusement. "I'm afraid that I must disappoint you, Lady Thalia. As I said, you would not find them at all interesting."

"Then may I inquire, sir, what you do when you are at home in America? We have heard so little of your life there."

Frustrated by her failure to extract any useful information thus far, she was quite determined to wrest something from him, but thus far it had been rather like attempting to prise open a particularly stubborn oyster.

"And may I inquire, ma'am, just *why* you are inquiring?" he asked, his eyebrows high. "As I said, I am greatly flattered by your interest, but you must admit that you have shown very little concern for my background until now."

"And for that, Mr. Thoreau, I must admit culpability." She had decided that frankness was the only possible response. "While in Paris, I should *indeed* have made a very thorough inquiry into your background instead of accepting you as what you appear to be—a gentleman of means. I thought, you see, that ours would be a transitory relationship, over in a few days. However, my only *real* excuse must be that I am not accustomed to being responsible for anyone except myself."

Mr. Thoreau's brow cleared. "Ah, you refer to Miss Lancaster! Now I understand your sudden intense interest, Lady Thalia." He executed a brief bow from his chair. "I apologize for failing to understand the reason for your questions."

She nodded an acceptance of his apology and waited for him to continue.

"My family has an importing business in New York," he explained, "and for the past ten years I have been in the habit of looking after some of the company's business interests abroad."

"And so you have traveled widely?" she asked, prodding him to say more. That his family was in trade scarcely surprised her. He was, after all, an American.

"Quite extensively," he agreed, "to the Orient and the Mediterranean and South America—and I have hopes of soon re-establishing our business ties in England."

"You believe that the war between our countries will soon end?" she inquired, momentarily diverted by his comment. "I had not heard as much."

"I am quite certain that peace will come quickly, and I plan to remain on the Continent until such a time."

Suddenly realizing that she had been successfully sidetracked, Lady Thalia took up her quest again. She was determined to learn more. "And are you not needed by your family at home or by your business there? After all, you have already been gone for quite some time."

He smiled at her, and she noticed again what an open, pleasant manner he had—precisely what she had warned

Lizzie to be wary of, and yet here she was, in some danger of succumbing to it herself.

"It is kind of you to be concerned, but my family is accustomed to my absences and they manage very nicely without me. The day-to-day business of our firm is largely run by people who have been in our employment for years."

He studied her face for a moment, then added, "If you are inquiring as to whether or not there is a young lady waiting at home for me, the answer is no. I am without romantic attachments."

"And since I am responsible for Miss Lancaster, I must ask you, sir, just what your intentions toward her are."

Here, most unexpectedly, he gave a brief shout of laughter, as he had on the night in Paris when Lizzie had announced that she was going to purchase a fan. Lady Thalia, who had been expecting a serious reply to her very serious question, looked mildly shocked.

Recovering quickly enough from that, she was irritated with herself for being caught by surprise, and more irritated with him for managing to throw her off guard once more. She prided herself upon being in charge of most situations, and she had planned to conduct this interview in a brisk and businesslike manner, discovering what she wished to know while putting the gentleman firmly in his place.

"*In loco parentis,* Lady Thalia?" he asked, his expression and his tone merry. "Forgive me for laughing, but I had no notion that you took your responsibility as seriously as that. You looked as stern and grave as any head of the family possibly could. Next you will be asking me what my fortune is and how much I plan to allot for quarterly pin money."

"A young lady's future does not seem to *me* to be a joking matter, Mr. Thoreau," she replied with some asperity, wondering how she had allowed herself to get into such a predicament. She had no desire whatsoever to play the role of a parent, yet here she was, as proper and prim as any careful matron of the *ton*. Her intimate friends would never believe their ears if they could hear her now. She who was prone to laughter reduced to a humorless watchdog!

"Nor do *I* consider Miss Lancaster's future a joking matter, Lady Thalia," he assured her, his tone more serious now. "I think that she is a most charming and courageous young lady. She faces a difficult situation, and I look forward to being of what assistance I can be to her while I remain in Vienna."

"So she informs me," said Lady Thalia dryly, "but I did not realize that she had made such a confidant of you, sir, in the *exceedingly* short time that we have known you. You must understand that I need to be certain that you will not take advantage of a young girl's vulnerability."

"Miss Lancaster is quite safe with me, I assure you, Lady Thalia. I must tell you, however, having seen some of the gentlemen that she will be meeting in Vienna, that you will need to be watchful. She is a lovely young woman, and doubtless will be a target for many flirts."

"How *excessively* comforting it is to have you put me in mind of my responsibilities, Mr. Thoreau! Since I have been so remiss in guarding her interests thus far, I daresay that I would *never* have arrived at such a conclusion myself, so I must thank you for cautioning me!"

Enjoying the tartness of her tone, he added, "And I would suggest that *you* take care yourself, ma'am. You also could fall easy prey to some of the gentlemen that I have encountered here."

Mastering the desire to pick up a book from the table

beside her and fling it at his head, she managed to reply with commendable restraint. "I comfort myself with the knowledge that we do not travel in the same circles, Mr. Thoreau."

Before he could respond in kind, the door opened and Lizzie hurried in. "I thought it must be you, Mr. Thoreau, when I heard the laughter. How very good it is to see you again—and you were so kind to leave me a letter. I cannot tell you how it cheered me to know that you were thinking of me."

He rose and bowed to her. "I am delighted to see you looking so well after a difficult journey, Miss Lancaster."

And she did, Lady Thalia noted with some concern, appear to great advantage today. Last night she had looked quite hagridden, but now, upon seeing their guest, her eyes were bright and her color good. Clearly she was in spirits as well. Lady Thalia frowned to herself as she watched the two of them together. Say what he might, Mr. Thoreau obviously found Lizzie quite as appealing as she appeared to find him. She could gladly have rattled his teeth for creating such a problem. *In loco parentis,* indeed!

It appeared quite clear to her that she had traveled hundreds of miles to a scene of glittering gaiety where she had planned to enjoy herself excessively, only to discover that she was going to be obliged to play mother hen to a pretty young woman. Without a doubt, countless days and nights of worry and watching lay before her. She sighed. It was all more depressing than she could abide.

Deep in her own dark thoughts, she glanced up and caught Mr. Thoreau's eye, bright with amusement. She could have sworn that he was reading her thoughts, and finding them most diverting. She found herself purposefully fingering a small crystal vase, and had to fight the impulse to do him immediate bodily harm.

"Dare I hope, Lady Thalia, that you too will save a waltz for me tonight?"

It needed only that, she thought bitterly, immediately attempting to mask her thoughts with a bright smile. He had asked her to waltz—and she actually wished to accept.

"I shall look forward to it, Mr. Thoreau," she assured him with a small, dignified nod. Gently, she restored the crystal vase to its rightful place on the table beside her.

Perhaps she might find other means, less violent and infinitely more satisfying, to cause him to regret making light of her.

Ten

By the time they left for the ball that evening, Lizzie was so tense that she had to make a conscious effort to relax her jaw enough to smile. Now that the time had arrived when she would undoubtedly see Matthew, she could scarcely bring herself to face the ordeal.

Both Beavers and Lady Thalia, knowing how difficult the evening would be for her, had helped her dress for the event, and she realized as she looked into the glass that she looked very well indeed. The new gold gown was most flattering, Beavers had tucked the golden ostrich feathers into her carefully dressed hair, and Lady Thalia had insisted that she also wear a diamond necklet and earbobs that belonged to her.

"They are the *very* thing that is needed!" Lady Thalia had exclaimed, as she had fastened them in place. "They are dainty enough so that they don't overpower you, yet they add *just* the proper touch of glamour! They will catch the candlelight and frame your face beautifully!"

"You are too kind," murmured Lizzie, not able to do much more than allow herself to be dressed like a doll. She felt absolutely frozen with fear. Not even her new seal muff nor the cashmere shawl could keep her from shaking as they prepared to leave.

Lady Thalia, seeing her state, regretted thinking for a

moment that Lizzie might be falling in love with Mr. Thoreau. It was obvious that her feelings for Matthew Webster threatened to overwhelm her at any instant. Indeed, Lady Thalia found herself wondering if she should even allow Lizzie to attend the ball in such a state. If she were to break down in front of Matthew and a roomful of strangers, the effect upon the child could be devastating.

Nonetheless, when Henry announced that Mr. Thoreau had arrived to escort them, she turned to Lizzie with an attempt at briskness. "Well, we had best be on our way. We don't want to keep our guest waiting for us—particularly when our first Viennese ball awaits us. Do you have your fan, my dear?"

She had hoped that this final pleasantry would lighten the mood somewhat, but Lizzie merely nodded, her movements as stiff as those of a marionette. Seeing Lady Thalia watching her closely, she added, "Yes, I've brought the gauze one—although I shall never be able to use it with such fatal effect as Miss Blackwell."

As they joined Mr. Thoreau, Lady Thalia murmured to him, "Do what you can to help her. She is so distraught that she can scarcely move."

Their carriage drive was not a long one, for the Redoutensaal was in the Hofburg Palace.

"It will doubtless be a crush," said Mr. Thoreau. "Not so dreadful as some, I have been told, but crowded nevertheless."

"Good!" said Lizzie desperately. "Perhaps I will not see Matthew there after all. Perhaps we should stay only a few minutes and then come directly back to the hotel."

"Think of your dragons, Miss Lancaster," he responded encouragingly. "One down and one to go."

"What dragons?" demanded Lady Thalia. "What are you talking about?"

Mr. Thoreau, who had hoped for at least a mild expression of amusement at the reference to Miss Blackwell as a dragon, was disappointed. Lizzie did not respond at all—or rather she did, but not in the manner he had expected.

"How can I slay my dragons? I cannot possibly face him!" she exclaimed, tears suddenly streaming down her cheeks. "*She* was wearing *my* St. George medal—the one I gave to Matthew before he went to the Peninsula! It was to protect him, but he gave it away without a thought of me!"

All of the unhappiness that she had kept dammed inside her for the past fortnight suddenly burst forth, and she collapsed into a heap on the seat of the carriage, sobbing as though her heart would break.

"That *miserable* boy!" murmured Lady Thalia through gritted teeth. "I hope that *I* see him tonight! I shall certainly tell him what I think of his behavior!"

This served to rouse Lizzie, who shook her head violently. "No! No, please, Lady Thalia, you *must* not say anything to Matthew! *Promise* me that you will not!"

"But why ever should I *not*, Lizzie?" she demanded. "Just look at yourself! You would not be so distraught if *he* had not behaved so badly! Why should *his* feelings be spared when yours have been lacerated?"

Lizzie scrubbed her cheeks with her hands and sat up. Although she hated having lost her composure in front of others, even friends like the two who were with her now, she was surprised to discover that she felt better after the sudden outburst of pent-up emotion.

"Because your fussing at him for me would make me look like the pitiful little squab that he thinks I am. *I* will let him see that I can manage *wonderfully* well without him, and I shall make him regret the day that he wrote that letter to me!"

"Brava, Miss Lancaster!" applauded Mr. Thoreau, taking

out a large white handkerchief and handing it to her. "Repair the damage that you have done with your tears, and we will escort you into the ball to slay all the dragons present! You have no need of St. George to help you. You can do it very well on your own!"

Giving him a watery smile, she patted her cheeks dry and Lady Thalia helped her to smooth her hair and readjust the feathers, which had been knocked awry. "The air is cool, my dear. If we walk for just a minute or two before we go in, you will have a little color in your cheeks."

By the time they made their entrance, Lizzie was firmly in control of herself and no one seeing her would have suspected that just minutes ago she had been sobbing. She glanced coolly about the room, her hand resting securely on Mr. Thoreau's arm. Lord Danvers appeared to collect Lady Thalia for his dance, and Mr. Thoreau led Lizzie onto the floor.

"It is quite a striking scene, is it not, Miss Lancaster?" he inquired, glancing up at the orchestra playing in the gallery above them, where fashionable guests strolled or sat on small gilt chairs to watch the dancers below. A magnificent double staircase rose to the gallery, which was lined with tall Palladian windows. From the high ceilings hung huge crystal chandeliers, the candlelight gleaming on their lustrous pendants and reflected in the countless windowpanes. Around them whirled the other dancers, and Lizzie found that the best way to keep from growing too dizzy in the crush of colors and movement and sound was to focus firmly upon her partner's blue eyes.

"Should you wonder what I am doing, Mr. Thoreau, I shall tell you. I am not merely staring at you, mesmerized by your gaze. I am taking your advice."

"My advice?" he inquired lightly, pleased to see that

she had so completely regained her composure. "And what advice was that?"

"Why to focus on the scene before me, of course," she replied, surprised. "To focus outward. Do you not remember?"

"I do indeed, and I am delighted to see that the advice is having a beneficial effect, ma'am. I confess it is a little disconcerting to me to find myself the focus. I feel rather like a bug caught on the end of a pin for a naturalist to study."

Lizzie laughed. "I am sorry that I make you so uncomfortable. I promise that I shall look away now and then—as soon as I have found my balance in the midst of this sea of movement."

She was pleased to discover that she was feeling almost lighthearted, and she gave herself up to the enjoyment of the final measures of the dance. As the last notes faded and Mr. Thoreau led her toward the edge of the throng, she looked away from him at last, and the first person that she focused upon was Matthew.

"Lizzie!" he gasped, looking her up and down in disbelief. "It *is* you, Lizzie! I did not believe Mansfield when he told me that you were here. You had not written to tell me that you were coming."

"No, I had not." Lizzie smiled at him sweetly. "But Mr. Mansfield was quite correct, Matthew. I am most certainly here."

She turned toward Mr. Thoreau. "Mr. Thoreau, this is Matthew Webster. And, Matthew, I should like for you to meet Mr. Daniel Thoreau, a most particular friend of mine."

Matthew bowed briefly in Thoreau's direction, although he did not take his eyes from Lizzie. "Your servant, sir," he muttered.

Mr. Thoreau bowed in return and nodded to acknowledge the greeting. Then he offered his arm to Lizzie. "Miss Lancaster, would you care for some refreshment after our dance?"

She slipped her arm confidingly through his. "That would be delightful, Mr. Thoreau."

As they took a step to move away, she glanced up at Matthew and smiled. "It was good to see you, Matthew. Perhaps our paths will cross again before the end of the evening. If not, I am certain that we shall meet elsewhere. I shall be in Vienna for at least the next few weeks."

Matthew stared at her, astonished. "But, Lizzie, I wished to speak to you—It is very important and we've had no opportunity to talk to one another in so long!"

"I have discovered that balls are poor places to attempt a serious conversation, Mr. Webster," said Thoreau over his shoulder. Then he winked at Matthew. "But they are wonderful for flirtations."

As the pair strolled away together, Lizzie realized that her fingers were digging into the sleeve of her partner's jacket. "Forgive me, Mr. Thoreau," she apologized, releasing her grip, "but thank you, too. You were wonderful with Matthew!"

"I must confess that I thoroughly enjoyed myself. I was half afraid that he was going to run after us as we walked away."

"Yes," said Lizzie, satisfaction thick in her voice, like the purr of a cat that has just been into the cream pot. "I thought that myself. I daresay that we shall see him again very soon."

"I have no doubt of it," replied Mr. Thoreau. "And I see that Lord Danvers is coming over so that we can switch partners. I fear that we shall have to wait for refreshments—and Matthew will have to wait until after this dance before he can try his luck again."

After Lord Danvers had claimed Lizzie's hand and they had glided away to another lilting melody, Lady Thalia took Mr. Thoreau's arm and shook it lightly.

"Well?" she demanded. "Tell me what happened! I could see the three of you from across the floor, but I couldn't tell just what was taking place."

"It was brutal," he assured her, guiding her to a place among the other dancers. "Webster never knew what had hit him. He didn't know that she was not still in England until Mansfield told him this evening. And Miss Lancaster handled the situation masterfully—she was as cool as a cucumber, treating him as though he were a distant acquaintance. She dismissed him very casually, saying that they might cross paths again during the next few weeks. He wanted to speak with her at that very moment, and insisted that it was most important—but she strolled away without a backward glance."

"Good for her!" said Lady Thalia with satisfaction. "I hope that he is *completely* overset by this evening. It would please me *tremendously* to know that he is suffering."

"Oh, I think there can be no doubt of that. Only look." Here he nodded toward Matthew, who was standing where they had left him, quite frozen in place as he watched Lizzie whirl around the floor with Lord Danvers. "Miss Lancaster is getting a little of her own back again this evening."

"And this is only the beginning," responded his partner, smiling. "And it only just occurred to me that Matthew probably does not even know positively that Lizzie has received his letter. He must suspect it, of course, because she was so cool toward him, but since she has not mentioned it, he cannot be certain. *He* will be forced to speak of it himself!"

"If I were not personally involved, with my allegiance naturally given to Miss Lancaster, I would almost find it in my heart to feel sorry for Webster," said Mr. Thoreau, looking at Lady Thalia's expression. "He will be shown no quarter."

"Most certainly not!" she agreed. "It is quite time for *him* to discover just how it feels to suffer!"

"Miss Lancaster is a charming girl, Webster," said Mr. Mansfield, clapping his friend on the back as Matthew watched her dancing. "You must be delighted to see her again!"

"Oh yes, yes, of course I am," murmured Matthew.

"You should have seen your face when I told you! I'm delighted that I was the one who got to surprise you with the news of her arrival."

"Yes, I was most certainly surprised," Matthew agreed unhappily. "I believed that she was still at home in England."

"She was disappointed not to find you in Paris, of course, but it cheered her, I think, to be able to meet Miss Blackwell. I was pleased to be able to introduce them to one another."

"She met Teresa?" demanded Matthew in horror.

Mr. Mansfield looked at his companion with concern. "Are you feeling quite the thing, Webster? You are as pale as megrims."

"I am fine!" He glared at poor Mansfield with ferocious intensity. "Tell me about their meeting! What did they say to one another?"

Mansfield began glancing about him, hoping to see a

friendly face, for Webster was clearly feeling unwell. His tone was carefully conciliatory as he answered.

"Only what young ladies say to one another upon such an occasion. Miss Blackwell told Miss Lancaster that she was glad to meet a friend of yours from home, and Miss Lancaster wished Miss Blackwell very happy—then we all chatted."

Webster clutched his arm, and Mansfield watched him nervously. "Lizzie wished Teresa happy? Are you certain of that?"

"Yes, of course I am! What could be more natural than that?" demanded Mansfield, who was beginning to grow slightly indignant. "That is quite usual for one young lady to say to another who has become engaged."

"Yes—yes, of course," murmured Webster, his gaze fixed once more on Lizzie.

"As to what we talked about the next night, I'm not certain I can remember—"

This was an unfortunate observation on Mr. Mansfield's part, because he discovered that Matthew once more had him by the arm.

"The next night? They saw one another again?"

"Yes—naturally, that was to be expected since they attended the same *soirées*—and of course I had gotten to know Miss Lancaster and Lady Thalia so well on our journey to Paris."

Webster stared at him, trying to piece all of the information together. "Lizzie is traveling with Lady Thalia Stanhope?"

Mansfield nodded happily. "Yes, she is a lovely woman. I quite enjoyed our conversations in the carriage."

"You traveled in their carriage with them?" It seemed to Matthew that his world had suddenly been turned upside down.

Again Mansfield nodded. "And Mr. Thoreau was already in their company, of course."

"Thoreau also traveled with them?" Matthew's voice was growing somewhat hollow.

"Yes, it was one of the most enjoyable trips that I have made, despite the discomforts of the carriage and of all of us sleeping in the taproom of the inn. We—"

Here he suddenly snapped his fingers, his eyes aglow. "And I *do* remember what we talked of the second time Miss Blackwell and Miss Lancaster met! Miss Blackwell was wearing the gold medallion that you presented to her, and Miss Lancaster was admiring it!"

He looked brightly at Matthew, proud that he had managed to remember the conversation at last.

Matthew, however, looked even paler than before, and Mr. Mansfield steered him carefully to the nearest chair.

"It's doubtless the heat in here, old fellow!" he said reassuringly. "I shall just go and find you something cold to drink and that will set you to rights."

He hurried away and Matthew remained in his chair. In the distance he could see Lizzie, smiling in the arms of Lord Danvers as they waltzed. She no longer looked like his Lizzie, he reflected—but then, of course, she was not *his* Lizzie any longer at all. He was engaged to Teresa Blackwell now, and Lizzie had no part in his life any more. Still, he sat and watched her, hoping for an opportunity to speak with her. He needed very badly to talk with her, to tell her how sorry he was for the pain he had caused her.

Except that she did not appear to be in any noticeable pain.

Eleven

The next morning Lady Thalia was pleased to see that they had received flowers from Lord Danvers, Mr. Mansfield, Mr. Thoreau, and two other young men with whom Lizzie had danced at the ball. The drawing room had become a veritable bower of roses and lilies, and their fragrance and color filled the room. She was delighted to think that Lizzie would begin her day with these visible signs of her success. Despite its inauspicious beginning, the evening had, on the whole, been a very satisfying experience.

Her pleasure was considerably diminished when Henry announced that Matthew Webster had come to call. Although she had been very pleased with the way in which Lizzie had dealt with him last night, she could not forget nor forgive the pain he had caused the girl. She nodded to him very coolly when he walked into the room.

"Good day, Mr. Webster. I had not expected to see you here."

Matthew flushed at this somewhat daunting greeting, but he bowed and took the chair that she indicated with another brief nod. He decided that he must dispense with the civilities and be direct, even though he had always stood in considerable awe of the lady before him. He felt an overwhelming need to speak with Lizzie, and he was willing to brave Lady Thalia's wrath in order to do so.

"I am certain that you know why I am here, Lady Thalia," he said earnestly. "I had hoped to speak with Lizzie at the ball last night, but she gave me no opportunity."

"Nor can I think why she *should* have done so, sir," replied his hostess, her tone growing arctic. "Your behavior has scarcely been such that she should feel *any* obligation to speak with you."

He sat there rigidly, distressed by her words but recognizing that she spoke no more than the truth. Watching him, Lady Thalia thought regretfully that it was a pity that such a promising young man should have proven to be such a disappointment. He had been an engaging, handsome boy and, although she had not particularly wished for Lizzie to form a serious attachment at so young an age, at the time she had been forced to admit that she could see no harm in the boy. It had seemed to her then that, though Matthew was not as highly intelligent as she would have liked Lizzie's partner to be, he atoned for that lack with loyalty and a pleasant, easy manner. She had believed that he understood Lizzie's worth and could be trusted to be a faithful and loving companion. "Which is more than most marriages achieve," she had told Beavers one evening just before he had left for the Peninsula, "so we must be grateful for that, I suppose."

"No, she owes me nothing, Lady Thalia," Matthew answered quietly, his gaze steady. "I quite realize that—but I feel that I owe *her* an explanation of my behavior."

She could see that his pain was genuine—but then so was Lizzie's, she reminded herself, and he was the cause of it. She hardened her heart against the appeal in his anxious gray eyes and the nervous twisting of his hands.

"I believe that you have already explained your behavior in a letter to her, sir. As I recall, you told her that you have fallen in love with someone much more sophisticated than she, someone better suited to the life you now lead. I am certain that you made the reasons for your rejection of her *perfectly* clear, and I cannot imagine what you would be able to add to what you have already told her, Mr. Webster."

Matthew looked at her miserably. "Your choice of words is harsh, Lady Thalia. I assure you that I didn't mean to reject Lizzie, for I shall always love her. I *do* sound like the most awful cad in your version of the matter."

Lady Thalia's eyebrows arched nearly to her hairline at this comment. "In *my* version of the matter? Are you suggesting that there is a second version and that I have in some way altered the facts of the situation, Mr. Webster? Did you *not* write to her that you had found another young lady—a Miss Blackwell, I believe—whom you wished to marry in preference to Lizzie? That *is* what is commonly termed a rejection of your fiancée."

"No, what you say is true," he admitted, "but you make it sound so very heartless when I did not mean for it to be so. That is why I *must* talk to her!"

"And just how do you think that you can make your behavior appear *less* heartless, Mr. Webster?"

"By telling her that I still *do* love her—just not as a husband should love his wife." Matthew was extremely pale now, rather than flushed, but she could see that he was in earnest.

"In fact, I suppose that you mean to say that you love me as you would a sister, Matthew." Lizzie spoke quietly, standing just inside the door that she had closed silently behind her.

Both Matthew and Lady Thalia rose and turned toward her, Matthew going eagerly to take her hand.

"Yes, yes, that is precisely what I mean, Lizzie! You *must* know that I will always love you—you are a part of my life."

Lizzie gently removed her hand from his. "Not any longer, Matthew. You have a new life. You told me so in your letter."

"Well, yes—naturally I have a new life, Lizzie," he answered, looking at her unhappily. "But I mean that you are a part of my *old* life, which I must always remember with fondness, and that I wish to remain your friend."

"I see." Lizzie sat down on the sofa, calmly folding her hands in her lap. Both of the others returned uncomfortably to their chairs and watched her uneasily, Lady Thalia worried that Lizzie might give way to tears once more, Matthew hoping that she would smile at him and forgive him, making him feel easy once more. He had discovered that he did not like living with guilt, and here sat the one person who could assuage it.

"And just what would you have me say, Matthew?" she inquired, after the silence had continued for a painful minute or two. "That I shall dance at your wedding?"

Matthew, seeing no irony at all in her question, nodded eagerly. "Yes indeed, Lizzie! I should like it above all things to have you there—and to hear you say that you wish me happy."

"But of course I wish you happy, Matthew," she answered mildly, her tone and expression that of someone ordering a cup of tea instead of speaking of an event that had shaken her whole life. "How could I not when I have always cared for you? And naturally I plan to attend your wedding."

Lady Thalia stared at her as though she had taken leave of her senses, but Matthew leaped from his chair and hurried over to take her hand once more.

"Thank you, dearest girl!" He leaned over and kissed

her forehead. "How good you are to forgive me and make things comfortable between us once more!"

He took her hands and pulled her to her feet, enveloping her in a hug that she did not return. "I cannot tell you, Lizzie, what a weight you have lifted from my heart! I have wished to talk with you for the longest time! Do say that you will come out with me today so that I may show you Vienna!"

"Not today, I fear," she replied, slipping smoothly from his embrace. "Mr. Thoreau has already engaged me for an excursion and he will be calling for me at any moment."

"Thoreau? The fellow whom I met last night?" His voice was sharp.

She nodded, and he frowned at her. "Are you not spending too much time with him, Lizzie? How long have you known him, after all?"

Lady Thalia responded quickly so that Lizzie would not have to do so. "You must remember, Matthew, that Lizzie is traveling with *me*, and that *I* have given my approval to her outing with Mr. Thoreau."

"Will you be there to chaperone her?" he asked, his concern for Lizzie overriding his reticence with Lady Thalia.

Lady Thalia bristled visibly at his abrupt question. She had been planning to send Henry with them once again, as she had in Paris, but she greatly disliked being dictated to by anyone—particularly someone she considered little more than a beardless youth and someone who had jilted Lizzie to boot. Her rejoinder was quick.

"There is no need for me to do so. I have *absolute* confidence in Mr. Thoreau. You must remember, Mr. Webster, that you no longer have *any* claim on Lizzie other than friendship."

"Yes, but as a friend, I must—"

"As my friend, you wish what is best for me," inserted Lizzie smoothly. She was well pleased to hear that she was to have no chaperone. She disliked the awkwardness of worrying about Henry, who was forced to tag along behind them. "I quite understand, Matthew. And perhaps you can show me Vienna another time."

"Of course I will," he replied, happily reminded that they were friends once more and that he no longer had to carry his heavy load of guilt. As she turned toward the door, he remembered her engagement and took the hint, bowing to both ladies and taking his leave cheerfully.

"It is so *very* good to feel comfortable with you once more, Lizzie," he said before closing the door behind him.

Lizzie looked at Lady Thalia for a moment, then smiled. "Do not worry about me, Lady Thalia. I am perfectly well. I have not, as your expression indicates, lost my senses. I *do* plan to dance at Matthew's wedding, as I promised. Only I plan to be dancing with him as his bride."

Lady Thalia was watching her with concern, and it did not comfort her when Lizzie added, "But between that time and this, I plan to make Matthew Webster the most *un*comfortable young man in Christendom."

And then she smiled—but it was a smile of grim determination, and the expression in her eyes was one that Lady Thalia had not seen before.

By the time Mr. Thoreau arrived, Lady Thalia was deeply grateful to see him. Although she would not have thought it yesterday, she was delighted that he would be spending time with Lizzie, hopefully diverting her thoughts from taking vengeance upon Matthew Webster. She would not even mind now if there were a mild flirtation with Mr. Thoreau. Lizzie's statement about making Matthew the most uncomfortable young man in Christendom—and her expression as she said it—had made her profoundly uneasy.

"The flowers that you sent are lovely, Mr. Thoreau," remarked Lizzie as they walked downstairs to the waiting chaise. "But I thought that you told me that you never sent nosegays."

"That, Miss Lancaster, was before I met you," he answered cheerfully. "And it seemed to me that you deserved some sort of accolade after your performance yesterday evening. You were remarkable."

She dropped him a curtsey, smiling. "Matthew has already come to call this morning," she informed him, offering a brief account of what had happened. She did, however, omit her final comment, feeling that Mr. Thoreau might inquire into it more closely than she wished.

He offered no comment about Matthew's revelation that he wished to be friends again, but he gave her a comforting pat on the arm and turned the subject to happier topics.

"I am glad to see that you and Lady Thalia have such delightful accommodations, Miss Lancaster. You appear to have all the comforts of home."

"Yes, we were most fortunate that Lord Danvers had room to spare. I suppose not everyone has been so fortunate."

"That is undeniably true," he agreed. "I have discovered that there are far more visitors than there are beds in Vienna. Too many people have tried to crowd into the city for the Congress."

"Do you think most of them are attending the Congress?" she asked curiously. "Or are many of them like us—just come to see it all?"

"A great number have come chiefly to enjoy themselves,

Miss Lancaster—which means, of course, that you shall have a very fine time because there will be countless dances and entertainments of all sorts."

"Yes, Lady Thalia had promised that we shall have quite a wonderful time here." She glanced at him curiously. "What about *your* rooms, Mr. Thoreau? Where are you staying?"

He grinned at her. "It would be more accurate to speak of my *room*, Miss Lancaster—or rather, my *portion* of a room."

"Do you mean that you have to share a room with someone?" she demanded.

"Indeed I do. Fortunately, he is a very pleasant-tempered Greek and we get along well. He also wished to be present as the future of the Continent is decided—the Greeks, after all, have a vital interest in all of these proceedings."

"I'm glad that you like him, but I'm certain that it must be very uncomfortable for the two of you to live in one room."

"George and I get on very well together," he assured her. "We have many interests in common."

"That is his name? George?" she asked. "How very disappointing! That doesn't sound in the least Greek."

"George Andronikos," he amended.

"Ah, much better," she said. "Now he definitely sounds Greek. Andronikos gives him an air of romance that plain George simply doesn't provide."

"He will be glad to hear that you approve," answered Thoreau. "I will be able to tell him so this afternoon when we meet him at the Prater."

"I am going to meet Mr. Andronikos?" she responded, pleased. "I shall enjoy meeting someone from Greece. And what is the Prater? A café?"

He laughed. "Not exactly. But I promise that you will like it even better than the Palais-Royal."

As they rode through The Inner City, she could see that the dwellings of the rich and poor were all jumbled together, palaces standing cheek by jowl with crowded apartment buildings, many of the dwellings as tall as five or six stories, all elaborately ornamented. It seemed to Lizzie that there were statues everywhere, and on the streets wandered singers and barrel-organ players and magicians, all stopping to perform at a moment's notice and taking full advantage of the golden autumn day.

The Prater, she found, was a world apart from the rest of Vienna, and Mr. Thoreau proved to be correct—she did indeed prefer it to the Palais-Royal. Not only was it far larger, but it also seemed to her a far friendlier, far more inviting place. Innocent though she was, she had been uneasily aware of the dark worlds that existed on the floors above the cafés and shops of the Palais-Royal. Although she had been fascinated by it all, she had also been a little afraid. Here everything was more open—there were meadows and gardens and woods—and scattered everywhere were cafés and taverns and entertainment of all sorts. The Prater was also decidedly rural in character—there were even beehives and, at the entrance, a dairy bar that served milk to passers-by.

They stopped at Herr de Bach's "gymnastics circus," where Lizzie was enthralled by the ease of movement of the young performers. She was amazed by it all, having never seen such a thing before, but Mr. Thoreau informed her that gymnastics was growing popular in Prussia and Switzerland as well.

"You are very fortunate," the Englishman seated next to Mr. Thoreau told them. "This has been closed for several weeks so that they could rehearse a new show that would be worthy of performing for the visiting dignitaries."

"Do they come to the Prater?" Lizzie asked. "I thought perhaps they would spend all of their time meeting together."

"Scarcely that, I should imagine, ma'am," he replied, laughing. "In Vienna, everyone enjoys life—and *everyone* comes to the Prater. You will find countesses and coachmen, duchesses and duelists—even royalty mixes with the rest of us."

It was with some difficulty that Mr. Thoreau coaxed Lizzie away from the gymnastics performance, for she would gladly have sat through everything twice. Finally, only a reminder that they would keep George waiting caused her to leave.

"That is very true. I should not wish Mr. Andronikos to think me rag-mannered," she agreed, and at last they walked briskly to a nearby coffeehouse. The gentleman they were to meet was already seated and drinking a cup of coffee, but he rose as soon as they appeared, making a deep bow to Lizzie.

"Good afternoon, Miss Lancaster. I am delighted to meet you, for I have heard so very much about you."

His bright, dark eyes were fixed upon her and his smile was, Lizzie thought in admiration, simply dazzling. Everything about him seemed intense and very much alive. She dropped a brief curtsey, then held out a small hand to him and he clasped it eagerly.

"You are as lovely as I expected, Miss Lancaster—so I must believe that you also possess the other qualities I have heard attributed to you—charm and intelligence and courage."

He pressed her hand for a moment before she could reclaim it, but she glanced quickly at Mr. Thoreau, surprised by his companion's words. It was a gratifying description, she thought, and it could only have come from Mr. Thoreau.

Thoreau merely raised his eyebrows and smiled at her in response. Then he pulled out a chair for her, and Mr. Andronikos called a waiter over to take their order.

When they were settled, the young Greek turned to her once more. "Miss Lancaster, I am most eager to hear what you think of Vienna. I understand that you are visiting here for the first time."

"It seems a lovely place," she said, "but of course I have only just arrived. I have seen only a very little of it."

"Daniel and I shall remedy that very quickly!" he assured her. He turned to Thoreau and clapped his hand on his shoulder. "It is good that this is such a warm autumn, my friend. We can take Miss Lancaster to the *Heuriger* tomorrow! I shall engage to bring the sausages and bread!"

"What is the *Heuriger*?" she asked, eager for another adventure.

"It is the name the Viennese have given to small vineyards where this year's wine is drunk," replied Mr. Thoreau. "There are many such places close by, and they are open in the spring and summer, serving only their own new wine. Even this late in the year, I believe there are a few with wine still left. We shall check the list that is published each day in the newspaper—and then we shall go!"

"Most definitely we shall! Tomorrow! And we shall have our supper there!" agreed Mr. Andronikos with great enthusiasm.

"Perhaps we should invite Lady Thalia to accompany us," said Mr. Thoreau. "Like you, Miss Lancaster, she has never visited Vienna before, and she might enjoy seeing something that is off the beaten track."

"That will be delightful! We shall most certainly invite Lady Thalia!" agreed Mr. Andronikos, who clearly had only the vaguest notion of her identity.

"Do you think she will come?" Mr. Thoreau asked Lizzie.

She looked at him doubtfully, a little surprised by his suggestion. "I don't know what she might say. However, I suspect that she might feel that I need a chaperone other than Henry for such an adventure."

"Well, we shall make it our business to find out what she will say," replied Mr. Thoreau, smiling.

Mr. Andronikos, seeing a friend passing by the coffeehouse, excused himself for a moment and hurried over to talk with him. Once he was gone, she could not restrain her curiosity. "You seem on very good terms with Mr. Andronikos. Did you know him before you came to Vienna?"

"Yes indeed. I have known him for a very long time, Miss Lancaster. My family owns an importing firm, and they have done business with the Andronikos family for decades. I met him first when we were just boys, and I was on a trip to Greece with my father. George and I are about the same age, and his father decided to send him to school in America for a few years."

"His father sent him to school in *America*?" demanded Lizzie, clearly astonished. "Why would he do such a thing?"

He looked at her with amusement. "Try not to make America sound like the back of beyond even though you believe it is, Miss Lancaster. We do have schools and people *do* receive educations there."

She colored. "Well, yes, I know that, of course," she replied hurriedly. "I mean, you yourself are clearly an educated man. It is just that I would not have thought of anyone in Greece sending his son specifically to America for an education."

"Yes, I can see that. However, times in Greece were very unsettled, and George's father wished for him to have a more stable situation. He also had a great admiration for our revolution and the government we have established in America. He thought that George could learn about those, as well as learning a little more about our business since he would one day be taking his father's place."

Lizzie nodded. "So that is why he speaks English with such ease. I had wondered about that."

"He had no difficulty in making the change because he found many connections between our countries. George was delighted to learn that the ancient Greeks had greatly influenced many of the men who framed our Constitution. It made him feel much more at home among us."

They sat in silence for a few minutes longer as she considered what she had just learned. "And so our Mr. Andronikos—George—is he like his father? Also very interested in establishing a democracy in Greece?" she asked.

Mr. Thoreau hesitated for a moment, then nodded. "Yes—he is, Miss Lancaster."

Lizzie thought that over for a moment. "But the Turks still rule all of that part of that world," she remarked, "so naturally they would never agree to such a thing. Creating a democracy would more than likely require a revolution like yours—or like that of the French, would it not?"

Again he nodded slowly. "It is possible. We must hope that it would be more like our own and less like that of the French."

She sat and studied him for a few minutes. "It appears to me, Mr. Thoreau, that you are much more actively involved in politics than I had realized. I had thought that you contented yourself with reading about such matters in the newspaper. You are not really in Vienna just to observe, are you?"

He smiled at her. "I am like the majority of people who have come to Vienna, Miss Lancaster—eager to see and hear firsthand what is taking place at the Ballhausplatz, and equally eager to enjoy myself."

"You sidestepped my question very neatly, sir," she observed approvingly. "Very nicely done."

"I am happy that you are pleased, ma'am," he returned, inclining his head in a brief bow.

"So I do not really know more than the fact that you are interested in politics, Mr. Thoreau," she said, "and, as you say, most certainly Vienna is filled with people who share your interest. I will be careful, however, not to mention to anyone that Mr. Andronikos wishes for a democracy."

"I only wish that Mr. Andronikos would be as discreet," responded Thoreau dryly. "That is why I felt that I could tell you about his beliefs—because he will undoubtedly tell you himself very soon. He is not as careful as he should be."

"But is it really so dangerous for him to speak his mind?" she asked. "After all, he is in Vienna, not within the Ottoman Empire."

"Metternich and the others are here to decide how they can establish a balance of power so that they can look forward to a long period of peace. They do not want to hear ideas that might bring about revolutions. That could upset everything that they are trying to achieve."

She found herself mulling over that conversation as she prepared for sleep that night. How exciting it was to be in Vienna at a time such as this, when powerful people were making decisions—many of them, she was certain, in secret—that would determine the shape and the future of the Continent. Just how an American and a Greek fit into the picture, she was less certain—but it was all very exciting, nonetheless.

Thinking about such matters with great concentration helped her to keep at bay unhappy thoughts of Matthew, who now wished to be her friend. As she drifted off to sleep, she thought with pleasure of his irritation when he discovered that she was going out with Mr. Thoreau. She had thought that perhaps she had caught a glimpse of him at the Prater, and it had crossed her mind that he might have followed them.

The thought pleased her. She would deal with Matthew in her own good time but in the meantime, as she had told Lady Thalia, she was going to make him exceedingly uncomfortable.

Twelve

Lady Thalia, overwhelmed by the passionate entreaties of Mr. Andronikos, who had returned with his companions from the Prater to beg her company on a visit to the *Heuriger*, had reluctantly agreed to become a member of the party. He had pleaded for the pleasure of sharing a charming aspect of Vienna with a charming lady, assuring her that it was a beloved institution of the Viennese people.

"It is *of* the people, dear lady!" he told her, taking her hand and fixing her with his glittering black eyes. "To see the *Heuriger* is to see the soul of the common people! You must see it now, Lady Thalia, for soon the winter winds will blow, and your golden opportunity will be swept away with the autumn leaves! I could not bear to see that happen!"

Seeing that she had no way of regaining her hand nor of ushering this vibrant but most insistent young man from her drawing room until she agreed that she and Lizzie would accompany them the next day, she gave way. She watched uneasily as they made their farewells and turned to go, fearful that Mr. Andronikos would descend upon her once more.

"But after *this*," she told Lizzie firmly when the door had closed safely behind Mr. Thoreau and Mr. Andronikos, and she was feeling somewhat stronger, "you must *not* be so involved with just *one* gentleman. Mr. Thoreau's attentions to you have been *very* particular and we would not wish to give the wrong impression. Besides," she added happily, gesturing to a tray upon which rested a gratifying heap of cards, "we have already been invited to so many *soirées* that after tomorrow you will have no time for junketing about with Mr. Thoreau and Mr.—with his Greek friend."

Wisely, Lizzie did not object, knowing full well that Mr. Thoreau would manage to see her whenever she asked him to do so—or whenever he wished to see her himself. Instead, she cheerfully joined Lady Thalia in going through the invitations and filling out their engagement calendar. Heartened by this demonstration of interest, Lady Thalia was confident that she had made her point.

"We *must* go shopping once again," she said, deeply satisfied by the promised whirl of activity and the interesting individuals she expected to meet. "Just look at the balls and breakfasts and theater parties we shall be attending! You most certainly will need additional outfits, Lizzie, and I am going to have to add to my wardrobe as well or I will be forced to appear in the same gowns so often that they will soon be in rags. I have made inquiries about a reputable dressmaker and we are going to see her tomorrow."

True to her promise, the ladies enjoyed a very satisfying shopping expedition the next day, and Lady Thalia was well pleased with the dressmaker she had selected. "Her work is absolutely exquisite!" she remarked to Lizzie afterward. "I have *never* seen ball gowns so delightful, even in Paris! And it is so *very* gratifying to know that when we attend Dorothée de Périgord's breakfast next week, we shall be impeccably gowned. Not having to think about what I am wearing because I am certain that all is as it should be is such a *great* comfort to me. A lady's attention should *never* be concentrated on her apparel. Now I shall be free to enjoy all that is going on about me."

Lizzie could not disagree with her. She too was learning to enjoy everything that was happening around her in this new place—and, like Lady Thalia, she had been impressed by this particular invitation. Dorothée de Périgord was the daughter of the Duchesse de Courlande and her husband was the nephew of Talleyrand himself. Separated from her husband now, she had come to Vienna with Talleyrand to act as his hostess. Lady Thalia was eager to inspect the lady in question, about whom she had heard much.

"She is said to be a *wit* as well as a beauty," she told Lizzie. "It is Danvers, of course, who has managed the invitation for us. It should be *most* amusing to see some of the notables that we have only heard about thus far."

Lizzie encouraged Lady Thalia to talk more about the coming breakfast, for doing so would keep her from fretting over their engagement with Mr. Thoreau and Mr. Andronikos. She did not wish for Lady Thalia to become distressed enough to cancel it.

"I *can* not imagine how I came to allow myself to agree not only to allow *you* to go with them but also to attend myself!" she had told Lizzie earlier that morning. "The two of us going out to some rustic café with two gentlemen we scarcely know does not seem at *all* proper."

"But we do know Mr. Thoreau," she had reminded Lady Thalia. "And you have often told me that you don't particularly care what others think of you or of what you do."

"And I don't—but I *do* care what *I* think—and that is my problem," Lady Thalia replied crisply. "While I am certain that our evening will be amusing, I am *far* less certain that it is suitable for us to be going. And what I might accept as appropriate for *myself* is not necessarily appropriate behavior for you as a very young lady, my dear."

"Pray don't fret over it, Lady Thalia," Lizzie had begged her. "You know that Mr. Thoreau would not do anything that would expose us to embarrassment—although I daresay that Matthew would disagree with that."

As she had intended, bringing up Matthew put Lady Thalia immediately in mind of his unfortunate attempt to interfere in that lady's affairs.

"Well, I suppose that *one* evening cannot do any lasting harm," she conceded after a brief pause, and Lizzie turned toward the window so that Lady Thalia could not see her smile. Matthew had unintentionally done her a kindness, and it pleased her to think how distressed he would be to know that she was making use of his error.

And so it was that the four of them set forth in the late afternoon, three of them in high spirits.

"Ah, Lady Thalia, you will love the *Heuriger*!" Mr. Andronikos assured her, blithely ignoring the fact that her expression indicated that she felt such a possibility was extremely unlikely. "And, just in case ours does not serve its own food, I have provided all the necessities for dining *al fresco*." Here he happily indicated a wicker basket, neatly covered with a checkered cloth.

"How do we know which vineyard we will go to?" inquired Lizzie. "Did you consult the newspaper, Mr. Thoreau?"

"Can you doubt it?" demanded Mr. Andronikos before he could reply. "Daniel lives with the newspaper in his hand!"

"Yes, I have noticed that he does," said Lizzie, amused.

"In other words, Miss Lancaster," said Mr. Thoreau, unruffled by his friend's remark, "I did indeed consult the newspaper, which listed several *Heuriger* as currently open. We will merely have to choose the one we prefer. As we drive by them, we will be able to tell at a glance which ones are open because a fir branch or a circle of straw will be placed above the entrance to the house. The owner takes it down once all his wine is gone."

"That seems a very curious practice," observed Lady Thalia without enthusiasm. "Has it always been done in such a manner?"

Encouraged by even this mild display of interest, Mr. Thoreau nodded. "The Viennese vine-dressers have done so for many years. However, Emperor Joseph II gave them the legal right to sell the wine that they had pressed, along with any provisions prepared on the same property."

His friend's expression darkened for a moment. "What a great kindness of the emperor," Mr. Andronikos noted bitterly, "to give them the right to sell what they themselves have made! Someday things will be different for the people."

Lady Thalia looked at him in surprise, and Lizzie glanced nervously at Mr. Thoreau, who changed the direction of the conversation immediately.

"It is unfortunate, Lady Thalia, that we are here so late in the season. During the spring and summer, people flock to the *Heuriger*, and you can see the trees in blossom and smell the perfume of the flowers as you sip your wine."

"Visiting the *Heuriger* is a favorite Viennese pastime," Mr. Andronikos assured her, managing to put aside his grievances for the moment. "Soon you will see why it is so, even though it is now autumn."

The vineyard where they finally stopped was a small one, no more than a few acres in size, and they were

soon seated at a rough wooden table in a diminutive garden, shaded by a linden tree glowing in the late
afternoon sun. The light that filtered through its bright
leaves washed the scene in gold, and Lizzie, noting this,
thought that until this trip she had never paid the least
attention to the powerful effects of light on a scene. She
glanced at Mr. Thoreau gratefully, for without him, she
might never have begun to appreciate such things.

Lady Thalia saw Lizzie's quick glance and, misinterpreting it, frowned. She looked around her in irritable
dissatisfaction. "Is this all that there is to it?" she asked
crossly. "It seems like a great deal of fuss about very little."

Embarrassed by her rudeness, Lizzie said hurriedly, "It
seems quite charming to me. Will you show us now what
you have brought in the basket, Mr. Andronikos?"

That gentleman stood and whipped off the checkered
cloth cover in a most theatrical manner, smoothing it
over a portion of the wooden table as a cloth, and then
he took out a small wooden cutting board.

"Behold! Here we have cheese!" And, with a flourish,
he lifted out two blocks of cheese, one pale and one
golden, and arranged them on the board. "And we have
sausage!" A long brown sausage, redolent of spices, joined
the cheeses. "And we must, of course, have olives! These,
dear ladies, are from my own trees and are like no other
olives that you will ever taste!" And he placed a brown
crock of brine-soaked dark olives on the cloth beside the
board.

Nor was he finished. A crusty loaf of dark bread and a
crock of fresh butter joined the rest and then he paused
dramatically until he had their attention once more.
"And now I present the *pièce de résistance*—an *apfelstrudel!*"
And he placed the golden pastry, lying on its own lace
doily, on the cloth.

"*How* delicious it looks!" exclaimed Lady Thalia involuntarily. She had not meant to express any pleasure in the meal or the wine or the trip so that she would discourage any further invitations, but her newly acquired fondness for *strudel* proved to be her downfall.

"I am so glad that you approve," replied Mr. Andronikos, bowing. "It was my desire to please."

"And indeed you have done so," Lizzie assured him. "It all looks delicious, and we shall probably have to leave the *apfelstrudel* entirely for Lady Thalia."

"Not *all*," Lady Thalia assured them, "but very possibly half." She decided that, having already spoiled the arctic manner with which she had intended to freeze the evening, she might as well enjoy herself. She was, at any rate, tired of playing the virtuous chaperone. For just this one evening, she would forget her responsibilities, allow herself a holiday from worrying about Lizzie, and be herself.

"Should you wish more, dear Lady Thalia, I shall leap upon my horse and ride back to Vienna to fetch it for you," said Mr. Andronikos gallantly.

"Very pretty, George, but you have no horse," Mr. Thoreau pointed out practically. "We came in a chaise."

His friend was not fazed. "I shall take one of those horses should it prove necessary," he assured Lady Thalia. "Or, if that fails, I shall take one from a passer-by."

"And then we shall all attend your trial and subsequent hanging," said Mr. Thoreau, slicing the pale cheese carefully and offering slices to the ladies. "Even the easygoing Viennese frown upon horse thieves."

Mr. Andronikos shook his head sadly. "Ah, my poor Daniel, you have no romance. You have no *soul!*"

He turned to the ladies. "That has always saddened me," he confided to them, ignoring Mr. Thoreau. "I must apologize for my friend, but it is true that I have found that many Americans seem to lack that sensitivity to romance that we Greeks possess. It is, perhaps, because their country is so new, and they have not had the opportunity to cultivate some of the more delicate feelings."

Unperturbed by his criticism, Thoreau responded cheerfully. "If I were to give my life, George, it would be for something I believe in—not for an *apfelstrudel*, no matter how delicious."

Mr. Andronikos continued to shake his head dolefully, as though all of his worst suspicions had been confirmed. "It would not be for the *apfelstrudel*, Daniel—that is not the point," he said patiently. "The point is that you are doing something gallant to serve a fair lady." And here he bowed to Lady Thalia, who acknowledged this pretty byplay with a smile and a nod.

Mr. Thoreau grinned at them. "An American would not be foolish enough to steal a horse in order to fetch a pastry for a lady—no matter how fair she might be. He is far too sensible for that. Now, he *might* be moved to appropriate a horse for a *truly* important cause—like warning other Americans that the redcoats are coming."

Mr. Andronikos put his head into his hands and groaned. Then, looking up at the ladies, he shook his head once more. "I must apologize for his appalling lack of gallantry, dear ladies."

"There is no need to do so, Mr. Andronikos," said Lady Thalia. "One cannot expect it of Americans. And I am pleased that Mr. Thoreau realizes that Americans *should* be worried if our soldiers are coming."

Mr. Andronikos threw up his hands in a gesture of despair, but before he could continue, they all looked up at the sound of new guests arriving. There were four other tables in the tiny courtyard, and only theirs was occupied. Two men entered, both of them obviously gentlemen, and Thoreau glanced sharply at his friend. Mr. Andronikos did not, Lizzie noticed, meet Mr. Thoreau's eyes. Instead, he bowed to her and to Lady Thalia, and murmured his profuse apologies.

"I must, you see, have a word with these gentlemen on a matter of business. It will take only a moment, and I will return to you immediately."

He joined the two men at their table, and they began to talk earnestly, their voices low.

"Well, so much for Greek gallantry," observed Thoreau lightly, but his eyes remained for a moment upon his friend. "I believe, ladies, that we should give our attention to our meal, and make George regret that he was gone from us for even a moment."

"Your friend seems to be very sociable," said Lady Thalia, watching Mr. Andronikos. "How unusual it is for him to stumble upon friends in such an out-of-the-way place."

"George knows many people in Vienna," returned Mr. Thoreau. "There has been a large Greek community here for years."

"Yes, but I don't believe those gentlemen are Greek," she said. "I am quite certain that they are speaking Russian. Princess Lieven acquainted me with some of the phrases from her language, so I do recognize the sound of it."

"Princess Lieven!" said Mr. Thoreau appreciatively. "You do move in rarefied circles, Lady Thalia—or at least the Princess would think so."

Lady Thalia smiled a little at his reference to Princess Lieven's pride. "I did not say that we are good friends, sir," she pointed out. "Merely that she taught me a few phrases of Russian. During a particularly boring house party, we both sought sanctuary in the library one afternoon, and she entertained me with tales of Russia and a brief language lesson."

"I am only surprised that she was satisfied with an audience of one," he observed. "From what I have heard, she prefers to hold center stage with an audience of hundreds."

"I did not say the lady was modest and self-effacing," Lady Thalia reminded him. She glanced again at the gentlemen talking with Mr. Andronikos and back to Lizzie and Mr. Thoreau. "It does seem to me that I have seen one of them before."

"Very possibly at the ball last night," suggested Mr. Thoreau.

She shook her head thoughtfully. "Not there. In London, I believe. Perhaps he was there for the celebration of Napoleon's defeat. There was quite a large Russian contingent present."

"Very naturally, I believe," he replied. "Drawn there, no doubt, by the charm of your Princess Lieven."

Lady Thalia laughed. "Or perhaps by that of the Grand Duchess Catherine—even Princess Lieven would have to give way to her."

Catherine was the younger sister of Tsar Alexander, and both she and her sister Elisabeth had accompanied him to Vienna. Each of them had private apartments in the palace of the Austrian emperor, while the Russian delegation had taken up residence at the Paar Palace. Catherine was much accustomed to admiration and considered it her due, just as Princess Lieven did.

"Very reluctantly, though, I should imagine," observed Mr. Thoreau. "I saw her in Paris, and she behaved very much as you have described. The lady is also very clever. She was, I believe, born for intrigue."

"Is she a schemer, then?" inquired Lizzie with interest.

Just then, a rustle of movement drew their attention back to the table they had been observing. The three men had risen and appeared to be saying their farewells. Lizzie and Lady Thalia were watching so intently that they did not realize that anyone else had entered the courtyard. Therefore, it came as a shock to Lizzie to realize that someone stood at the corner of their table, just between her and Lady Thalia.

It was Matthew, and he was gazing at her reproachfully. "I told you, Lizzie, that you must be more careful—yet here you are."

"How did you find me?" she asked blankly.

Matthew shook his head. "I had not expected to. I simply happened to come along at the right time."

It was Lady Thalia's turn to shake her head. "There is not the least prospect of your coming upon us like this by accident, Mr. Webster. You might consider telling the truth, sir."

Mr. Andronikos rejoined them at their table as the other two men left the *Heuriger.* Seeing Matthew there, he paused for a moment, then smiled and bowed briefly. "Good evening, Mr. Webster," he said pleasantly.

"Do you know each other?" Lizzie exclaimed in surprise.

"Indeed we do," said Matthew, returning his bow very briefly. "I have discovered that Mr. Andronikos is a gentleman with many interests, and our paths have crossed several times since he has been in Vienna."

Mr. Andronikos continued to smile. "But of course they have, and I look forward to the time that they will cross again, Mr. Webster."

Matthew did not appear amused, and he appeared still less so when the young Greek turned to Lizzie and offered his arm.

"Shall we take a stroll in the garden, Miss Lancaster? I believe a little exercise may be in order before we return to our picnic."

She placed her hand on his arm, and together they strolled through the gate that led from the courtyard and into the garden, which was now growing thick with shadows.

"Lizzie!" Matthew called after her. "Don't do this simply because you are angry with me! Come back!"

"Mr. Webster, pray remember your present relationship with Miss Lancaster, and conduct yourself accordingly," said Lady Thalia, her tone short. "It can be of no consequence to you whether or not she walks in the garden with Mr. Andronikos."

"She is doing so simply to annoy me," observed Matthew grimly, staring at the backs of the retreating couple.

"What complete rubbish you talk, Webster!" snapped Mr. Thoreau. "Miss Lancaster does not require your permission for anything that she does, and you place too great a value upon your own importance if you believe that she acts out of a desire to irritate you."

"You take a very great interest in her affairs," replied Matthew, looking at Mr. Thoreau with obvious dislike. "For one who has known her so short a time, you seem to have grown much too intimate."

Here he directed his gaze to Lady Thalia, who had been listening to his remarks with mounting anger. "As for you, ma'am, I fear that the Lancasters placed too much confidence in you when they allowed Lizzie to come here in your company."

"How *dare* you say such a thing to me, you impertinent boy? I will thank you to take your leave of us now, and I assure you that you will *not* be welcome to call upon us until you have mended your manners and given me an apology!"

Matthew looked at her for a moment, unmoved by her anger. Then, after glancing briefly into the dark garden at the sound of Lizzie's distant laughter, he bowed to Lady Thalia and to Mr. Thoreau, then departed without another word.

"He takes far too much upon himself!" said Lady Thalia, deprived of her quarry and still angry.

"Indeed he does," returned Mr. Thoreau pacifically, "and I only hope that you will not take out your anger upon me, ma'am."

She relaxed slightly at his words and forced herself to smile. "I hope that I am not so rag-mannered as that. I shall force myself to think of other things."

Lady Thalia took a sip of her wine and looked thoughtfully at Thoreau. After a few moments, she said, "It does seem *excessively* odd that Matthew would know Mr. Andronikos."

"In Vienna these days, everyone knows everyone," he answered. "I daresay that both of them have made countless new acquaintances during the past weeks."

"Mr. Andronikos smiled at Matthew, but they didn't seem to like one another at all," she observed.

"No," agreed Mr. Thoreau, "no, they did not."

After a moment he added, "Perhaps we should join the others in the garden, ma'am. Would you care to accompany me?"

Standing, he offered her his arm. To her own surprise, she rose and took it, and then the two of them strolled into the shadows.

Thirteen

After that evening, Lady Thalia put aside all thought of Matthew and Mr. Andronikos, for she and Lizzie were swept up in a whirl of social activities that scarcely left them time to sleep. Lizzie, however, did not dismiss the gentlemen from her thoughts. In fact, within hours of their disagreement, she had another meeting with Matthew that Lady Thalia fortunately did not discover.

The morning after he had encountered them at the *Heuriger*, Lizzie was awakened by a young maid who worked for the hotel. The girl dropped Lizzie a brief curtsey, then handed her a folded note, smiled, and hurried from the room. Puzzled, Lizzie opened it and saw at a glance that it was from Matthew.

A few minutes later, she slipped quietly from her chamber so that no one would realize she had awakened and then hurried downstairs and out the main entrance of the hotel. She was half afraid that Matthew was bringing bad news from home, but the greater likelihood, she knew, was that he planned to continue the scolding he had begun the night before. Although she had dressed quickly, she had chosen her dress carefully—a gown of gold merino, trimmed with ribbon and cord of deep emerald green, and a pelisse of the same green. Perhaps, she thought, he might see it and remember that other gown of green and how they had danced together to "Greensleeves." At least it could do no harm to try.

"Lizzie!" Matthew was waiting beside the entrance, and he swiftly tucked her hand into the crook of his arm and walked her across the street.

"Matthew, is there something wrong?" she asked. "You said that it was an emergency. I thought perhaps that there had been an accident or sickness at home."

That had been her first fear, but now she had had time to realize that such news would naturally come to Lady Thalia rather than Matthew.

He shook his head. "The emergency is here, Lizzie, not at home."

Annoyed with him for having frightened her, she glared at him. "And just what is the emergency, Matthew?" Then, giving him no opportunity to reply, she went on. "I suppose that the emergency is that I am seeing Mr. Thoreau and Mr. Andronikos and that they do not meet with your approval! May I remind you, Matthew, that you are no longer my fiancé?"

"I know that, Lizzie," he replied quietly, "but I cannot stop caring for you simply because—"

He hesitated a moment, and she finished the sentence for him. "Simply because you have inconveniently fallen in love with someone else. Yes, you have told me that, Matthew, but it does *not* give you the right to interfere in my life!"

"I'm not trying to interfere in your life, Lizzie. Truly, I'm not. Or at least I wouldn't be if you were seeing someone more worthy of you." His tone was earnest, and she knew that he meant what he was saying. Unfortunately, what he was saying infuriated her. He would apparently be completely satisfied to hand her over to some gentleman he deemed "worthy" of her. She felt like a package that could be handed from one to another—at Matthew's discretion, of course.

"Mr. Thoreau *is*, as you put it, 'worthy of me'—and I admire him and enjoy his company! It doesn't matter to me that he is an American. As for Mr. Andronikos, he is *most* amusing—and, as a friend of Mr. Thoreau's, he must be perfectly acceptable to me. Whether or not you think him acceptable is not of the *least* consequence to me, Matthew! Really, you *do* take too much upon yourself!"

Despite her anger, a part of Lizzie was secretly amused to hear herself speaking in exclamation points as Lady Thalia did. She was pleased, too, to see that Matthew was astonished that she had spoken to him in such a manner, for at home she had always been in agreement with all that he said and did. When they were children, she had been too young to quarrel with, and later they were too much in love—over too brief a span of time, she thought regretfully—to quarrel. Also, she had known he would be going away to war, and she would never have done anything to distress him under those circumstances. At any rate, he was not accustomed to such a reaction from her, and she discovered that she felt better after saying it. Lady Thalia's approach had much to commend it, she decided.

They had been walking briskly and by this time they had reached a coffeehouse, its large windows polished and proclaiming to the world its name—*Hoffmann's*—in elegant gold letters. Just inside the coffeehouse, she could see an enormous espresso machine of white and gold porcelain ensconced on a marble counter, and as the door opened, the heavenly fragrance of freshly brewed coffee and baking bread floated out to her. For a moment at least, her attention was diverted, and Matthew was able to guide her inside without resistance.

"This is *wonderful!*" she exclaimed, breathing deeply

and glancing about her at the customers, all happily engaged in drinking and eating. The atmosphere was friendly and conversation was brisk.

"I thought you would like it," he said, smiling at her.

His familiar, affectionate gaze gave her heart a sudden wrench, and she looked away quickly so that he would not suspect it. "And I do," she said, quite calmly. "Who could not enjoy such a place?"

"I could, of course, have taken you on down the street for a *Frühstückgulash*," he said casually, "but I thought that you would prefer Hoffmann's."

"A *Frühstückgulash*? What is that?" she demanded, just as he had intended she should.

"A breakfast goulash," he returned, as they settled themselves at a table.

Before she could inquire more closely into this, a waiter arrived to take their order, and she had to wrestle with the delectable decision. At last, after careful consultation, she settled upon *Faschingskrapfen*, lovely golden brown rounds of fried dough, filled with apricot jam and dusted with sugar.

After the waiter left, she spent a few minutes watching the other customers, particularly one frail little woman who was having as much trouble making up her mind as Lizzie had. After serious consideration, she ordered what appeared to be cherry *strudel*, and Lizzie reflected briefly that Lady Thalia should have been there with them. She would love Hoffmann's.

"This is really a charming place, Matthew," she said at last. "Thank you for bringing me here—even if it was in order to lecture me."

"I'm glad that you like it, Lizzie." He had been watching her carefully. "To be truthful, I am surprised that you have been enjoying yourself in Vienna. After all, you are hundreds of miles from home, and you said that you never wished to leave there."

She shook her head. "I was wrong," she replied. "I may well wish to return there after a time, but for the present I am, as you say, enjoying myself tremendously."

Remembering his letter to her, she would have said as much whether it were so or not, but as she said it, she realized that it was true. She was indeed having a wonderful time. She would not have wished herself at home without the experiences she had had during the past weeks. Without quite realizing it until now, she had become, in some ways, a different person.

Matthew was still studying her. "I can't quite place my finger on what is different about you," he commented, "but I know that you have changed. You are not the same Lizzie that I have always known."

"Well, I scarcely could be after all that has happened, could I?" she asked gently and was pleased to see that he looked uncomfortable. "But you still have not told me, Matthew, why I should not spend time with Mr. Thoreau and Mr. Andronikos."

Matthew looked even more uncomfortable at this. "I can't tell you just what I know, Lizzie. I wouldn't be permitted to do so because of my work—but I can tell you that you *must* be careful here in Vienna. There are all sorts of dangers you could fall into, and you are such an innocent that you would never see them coming. I don't want you to find yourself in trouble."

"I shall be careful, I assure you," she answered, cheerfully addressing herself to the apricot buns and her coffee. "And if I find myself in trouble, I know that I may always call upon you—or upon Mr. Thoreau."

He had nodded encouragingly at the first part of her

comment, but at the mention of Mr. Thoreau, his brows drew sharply together.

"You seem to think very highly of a man that you scarcely know!"

"You are wrong, Matthew," she said, keeping her tone level. "I have come to know him quite well. Sometimes, I have discovered, when you are thrown together with strangers, you can establish friendships that are quite as strong as those that have existed for years. I trust him absolutely."

He shook his head in disgust. "Very well, Lizzie! I see that you have grown headstrong and that you will do whatever you wish to do, and the devil take the hindmost! I have done my best to warn you!"

"Indeed you have," she agreed pleasantly, "and that must be a comfort to you—so now you may put me from your mind, Matthew. You have done your duty."

He put out his hands and took hers in them, including the last bit of apricot bun, whose stickiness he ignored as he looked into her eyes.

"Lizzie! Why must you be so infuriating? *Do* please listen to me!"

"Good morning, Miss Lancaster. How fetching you look this morning," said a familiar voice, and she looked up to see Mr. Thoreau smiling at her.

He turned his gaze to Matthew, and his smile faded. "You, Mr. Webster, look somewhat less fetching." Before Matthew could respond, he continued. "And it would seem to me, sir, that for someone who expressed such concern for Miss Lancaster's reputation, you are being quite irresponsible in your behavior this morning."

Matthew flushed darkly and started to rise from the table, but Mr. Thoreau put a hand on his shoulder and pressed him firmly back into place. "And making a spec-

tacle of yourself just now would compound the damage,"
he said gently. "You must know that you should not have
brought her out alone so early in the morning to such a
public place. Anyone who saw you and knew you might
well misunderstand the situation."

"You have no business to speak to me about appear-
ances nor about Lizzie—" began Matthew, trying to rise
again. Mr. Thoreau's hand, however, held him firmly in
place.

"On the contrary, Mr. Webster, unlike you, I have
every right. I am a friend of Miss Lancaster and *I* am not
engaged to another lady."

Lizzie could see that the muscle of Matthew's jaw was
quivering, always a certain sign of scarcely repressed
anger. She had seen it often when he and her brother
George had quarreled, and she recognized it now with
pleasure. It was satisfying to know that he was feeling at
least a portion of the distress that she had felt.

Mr. Thoreau again smiled at Lizzie. "Miss Lancaster, I
would like very much to escort you safely home."

"I would be delighted by your company, sir," she said,
tidying away the last evidence of apricot buns with her
heavy napkin.

"I brought you here, Lizzie, and I will see you home,"
said Matthew, finally rising successfully from the table
and glaring at Mr. Thoreau.

"And I am certain that you asked permission of Lady
Thalia before escorting her here, did you not, Webster?"

"You heard what Lady Thalia said to me last night!"
retorted Matthew.

"My point exactly, sir," replied Thoreau, holding out
his arm for Lizzie to take. She did so with what seemed
to Matthew an irritatingly trusting air.

"*I* shall also see you home, Lizzie," he informed her grimly, offering her his arm as well.

"I am overwhelmed by such attention," she said sweetly, delighted to see him so irritated.

Together, the three of them made their way out the door, and they paused in front of the coffeehouse window because Lizzie stopped in her tracks to admire the great espresso machine once more.

"What a lovely creation," she said. "I am *so* glad, Matthew, that you brought me here. I quite enjoyed it."

Matthew glanced at Thoreau with a trace of satisfaction. "I was certain that you would like it, Lizzie. After all, I have known you for so long that I must by now know your likes and dislikes."

Lizzie turned to Mr. Thoreau and her face brightened. "Do you remember our afternoon in Paris, Mr. Thoreau?" she asked.

He nodded, both of them acutely aware that Matthew was staring at them, his attention fully engaged. "I am not likely ever to forget it, Miss Lancaster."

"I told you then that you had presented me with the loveliest gift I had ever received. That will always be true."

"Gift? What gift?" demanded Matthew. "Lizzie, you know that you have no business accepting gifts from men you scarcely know!"

When she looked up at him, she was no longer smiling. "But Mr. Thoreau isn't a stranger, Matthew. I have told you that. In fact, I feel that I already know him better than I ever knew you."

Silence descended upon all three of them, and it was maintained until they reached the hotel once more. The gentlemen bowed their farewells outside the entrance, and Lizzie disappeared within, pausing on her way to stop and lift her hand in a tiny wave to Thoreau.

For the next two weeks Lizzie did not see Matthew at all, nor did she see Mr. Thoreau more than twice, each time at a party where she scarcely had the opportunity to do more than speak to him. Mr. Andronikos she encountered once at a ball, where he danced with her twice, assuring her that he had never met any woman who was not a Greek that so fascinated him. However, she noticed that he had also danced with Lady Thalia, and she wondered if he had told her precisely the same thing. Smiling to herself, she thought that he probably had. He was quite an incorrigible flirt, which was a part of his charm.

And so the time slipped by, with Lizzie staying too busy to give overmuch time to thinking of the three gentlemen in her life. The days and nights were filled with engagements, and she was so exhausted by them that when she went to bed, she fell immediately into a deep sleep.

"How *very* satisfactory this has been," sighed Lady Thalia, slipping out of her shoes very early one morning as their carriage was rolling home through the dark streets. "I had the most *interesting* conversation imaginable with Prince Talleyrand. I *do* think that having his niece invite us to her breakfast was the most fortunate occurrence. He may not be a handsome man, but he *is* a fascinating one."

Their invitation from Dorothée de Périgord had opened other doors for Lady Thalia and Lizzie, as well as begun a friendship between Lady Thalia and Talleyrand, who always had an eye for an attractive lady, particularly one no longer young.

"Yes, I have noticed that the two of you deal very well together," returned Lizzie. "You had best be careful or the Duchesse de Courlande may grow jealous." Everyone knew that the Duchesse had been Talleyrand's mistress for years.

Lady Thalia laughed. "Oh, she would not do so. She is *very* well aware of what he is and how well he manipulates people. I am certain that much of his political information comes from ladies with whom he has had liaisons over the years. He *always* keeps his contacts and I understand that they are astonishingly loyal to him."

"And what were you two laughing about tonight as we were preparing to take our leave?" inquired Lizzie idly, listening to the wheels of the carriage thump over the cobblestones.

"He was telling me about his preparations for Vienna. When he was conferring with the King, Talleyrand said to him, 'Sire, I have more need of *casseroles* than written instructions.' He *knows* how much can be accomplished at social events. *Most* of the political maneuvering takes place away from the meetings at the Ballhausplatz. He is nobody's fool."

"And what did King Louis say to that?"

Lady Thalia laughed. "He *agreed*. And so Talleyrand brought along his chef, prepared to entertain *lavishly*."

"And so he brought Carême? The one that Mr. Thoreau and Mr. Mansfield were discussing when we first met?"

"The very same. They no doubt have found that *most* amusing!"

Lizzie hesitated a moment before responding. "We have seen Mr. Mansfield several times, but it has been a week since we encountered Mr. Thoreau, I believe."

"I daresay it has," returned Lady Thalia with a marked lack of interest. "No doubt he has other obligations with *other* friends—perhaps with Mr. Andronikos."

"Perhaps," agreed Lizzie, trying not to sound too interested herself. Then she smiled. "I am surprised, Lady Thalia, that you remember his name."

"Why should I *not* remember Mr. Thoreau's name?"

she asked, sounding surprised. "After all, we have met him upon many occasions by now."

"Oh, I didn't mean Mr. Thoreau—I was referring to Mr. Andronikos," replied Lizzie mischievously. "But then, as I recall, you *did* dance with him recently."

"Yes, I really had *no* choice, but I was pleased to find that he was quite passable upon the dance floor—*except*, of course, that he does talk a very great amount of nonsense."

"Does he indeed?" said Lizzie, feigning astonishment. "What sort of nonsense?"

Lady Thalia sounded annoyed. "You know *very* well what I mean, Lizzie, so don't try to pretend that you do not. Precisely the kind of thing that he said at the *Heuriger*. If *ever* a young man dealt in false coin, it is George Andronikos."

She was silent for a moment, then added with laughter in her voice, "But he is still a *most* charming young man."

Lizzie laughed. "I knew that you thought so. Judging by your expression, I was only surprised when the two of you did not elope before the end of the dance."

Lady Thalia gave up all pretense of propriety at this point. "Yes, it is *all* very well to laugh at me, Lizzie. I *do* admit that I find both Mr. Andronikos and Mr. Thoreau very personable young men."

"You should not make them sound as though they are mere boys," objected Lizzie. "After all, they are your own age, ma'am."

"Yes, that is all very well," she replied, eager to change the subject. "What we *must* be planning for, Lizzie, is the fancy dress ball at the Spanish Riding School. We have only a fortnight to think of appropriate costumes and find what we need to create them."

"Two weeks is a world of time," said Lizzie. "We will

have no problem. I thought perhaps I might go as a shepherdess."

"Very pretty," returned Lady Thalia approvingly. "And I believe that *I* shall be Cleopatra."

Lizzie's eyes opened wide at this. "Why, your costume must certainly raise eyebrows, ma'am. You will be the talk of the evening."

"I should *greatly* enjoy that," she admitted. "I seem to have grown *dull* and I need to do something to stir myself up."

"Never dull!" denied Lizzie. "But if you would enjoy scandalizing Vienna, then you must by all means do so."

"Those are *my* sentiments exactly, my dear!"

Soon enough they arrived at their hotel, and the ladies retired to their chambers. Lizzie mulled over their conversation as she was preparing for bed. She had not wished to be a shepherdess, but Beavers had suggested it to her and, since she had not been able to think of anything else, she had accepted it. As she thought about it now, her choice seemed pitifully bland and unexciting. Surely, she thought, there must be something else.

She had just dozed off when she had a blindingly brilliant—or so it seemed to her—idea. She could picture herself in the costume. Better than that, she could picture Matthew's horrified expression when he saw her. She had only managed to aggrevate him a few times in the past weeks, and she needed to think of something that he would find completely unsettling.

Lizzie smiled. He would be thoroughly unsettled. She pulled the bedcovers up to her chin with a satisfied sigh.

She would send for Mr. Thoreau in the morning—or, she thought, remembering the time and correcting herself—later this very morning.

Fourteen

Only a few hours later, Lizzie wrote her billet and sent it to the inn where Mr. Thoreau was staying. In it, she told him that she would be in attendance at a ball at the Redoutensaal that evening and asked him to meet her there, telling him that she had a favor to ask of him. Satisfied that he would come, for she had acquired great faith in his reliability, she then gave her attention to the activities of the day—a late breakfast given by the Countess von Veermann, a ride in the Prater with Lady Thalia and Lord Danvers, the ball—and finally a late supper given at the Palm Palace by the Duchess von Sagan, the older sister of Dorothée de Périgord.

Lizzie had discovered that life in Vienna was rather more complicated than anything she could have imagined when she lived safely at home at the Lodge. For instance, she had been astonished to learn that the Duchess von Sagan was the lover of Prince Metternich of Austria—but then so was the Princess Bagration, who occupied the other wing of the Palm Palace. And both ladies also apparently received payment from Tsar Alexander for their assistance with Russian political interests. She looked forward to the supper that evening, for she very much wanted to see the Duchess more closely than she had thus far—and she was also very curious to see just who would be in attendance at the supper.

She arrayed herself carefully for the ball, choosing the diaphanous gown she had feared so greatly when Madame Delacroix had made it for her. She had not yet worn it, both because Lady Thalia had ordered so many new gowns for her after their arrival in Vienna and because she had still been uncomfortable at the thought of wearing it. Tonight, however, having made up her mind about her costume for the approaching fancy dress ball, she felt that she could face the gown, a gauze-like confection with the same soft golden glow of the late afternoon sun in the Place du Carrousel in Paris. She surveyed herself in front of the cheval glass in her chamber and smiled at what she saw. If she were fortunate, Matthew would be present this evening, too. She was certain that he would disapprove.

Lord Danvers escorted them to the Redoutensaal that evening, and he led Lady Thalia out to dance first. Lizzie's hand was requested by a pleasant-faced young man on Metternich's staff, but their conversation was difficult, for Lizzie's mastery of French was far from perfect, and she knew no German whatsoever. She was distracted, too, by her desire to see Mr. Thoreau. Given his dependability, she had really expected to be dancing first with him, but as yet she had not caught any glimpse of his sturdy form.

She was rescued from the young Austrian by Mr. Mansfield, who claimed the next dance. When she explained her language predicament to him, he laughed.

"Then you find yourself in the same predicament as most English," he laughed. "We have the same problem even in our delegation to the Congress."

"But you speak French, Mr. Mansfield," she protested.

"I remember being very impressed when you spoke to the French postilions when we were on our way to Paris."

"Oh, I do well enough with speaking it," he said lightly, "but writing it is quite another matter. We could do with having Wellington here, for not a one of us in the delegation can manage to write it well enough to maintain our correspondence."

"But then what do you do?" inquired Lizzie, surprised by his comment. French was the language of diplomacy, so it appeared to her that they labored under a great handicap.

"We have Gentz, Metternich's assistant, to help us. He comes around regularly to do our translations for us."

She looked at him doubtfully. "But is that quite safe, Mr. Mansfield? After all, English interests and Austrian interests are different—even I know that."

Mansfield laughed. "You are correct, Miss Lancaster, but you worry far too much, I assure you. Lord Castlereagh is a cautious man, and he keeps our affairs secure and, amazingly enough, running quite smoothly."

The movement of the dance separated them just then and when he joined her once again, he said, "I am delighted that you finally got to see your good friend from home, Miss Lancaster."

"Yes, I was pleased, naturally, to see Matthew once more," she replied smoothly. "He appears to be staying very busy in Vienna."

Mansfield nodded. "One sees him everywhere. It is just as well that he remains occupied, of course. Otherwise he would doubtless be troubled by his long separation from Miss Blackwell."

"Yes, I am certain that he is grateful for his schedule," said Lizzie, not betraying her thoughts by even the slightest change in expression.

"I had hoped that Miss Blackwell was sincere when she said that she might come to Vienna," he continued, "but I suppose that was too much to hope for."

"Yes," Lizzie agreed, thinking how very glad she was that Miss Blackwell was safely contained in Paris. She thought of her oftener than she would like, even at that distance. Having to see her with regularity would be still less pleasant. "It is a pity, but perhaps Matthew will be able to go to Paris soon and see her."

She was grateful for the end of the dance, and more grateful still for an interruption that saved her from Mr. Mansfield and further discussion of Matthew and Miss Teresa Blackwell.

"Ah, Miss Lancaster! How delightful it is to see you once again," said Mr. Andronikos, appearing suddenly beside her and bowing low over her hand. "I am devastated to be late! I had so wished to dance with you first this evening!"

"You are very kind, sir," she replied, smiling. She found it impossible not to enjoy him, even though she knew that he spoke only in hyperbole.

She turned to introduce him to Mr. Mansfield, but she was forestalled.

"Mr. Andronikos," he said, bowing. "I did not realize that you were acquainted with Miss Lancaster."

The Greek smiled and returned the bow. "And how could I fail to be acquainted with the loveliest lady in Vienna?"

Mansfield, clearly not wishing to converse with Mr. Andronikos, turned to Lizzie and bowed. "I thank you for the dance, Miss Lancaster. I can see that I leave you in good hands." And then, having inclined his head slightly in the other gentleman's direction, turned and walked across the floor to join another group.

Lizzie glanced about them, then asked, "Did Mr. Thoreau not accompany you tonight?"

He shook his head regretfully. "I fear that Daniel was called away unexpectedly and will not return for at least another sennight."

"But he did not tell me that he was going!" she exclaimed before she could stop herself.

Mr. Andronikos regarded her seriously, still holding her hand in his own. "And I must bear the blame for that, Miss Lancaster, for Daniel left with me a letter to deliver to you so that you would know of his absence— but I myself had to leave Vienna soon afterward. I have only returned this very afternoon, and I found your note waiting for Daniel."

She stared at him for a moment. "And did you open my letter to Mr. Thoreau?" she demanded.

He nodded guiltily. "I felt that I must, you see, for I had been remiss in getting his letter to you. I feared that you might have an immediate problem with which I might be able to help."

Forgetting for the moment the danger of wrinkling her gown, Lizzie sat down abruptly in one of the tiny gilded chairs that edged the dance floor. Concerned by her suddenly forlorn expression, Mr. Andronikos sat down next to her.

"What is wrong, Miss Lancaster? In what way may I be of service to you?" His voice was coaxing, but it took a minute for her to think about what he was saying.

She stared at him for a moment. Her problem was not really such a great one after all, she reflected. She should not feel so suddenly empty at discovering that Mr. Thoreau was far away instead of here in Vienna where she could call upon him whenever she needed him. And here was his friend, graciously offering to help her. The difference between depending upon Mr. Thoreau and depending upon Mr. Andronikos, however, seemed the difference between a rock and a grasshopper.

Mr. Andronikos was still watching her closely. "Shall I bring you something to drink? Do you have your smelling salts in your reticule?"

Lizzie smiled. "Thank you, sir, but I have no need of either. I am really quite well—only surprised, you see."

He nodded in relief. "Yes, of course it must be a shock to you to see me instead of Daniel—but I assure you that I will do my humble best to help you with any problem that you may face, Miss Lancaster!"

He straightened his shoulders and stood taller still. "Merely ask of me what you will, dear lady, and I will do my best to satisfy your request!"

In spite of herself, Lizzie laughed at his serious expression and pose. "And I assure you, Mr. Andronikos, that my request is not one that will threaten your health or well-being! I have a very small problem that I wished for Mr. Thoreau to help me with."

He sighed and relaxed his military stance. "I can only wish that it were a difficult one, Miss Lancaster, so that I could show you my devotion. What is it that you would like for me to do?"

"Do you plan to attend the fancy dress ball at the Spanish Riding School a fortnight from now? The one given by the English delegation?"

"But of course! Everyone will be there!" he responded.

"Exactly so! But, you see, I need help with my costume, Mr. Andronikos. I need to travel to another part of town to find it, and I have no one to take me there."

"But where do you wish to go, Miss Lancaster?" he asked. "What is the costume you have in mind?"

Lizzie laughed. "I shall be a gypsy!" she responded. "You

need to take me, I think, to the Prater, where I heard a
gypsy fiddler playing when I was there this afternoon with
Lady Thalia and Lord Danvers. I heard the music when I
was there with you, too."

Mr. Andronikos stared at her in astonishment. "You
wish for me to take you to see the gypsies, Miss Lancaster?"
he demanded. "But you must know that I cannot do that.
Lady Thalia assuredly would not allow it!"

"Well, we need not tell her," Lizzie pointed out. "I can
make arrangements to slip away and you can meet me
outside my hotel."

She glanced at him and he still looked extremely
doubtful, so she added, "I knew that I would be able to
rely upon Mr. Thoreau to help me with this, but perhaps,
Mr. Andronikos, you feel that this would be asking too
much of you. If that is so, I certainly understand. After
all, this is not at all like stealing a horse to fetch another
apfelstrudel for a lady."

Thus forcibly reminded of his offer at the *Heuriger*, as
well as his ragging of Daniel Thoreau for his lack of gallantry, Mr. Andronikos straightened his shoulders, took
a deep breath, and bowed to Lizzie.

"Dear lady, I will most certainly do as you request—
although I am quite certain that I shall be reproached
not only by Lady Thalia, but by Daniel as well."

Lizzie did not try to conceal her delight, and she
leaned toward him, rapping his arm lightly with her fan
without even realizing that she was doing so and causing
him to bend down, since he expected her to say something private. Instead, she kissed his cheek lightly.

"You are a dear man, Mr. Andronikos," she said lightly,
smiling at him. "And you are truly helping me, whether
it seems so to you or not. In time, you will see."

He had no opportunity to respond because Matthew

bore down upon them just at that moment, bowing stiffly to Andronikos and glaring at Lizzie.

"May I request the pleasure of the next dance, ma'am?" he asked, his tone closer to that of a command than a request.

Mr. Andronikos frowned, but Lizzie again tapped him lightly on the arm, saying, "Then I may count on you, sir?"

He bowed to her deeply. "Indeed you may, dear lady. I shall see you very soon." Then, casting a dark look at Matthew, he added, "And I trust, Mr. Webster, that you will address Miss Lancaster in a more gentlemanly tone."

He turned and walked away before the startled Matthew could reply.

"Andronikos certainly takes too much upon himself!" he said sharply.

"Does he indeed?" inquired Lizzie mildly. "Asking you to treat me as you would a lady and not to speak to me as though you were giving me a command instead of making a request? You think *that* is taking too much upon himself, Matthew?"

"You know very well what I mean, Lizzie!" he snapped. "Don't start trying to play word games with me. You know precisely why I spoke to you like that!"

Lizzie paused for a moment, surveying the young man before her. He was still her Matthew, and he presented a well-dressed, polished façade to the world, but in his gray eyes she could see none of the old tenderness. She had seen it there when he took her to Hoffmann's to talk to her, and she had seen it at odd intervals since then— twice when he had danced with her, once when he had encountered her by accident upon the street. Now, however, it seemed to have disappeared all together. The only warmth there was clearly the result of irritation.

"What do you mean, Lizzie, by getting yourself in-volved with Andronikos and Thoreau after I expressly told you that you should avoid them?" he demanded. "You are behaving no better than Alice would, and we have always laughed about how headstrong she is!"

"Perhaps we simply see the whole situation differently, Matthew," she replied, not allowing herself to become ruffled in the least. "I, naturally, know none of the secret things about them that you claim to know, but I *do* know that I like them immensely—and that *they* go out of their way to befriend me."

"Of course they do!" he retorted.

"And what does that mean?" she demanded, her irrita-tion beginning to get the better of her. "Is that supposed to imply that there is a reason that they would be kind to me, other than the fact they enjoy my company?"

They were beginning to attract a little attention from those about them and, noticing that, Matthew said in a lower voice, "Come along, Lizzie. Let's find a place where we can talk. We cannot possibly dance and discuss this."

"And if I don't wish to talk to you?" she asked sharply, thoroughly annoyed that he was once again trying to take command. "What will you do then? Drag me along with you?"

"Of course not, Lizzie! Please don't act so missish! It doesn't become you!"

"*Missish?* Because I disagree with you? I *never* thought I would say such a thing to you, Matthew, but you have become too set up in your own esteem! You were always such a merry, loving boy, and look what you've become! High-handed and completely careless of my feelings!"

They had been walking briskly, his hand at her elbow, guiding her, as they talked. Both of them were flushed and angry, but they paused for a moment in their argument because they could see that they were still drawing interested glances from passers-by.

"Where are we going?" she finally demanded, as they grew close to the entrance.

"To my carriage," he said.

"Without telling Lady Thalia?" she asked, shaking his hand loose and stopping to look at him.

"We will not be gone so long that she will miss you—unless, of course, Andronikos makes it his business to tell her that we left together." Once again he took her arm and guided her toward the door.

"Well, it doesn't seem to me that I should be going anywhere alone with you in a closed carriage, Matthew. It certainly has the appearance of impropriety."

"Honestly, Lizzie, if that is not being missish, please tell me what is!"

Fighting down the impulse to box his ears, she swallowed hard and forced herself to sound at least moderately calm. "And so you would not object if Miss Blackwell were to ride alone with a gentleman? At night and in a closed carriage?"

"Certainly I would object, but that would be quite another matter from the two of us getting into a carriage together. You know that, Lizzie."

They had by then walked out onto the street, and Lizzie suddenly realized that she had left without her wrap and the night air was sharp. Matthew noticed that she had begun to shake, and, without a word, he stripped off his jacket and put it around her shoulders. They turned a corner and continued to walk, the line of waiting carriages still stretching some distance. To her relief, they finally stopped beside one of them, and he opened the door and handed her in, calling to the coachman as he did so.

"You keep a carriage of your own in the city?" she

asked, curiosity for the moment overcoming anger. "Isn't it very expensive?"

"Emperor Francis is paying for it. He provided 300 carriages, complete with liveried servants for visiting royalty and dignitaries."

"But you're neither of those things, Matthew, so why do you have one?"

"Because I am here under Wellington's orders, and I occasionally have need of one," he replied briefly.

She was mulling that over as they started down the street. "It is still very cold, Matthew," she pointed out. "And I am most uncomfortable."

He picked up a carriage robe and started to lay it over her knees.

"Don't do that! You'll crush my gown and probably get it dirty as well!"

He dropped it back on the seat. "Very well. But you wouldn't be nearly so cold if you would wear sensible gowns instead of one made of fabric so thin that you might as well not be wearing a gown at all! I can't imagine why Lady Thalia allowed you to wear it!"

Lizzie ignored for a moment the fact that she had had her own private doubts about the gown, but she had certainly seen those that were much more daring than hers. And then she thought of Miss Blackwell, who appeared to live in diaphanous gowns.

"And I suppose you point that out to Miss Blackwell, too," she ventured.

"Of course not," he returned. "She always looks most attractive and it is scarcely my place to tell her what she should wear."

"But you are telling *me*. And you are about to be *her* husband, not mine, Matthew. The things that you are saying do not fit together very logically."

He sat in silence for a few minutes, and Lizzie, feeling that she had made her point, decided to press it. "And why should it be acceptable for *us* to be alone together in a carriage when you do not think it would be proper for Miss Blackwell to do so?"

He reached over and took her hand. When she tried to withdraw it, he held it still more firmly.

"I *do* owe you an apology, Lizzie," he said at last.

It was her turn to sit in silence as the carriage creaked through the dark streets.

"For jilting me?" she asked finally, her voice flat.

"Don't use language like that, Lizzie. It isn't becoming— and it isn't like you at all."

"And just how would you *like* for me to say it, Matthew? That you discovered someone else whom you loved and just dismissed me? That I am too much a homebody for you to marry and that you very much wish that I had stayed at home?"

She was furious, and she was determined that her anger would sustain her so that she wouldn't give way to tears. This was the first time that they had mentioned Miss Blackwell, and she longed to tell Matthew just what she thought of his giving away her St. George medal to his new love. She could not do it now, however, for she knew that she couldn't speak of it without crying at his betrayal, and she refused to do so.

"In truth, I *do* wish you had stayed at home, Lizzie! You have done nothing but complicate matters for me here! I cannot be worrying about you and still give all my attention to the work that I am here to do!"

"And why *should* you be worrying about me?" she demanded. "What have I done that should cause you such concern?"

"I have already told you, Lizzie," he replied, his voice

sounding as though he were trying to retain a semblance of patience. "I *warned* you that you should stay away from Daniel Thoreau and George Andronikos, yet you have clearly done nothing of the sort. If anything, you have made a point to stay in touch with them—as you demonstrated tonight."

"They are both perfectly gentlemanly in their conduct, Matthew, so why should you be so worried about my seeing them?"

"Thoreau is as wealthy as Croesus, so he *should* be able to play the part of a gentleman perfectly well!" he retorted.

"As you very well know, it is his behavior that I am referring to, Matthew, not his pocketbook! And I know that his family is in trade, so you needn't mention that either! He is a delightful man!"

She paused a moment and then, before he could reply, she added, "I knew he was well-to-do, of course, but I had no notion that he was so very wealthy." She glanced at Matthew from the corner of her eye. "Perhaps I shall set my cap for him! It is not often that one finds such a happy combination of fine appearance and disposition linked with a fortune."

She was aware that Matthew had no knowledge of her family's present precarious financial situation, for her father had been careful to keep the matter secret. However, he also knew that their circumstances were modest and that a comfortable marriage settlement for Lizzie would be more than welcome.

"Yes, that would be perfect, Lizzie! Choose someone from a country with which we are at war! Marry a wealthy American who believes in revolutions and supports them! The two of you can trundle around the world together, throwing money to the lower classes in order to encourage sedition! What a pretty life you would make for yourself by marrying him!"

"Naturally he believes in revolution! As you say, he *is* from America! As for supporting revolutions, the French one is over!"

"So we would like to believe," he replied.

Before he could continue, she said, "And Mr. Thoreau detests Napoleon for betraying the cause of the French people and making himself emperor, so don't think for a moment that he would support him! If Napoleon comes back with the violets as he promised, it will not be with Mr. Thoreau's assistance!"

He looked at her sharply. "You seem to know a great deal about all of this, Lizzie. I did not realize that you were so much in Mr. Thoreau's confidence."

She was somewhat taken aback by this, and quickly reviewed her words. She had not, as far as she could see, said anything that could damage Mr. Thoreau. "Not at all," she said stiffly. "It is simply that he is my friend, and that we *do* talk about things that are of interest to us both. And as for Mr. Andronikos, he has also stood my friend— even if he is the most accomplished flirt in Vienna."

"I cannot believe that you could call a man your friend and in the next breath admit him to be a dedicated flirt. What has happened to you, Lizzie?"

"Perhaps I've begun to grow up, Matthew. You told me in your letter that we had grown apart and should not marry. I know now that you were right and that we would no longer suit." As she said it, she realized with a flicker of pain that she might be speaking the truth. "As it is, we are both free to go our own ways—and it appears to me, Matthew, that you yourself have chosen a most accomplished flirt as your fiancée, so your own tastes have clearly changed as well."

She had not been able to resist that final jab, and Matthew bristled indignantly just as she had known he would. "How unjust you are, Lizzie! You have scarcely done more than meet Teresa, and yet you judge her in such a manner! Such behavior does not become you!"

"Miss Blackwell is not a flirt, then? If I spent more time in her company, I should see that she is nothing of the sort?"

He hesitated a moment before answering. "Teresa has a natural buoyancy of spirit—and a pleasure in others—that might make some who do not know her feel that she is a flirt. Anyone who truly knows her as I do, however, realizes that taking such pleasure in others is merely a part of her nature and not an artificial behavior."

"I see," said Lizzie, as though she had made a sudden startling discovery, "so a natural flirt is not to be criticized, while one who has learned the art should be. In that case, Mr. Andronikos is not to be condemned either, for he has undoubtedly had his happy manner from the cradle. I am certain that it was not acquired later."

"Miss Blackwell and Mr. Andronikos are not to be compared in any way. She is a refined young lady, a lady of quality, while Andronikos is—" He broke off, as though searching for words.

"A gentleman of quality?" she offered helpfully.

"A revolutionary who can be trusted to do nothing except foment trouble for all connected with him!"

Lizzie, remembering her conversation with Mr. Thoreau about his friend George, made no immediate reply.

The carriage paused for a moment in the light offered by an uncurtained window above it, and Matthew turned to look at her. "You know that is true, don't you, Lizzie?" he asked, his voice filled with disbelief. "And yet you like him and spend your time with him."

"I know nothing of the sort!" she said quickly, but she did not sound convincing, even to herself. "But even if what you say were true, how could it be so terrible for someone to long for freedom?"

"It depends very much upon what that person is willing to do to achieve it," he responded grimly. "And also how his actions might affect others. After all, Lizzie, the reason that we are here is to try to establish a lasting peace."

"And all of Vienna knows that every country represented here has its own notion of how that should happen—and they all have to do with carving up other countries, whether they agree to it or not!"

Even at the social gatherings, she had not been able to miss the rumblings of discontent from the Poles, who wanted their country back; from displaced German nobility, who wanted their estates back; from the Prussians, who wanted Saxony; from the Austrians, who wanted to limit the power of Russia and France; from the Russians, who wanted to keep Austria and France under control; from the French, who did not want an alliance of Russia and Prussia. And of course there was present an assortment of tiny kingdoms and principalities, all lobbying for their own concerns. Among the British, feeling blissfully that the war was over and they were safe once more, only Castlereagh and some of the members of his delegation appeared to have any notion of what the interests of their own country were. Lizzie had reflected that attending parties in Vienna sometimes felt like being in the midst of a bubbling pot, one that was about to come to a rolling boil.

"Lizzie, matters are growing more serious than you know. The French are increasingly unhappy with their king, and they feel that we are the ones that are keeping him in power. There is talk of insurrection there, and attempts have already been made on Wellington's life."

She stared at him in horror. "The Duke has been attacked?"

He nodded. "The problem is a very real one—which is precisely why you must not be mixing with those who support revolution in any form."

"But surely you are not saying that Mr. Thoreau and Mr. Andronikos are involved in encouraging France to rise again or in attacks against Wellington?"

Matthew shrugged. "There is always that possibility," he said gravely.

"Possibility? In other words, you have absolutely no proof that they are connected to the affairs you have been telling me of!" Anger came boiling up again as she realized that he was trying to control her and that his accusations had no foundation. "If you did, you would tell me so, instead of giving me ominous warnings based on nothing save your own suppositions!"

"You know very well, Lizzie, that all I wish is your safety." He sounded weary now, as though tired of arguing with a child who could not follow his reasoning.

"We are no longer engaged, sir, so you have no business at all to be concerned in my affairs!"

"But I still care about you, Lizzie, even though we aren't engaged! I feel that you are in some sense still my responsibility and I have told you that! I cannot stand by and see you involve yourself in matters that you do not understand!"

"I am not involved in *anything* save having a good time, Matthew—and you seem determined to keep me from having one!"

"Honestly, Lizzie, you would try the patience of a saint!" he exclaimed, giving way to anger once more. "It is a blessing twice over that we are not to be married!"

"I believe that we are quite in agreement with your last

statement, Matthew! And it is you who is interfering in my affairs without so much as a by-your-leave! I should like to see you try to treat Miss Blackwell in this high-handed manner!"

"Teresa has no need of being reprimanded! She knows how a lady should conduct herself—and you are either too young or too headstrong to behave sensibly!"

"And I am delighted to hear that you are marrying such a paragon, sir! But I will tell you now that if you don't take me back to the Redoutensaal immediately, I shall open the door and jump from this carriage!"

"That would be sheer idiocy, Lizzie. You would only hurt yourself and create a scene."

"And you would be the one who would have to explain that to Lady Thalia—and to any interested passers-by!"

"I *can* not believe the change in you, Lizzie. It is most disheartening. You used to be so reasonable."

However, he apparently took her at her word, for he ordered the coachman to turn back. They rolled back to the Hofburg in silence, each of them too angry to speak. Lizzie was profoundly grateful for the anger, since it kept the tears at bay.

After reclaiming his jacket and escorting her back into the ballroom, Matthew bowed to her, turned, and walked away without a word.

Lizzie, in the meantime, smiled mechanically at the eager young Frenchman who asked for the next dance and laughed as they tried to talk, using his limited English and her limited French. She was determined that she would enjoy the evening. After all, she still had the Duchess von Sagan's supper to look forward to—and Mr. Andronikos would soon be taking her to see the gypsies.

She had intended to make Matthew excessively uncomfortable and she had clearly managed to do so. Now, however, she could no longer determine just how her pleased she was with her success, and she was very grateful that she was too busy to be able to think about it.

The supper given by the Duchess von Sagan was fully as interesting as she and Lady Thalia had expected it to be. Even Prince Metternich came for a short time, although it was whispered that he went immediately across the courtyard to the wing of the palace belonging to Princess Bagration. They saw, too, the men that Mr. Andronikos had met at the *Heuriger*.

"They are Russians, just as I thought," Lady Thalia whispered. "Why do you suppose he is interested in them?"

Lizzie, naturally, had not the slightest idea, and they had no time to discuss the matter because she soon found herself engaged in conversation with a lanky young Englishman. Mr. Bakersfield had no official reason for being in Vienna, but he was well connected and had thus managed invitations to many of the most exclusive gatherings.

"This is the most marvelous place!" he informed her enthusiastically. "Always something going on or something new to see! And riding in the Prater is grand! Do you ride, Miss Lancaster?"

She was forced to admit that she was an indifferent horsewoman, and he looked mildly deflated for a moment. "I had thought perhaps we could ride out together," he said, "but if you would not be comfortable—"

"I'm afraid that I should spoil it for you," she replied.

For a moment she thought longingly of the velvet riding habit that Lady Thalia had insisted upon having made for her, despite her protests that she would never use it. Still, she did not wish to go riding, and most particularly she did not wish to go riding with Mr. Bakersfield.

"Nonsense, Miss Lancaster. I am certain that you are

being too modest," he assured her. "And if you were in need of help, I should assuredly be there to offer my assistance—and I can supply you with a very gentle mount."

"You are very kind," she said, "and I am certain that seeing the Prater from horseback is delightful. Tell me, sir, have you ever seen gypsies during your rides?"

If he was slightly taken aback by this turn of the conversation, he did not show it. "Have indeed," he told her. "Saw an encampment just at dawn a few mornings back. They were cooking their breakfast and grooming their horses."

"Have you seen them since then?" she asked.

He shook his head. "But I know that there are some gypsy fiddlers that play now and then at the cafés in the Prater, or at places around the city—sometimes in the little wine cellars, I believe. Interested in gypsies, are you?"

She nodded. "Yes, they are such romantic figures, are they not?"

Mr. Bakersfield's expression revealed both his doubt about that and his reluctance to disagree with a lady. Honesty won out, however. "Seem a little shiftless to me," he said, "and perhaps not as clean as they could be."

"But think of their music, Mr. Bakersfield! Think of their dancing and their joy in life! Think of their freedom!"

"Well, yes, there's that, of course," he admitted reluctantly. "Still, not to my taste, you see."

"Yes, naturally tastes differ, Mr. Bakersfield." Then, turning the conversation before he could return to the matter of the ride, she indicated with a nod of her head one of the gentlemen she had seen with Mr. Andronikos at the *Heuriger*. "Do you know the tall gentleman in the green waistcoat?" she asked idly. "He looks rather familiar to me."

"Yes, one sees him a great deal," agreed Mr. Bakersfield. "I can't remember just what his name is, though—a Greek chap, it seems to me. Difficult name."

"Greek?" she asked in surprise. "I had thought that he was Russian."

Mr. Bakersfield shook his head. "From Corfu," he said. "But he works for the Tsar. Quite a favorite, I hear."

"Indeed?" responded Lizzie thoughtfully. "That is very interesting."

Mr. Bakersfield looked doubtful. "Suppose that it is, but I haven't the least notion why."

Lizzie laughed. "How very enjoyable it is to talk with you, sir. It is refreshing to speak with someone from home."

"How relieved I am to hear you say that."

Lizzie and Mr. Bakersfield both looked mildly startled by this statement since neither of them had made it.

"Webster!" exclaimed Mr. Bakersfield. "Didn't see you come in. Miss Lancaster, allow me to present Mr. Matthew Webster." He paused a moment, looking puzzled as he thought about Matthew's comment. "Do you know each other then? Were you speaking to Miss Lancaster when you sneaked up on us?"

"I confess that the lady and I are acquainted," replied Matthew. "For many years, in fact."

"Indeed!" said Mr. Bakersfield, his brows rising and his voice teasing. "And what will Miss Blackwell think of your having a friendship with such a striking young lady as Miss Lancaster? I daresay she will be so jealous as to set a watch on you."

Not waiting for Matthew to reply, he turned to Lizzie

and added, "I met Webster's fiancée when I stopped off in Paris. I daresay you know what a prize he has won."

"Indeed I do," replied Lizzie. "They are, I think, very well suited to one another." She looked directly at Matthew as she said that, then turned back to Mr. Bakersfield and smiled. "If you will excuse me, sir, I see someone whom I need to talk to just now."

They scarcely had time to bow before she left them, walking boldly across the room to introduce herself to the Greek gentleman in the service of the Tsar.

Fifteen

By the time a few days had passed, Lizzie had managed to put Matthew out of her mind so that she could concentrate on the pleasures at hand. She and Lady Thalia had been engaged on a daily round of engagements, including as many Russians as possible since she felt that doing so would cause Matthew the maximum amount of distress (although she naturally was not thinking about him). Walking across the room to receive an introduction to the Greek Kapodhístrias that night at the Duchess von Sagan's supper had appeared to inflame Mr. Webster quite satisfactorily, and she could think of no reason not to fan those flames.

She kept herself busy, always smiling and enjoying every moment so that when she went home to England, she would have stored enough memories to keep her warm through her declining years—which she felt she would most certainly face when she went home, for no eligible young man would be likely to marry a young woman with no dowry. A letter from her mother had disclosed the unhappy news that her father had been obliged to use the money set aside for that purpose in order to solve some of their financial woes.

Perhaps she would have to go home and face life as a spinster, perhaps even become a governess, with Lady

Thalia's help. It was even possible that if she became desperate enough, she might marry some poor man who had no expectations of a dowry. Naturally, her life would be a much more difficult one under those circumstances, but it did not appear to her that she had many choices. In the meantime, she intended to make the most of each present moment.

She had discovered, to her amazement, that here in Vienna she had a following of young men—and of some older ones, as well—and she had begun to enjoy herself tremendously. So, for the moment at least, she put depressing thoughts away and reveled in the attention she was receiving—although knowing very well that there was no chance that any of them were thinking of making her an offer. They were simply doing what all the other visitors to Vienna were doing—enjoying themselves. It was, Lady Thalia had said, rather like attending a vast, extended house party.

She had almost given up hope of hearing from Mr. Andronikos and had resigned herself to attending the fancy dress ball as a shepherdess when he appeared one morning to call upon her, bearing a large bouquet that he presented to her with his customary flourish.

"Ah, dear lady, a thousand pardons for making you wait so very long," he said, bowing low over her hand. Then he lowered his voice and asked, "We are quite alone, are we not?"

"Yes, Lady Thalia is recovering from influenza and is still in her chamber, so we shall be able to speak privately, Mr. Andronikos. Have you had any success?"

He nodded, his dark eyes glowing. "But of course! How could you think otherwise, Miss Lancaster? It took somewhat longer than I had expected, since the weather has turned and the rain had caused the gypsies to move their camp. But tonight we shall meet them!"

"Are we going to their camp?" she asked, feeling slightly overwhelmed by his success and wondering if she really wanted to do this. Riding out to their camp in the dark and the rain suddenly held very little appeal. It did not seem nearly so enticing as going to see them on a sunlit afternoon.

Mr. Andronikos shook his head. "I did not think that would be suitable. I have made arrangements for them to play and dance at a tavern I know, and we shall talk to them afterward."

"At a tavern?" Lizzie faltered. This also seemed to her more than she had bargained for. Then, however, she had a sudden vision of Matthew's disapproving expression should he hear of such an excursion and that caused her to straighten her shoulders and continue. She wished to see how horrified he would be when she appeared in her gypsy regalia at the fancy dress ball.

"Yes. It is, of course, not usually appropriate to take you there, but I have also arranged for a private place for you. We will sit where you can see them perform, but there will be a screen so that you have some privacy from the others in the room—and naturally I shall remain at your side."

"Thank you, Mr. Andronikos," she said gratefully. "I know that this must seem foolish to you, but it will give me great pleasure."

"You could never seem foolish to me, Miss Lancaster—and if doing this gives you pleasure, that is all that I must know. And I assure you the tavern is safe. I often go there, as do many Greeks."

They settled their plan quickly. He was to meet her at a ball and supper being given that evening by a wealthy young Viennese couple. The couple appeared to have invited a goodly portion of the better-known visitors to their city, and the crush at the party would be tremendous. Lady Thalia, improved but still not feeling particularly well, had elected to stay at home resting. Lord Danvers had agreed to escort Lizzie.

"Nothing could be better," she told Mr. Andronikos, "for Lord Danvers will disappear into the card room immediately and stay until it is time to leave. No one will notice if I am gone for hours."

In fact, before Mr. Andronikos had come, she had been thinking of staying home that night. Even though she knew a number of people by now and never lacked for partners in the dance, she had not been happy at the thought of a long evening spent in a large crowd with no particular person accompanying her. Now, however, she had a reason to go.

All went as they had planned, and very soon after Lizzie's arrival, the two of them slipped out to the carriage that Mr. Andronikos had procured. This time she took her wrap with her, so the cold was not such a problem. The rain had abated for the moment, and the carriage rocked comfortably through the streets. Although she did not feel as absolutely secure as she did with Mr. Thoreau, she was assured that her companion would look after her well, and she was anxious to watch the gypsies perform.

When they arrived at the tavern, he helped her down and guided her quickly through the main door. The room was rather dark and smoky, but she could see that it was quite full. The others paid no particular attention to them, however, for they were talking and laughing loudly, and through it all was threaded the haunting strains of a gypsy tune. He led her down one side of the room to a small table behind a carved wooden screen. Although she was hidden from the eyes of the rest of the audience, she could see the pair of gypsy fiddlers. One was an older man, his hair shining white in the flickering candlelight as he bent over his fiddle, intent upon his music; the other was a thin, dark young man whose features and manner made her think of a hawk.

"May I bring you something to drink, Miss Lancaster?" Mr. Andronikos asked her in a low voice.

She shook her head, smiling. She felt that drinking something here would be tempting fate. Besides, all that she really wanted to do was to listen to their music and watch the dancer when she performed.

In only a few minutes, a young woman stepped out onto the floor where the fiddlers were. A few tables had been cleared away so that she would have space to move, and she swept into a sinuous dance, her movements more graceful than Lizzie could ever have imagined. All conversation stopped now, and she became the center of attention. Her dark hair hung loose, and her body seemed to follow every note of the music, responding to the shifts from joy to sorrow and a deep longing. Her eyes were bright and her gold earrings and bangle bracelets glowed against her dusky skin. Sometimes she whirled so quickly that the bright turkey red of her skirts and kerchief seemed to merge with the gold, so that it seemed to Lizzie that she resembled one of the gleaming tops that children played with at holiday time. Her feet were bare and around one ankle she wore a gold anklet hung with tiny bells.

There was applause when she finished and the three of them bowed under a shower of coins tossed by the audience. The older man looked toward Mr. Andronikos, who nodded and rose. Bending over Lizzie, he said, "I shall be back in just a moment, Miss Lancaster. You will be quite safe here."

He followed the three of them out of the room as soon as they had collected their money, and on the far side of the screen, the conversations resumed. She could follow none of them, for they were, she assumed, mostly in Greek. After a few minutes, however, they began a song of their own. She could see through the screen that they were standing and they sang with such fervor that the very room shook. Lizzie saw Mr. Andronikos slip back into the room. He nodded at her, but he stood with the others and sang until the song was over. Then he came to join her once more.

"What was the song, Mr. Andronikos?" she asked. "What were you singing about?"

"It is a song about freedom," he said. "Not just freedom from the Turks for us, but freedom for everyone. It is a clarion call to men to remind us of what we are and of how we should live. It is an oath never to act as a tyrant and never to allow ourselves to become slaves. Rígas wrote that it is better to live one hour in freedom than to live forty years as a slave."

Lizzie was shaken, both by the forceful singing and the intensity of Mr. Andronikos' words and gaze. "And it was a man named Rígas who wrote the song?" she asked.

When he nodded, she added, "Is he here tonight?"

"Dead," he replied, shaking his head. "Murdered!"

Lizzie stared at him, and he leaned toward her, taking her hand. "Forgive me for speaking so abruptly of such a terrible thing, Miss Lancaster, but, as you see, this a matter of great importance to me—to all of us who come here."

"Who murdered him?" she asked, horrified. "And when did it happen?"

"He died sixteen years ago," he replied. "He was born in Thessaly, but he did much of his work here in Vienna during the last nine years of his life. He studied the rights of man as they were proclaimed in America and in France, and he worked to write a constitution for the Greeks. All of his work, including his call for revolution against the Turks, was printed here in Vienna, but it had to be done secretly because this government would crush anything that threatens stability."

"And so what happened?" she demanded. "Did they find him out?"

"He was betrayed. He and a companion traveled to Trieste, and he had sent ahead to a friend boxes containing copies of his constitution, his freedom hymn, and his call for revolution. His friend was away and the boxes were opened by someone else, who reported him to the authorities. He, along with a number of others, was arrested and brought back here to be questioned. Those like Rígas, who were Turkish nationals, were sent to Belgrade, where they were murdered and their bodies thrown into the river. The authorities said that they drowned during an escape attempt, but we know it was not so."

Lizzie sat in silence. Anything that she could think of to say seemed too inconsequential a response to such a story. After a few moments, Mr. Andronikos appeared to remember that she was still sitting there and that he was holding her hand. He gave it a quick pressure, then released it.

"Forgive me, Miss Lancaster, but he was a great man. It still grieves me to think of it."

"And so it should," she responded, "but at least you still sing his hymn."

"It is sung everywhere there are Greeks," he assured

her, "and his work is widely read. Soon we will be able to establish the constitution that he wrote for us."

Lizzie glanced around them nervously. "But, Mr. Andronikos, should you not be careful what you say? After all, you have just said that the government here does not want anything happening that threatens the stability in this part of the world."

He smiled at her. "Do not worry for me, dear lady. There is always danger for men who wish to change the way of the world, but soon I will be gone from here."

"Gone? Where are you going? May I know?"

"Assuredly you may know. I need to learn more about being a soldier, so I am going to Paris to join the French army. There can be no finer training ground for me."

"But you are not a royalist!" she protested. "Will it not distress you to serve a king?"

"Ah, but for how long will there be a king, Miss Lancaster? That is what we must ask ourselves."

Lizzie had no desire to question him any more closely upon that point while they were in such a public place, but she did venture one more comment. "But the French army was defeated, Mr. Andronikos, and although other countries helped us, it was our English army that brought that defeat. Does that not make our army superior to the French?"

He smiled at her and shook his head. "That army is gone, dear lady—disbanded once the war was over. Some were sent to America for the war in progress there, others simply went home. There is only a skeleton of the original left."

Lizzie had not ever considered the fact that Wellington's army no longer existed, and she discovered that it was not a comfortable thought. Particularly not when thinking of Mr. Andronikos' comments about the French.

She remembered, too, what Mr. Thoreau had said about Napoleon's promise to return with the violets. She did not wish to discuss that publicly, however, so she turned the conversation back to the gypsies and what had transpired between them and Mr. Andronikos.

Smiling, he held up a paper-wrapped bundle. "I have in here, Miss Lancaster, golden jewelry such as the dancer wore, and a bolt of bright cotton. I shall leave the bundle at the desk of your hotel. Also, as you wished, I have engaged the fiddlers for the night of the ball."

She smiled at him. "You have been wonderful to me, Mr. Andronikos. I shall never forget it—nor shall I ever forget you."

"What more could I ask, dear lady?" he asked, leaning over to kiss her hand.

Once they were safely back in the privacy of the carriage, she once more turned the conversation to her fears. "Do you believe what Napoleon said?" she demanded. "That he will return with the violets?"

"Who can know?" he shrugged. "One may only hope."

"Hope?" she said in disbelief. "He would bring war and chaos once more!"

"He would bring an opportunity," said Mr. Andronikos gently. "And for people who wish the world to change, that would be an opportunity to be seized."

Lizzie sank into silence. Much as she had looked forward to seeing the gypsies and acquiring what she needed for her costume, she could not work up any enthusiasm now for enjoying herself as a gypsy and striking back at Matthew. What Mr. Andronikos had told her had suddenly thrown her off balance and she felt as though she was teetering on the edge of an abyss. If Napoleon were to return, war was inevitable.

And she was far from home.

And if there were a war, Wellington would unquestionably lead the English. And so Matthew would also go once more to war.

Sixteen

That desolate feeling was still haunting her when she awoke the next morning, and Lady Thalia was still in bed recovering from influenza. Everything in life seemed as gray as the weather, and Lizzie could feel herself slipping into the slough of despair. She was haunted by thoughts of a war and felt more than a little homesick. She sat by the fire and drank a cup of chocolate, thinking fondly of the Lodge and her family—even of her laughing, careless brother who had caused the family such distress. Despite his thoughtless ways, he was a kindly person, never mean-spirited nor miserly when he was flush with funds. She had received a letter from him, telling her how ashamed he was that he had cost her the precious dowry and promising to make it up to her. She had not responded yet, not for lack of time, but because she hadn't been able to think of the best way to phrase her thoughts. She did not wish to let him see how bleak her future appeared to her. Alice, of course, was in no better state with regard to her dowry, although she doubtless knew nothing of the matter yet.

Finally, she gave herself a shake and determined to go right along with her plans. After all, how could it help anyone if she became as blue as megrim? It could not help her family, her concern meant nothing to Matthew, and she certainly could do nothing about a possible war. Since she could not help, she decided that she would enjoy herself and do what Mr. Thoreau had advised her to do—focus on the world outside herself.

She went down first to see the concierge and pick up her package from Mr. Andronikos. She decided that she would tell Lady Thalia about her costume idea because she was bored and sickly and she too needed something more cheerful to think about. She would not, of course, tell her about going with Mr. Andronikos to pick up the materials.

As she had hoped, her gypsy costume was just the medicine that Lady Thalia needed. She sat up in bed, demanded a cup of tea from the long-suffering Beavers, and commanded Lizzie to lay out on her bedcovers what she had acquired thus far.

"*Very* dashing!" she murmured, looking at the jewelry. "I shouldn't let you do this, of course, but then *I* am going as Cleopatra, so I can scarcely criticize."

She held up the golden anklet strung with bells and examined it with interest. "Lizzie! Are you wearing this just for the sound of the bells, or are you planning on showing your ankles in public?"

"If I dance as I enter the ballroom, even for a moment, my ankles shall undoubtedly be seen," Lizzie pointed out practically.

"*Dance?*" Lady Thalia regarded her with mesmerized horror. "Do you mean that you plan to dance like a *gypsy?*"

Lizzie nodded, then did her best to imitate a few of the gypsy girl's movements. "Well, you can see what I mean, at any rate. I shall only do a couple of quick turns to make my skirts twirl as I enter the ballroom, and of course having the gypsy fiddlers playing will help with the effect."

Lady Thalia's expression had not changed. "Gypsy fiddlers?" she demanded, waiting for more information.

Again Lizzie nodded with satisfaction. "Mr. Andronikos has arranged for a pair of them to be there with me. He will manage our entrance."

"*Will* he indeed?" said Lady Thalia, collapsing back against the pillows. "Why, this sounds for all the world like a *stage* performance, Lizzie! Beavers, are you attending to what she is saying?"

Beavers, who was opening the draperies and putting the room to rights, nodded comfortably.

"I suppose that a stage performance is really what we are planning," Lizzie agreed. "I want to have an effective entrance, and I should like very much to be noticed for at least the first few minutes I am there."

"Oh, I have not the *least* doubt that you will be!" Lady Thalia assured her. Her horror had faded and had quickly become fascination. "But why, Lizzie, *why?* For whom are you performing?"

"For Matthew," she replied simply. "And, at least in part, for myself."

"I suppose that you wish to set Matthew's back up once again," said Lady Thalia, "and I am *certain* that I understand why you wish to do so. But in what way is this for *yourself*, my dear?"

"The gypsies make me think of everything that I am not—wild and free and careless of what anybody thinks of them. I should like to be that way for just one evening, I think."

She paused a moment before she went on. "When we go back to England, I shall more than likely have to marry someone who will accept a dowerless girl or, if I think that I cannot face that, I mean to be a governess.

I thought perhaps you might be able to help me find a position, ma'am."

Lady Thalia, who had been unaware of how serious the family's financial straits were, sat silent for a moment before answering. Lizzie suddenly looked, she thought, quite desolate, and she made up her mind to think of some means to help her without injuring her pride.

"But of *course* I will help you, Lizzie, if that should be what you decide to do—but we need not think of that until later. Now we have *much* to do if we are to have our costumes ready."

"But you are still not well, Lady Thalia—and the doctor told you to rest. You may not be able to attend the ball."

"I *am* resting! As for not attending, that is a nonsensical notion! Of *course* I shall attend! And I feel *immeasurably* better now that we have your costume to prepare! You were absolutely correct that it is good to focus on something cheerful."

Lizzie started to protest, but Lady Thalia wagged a warning finger at her. "I shall *not* get out of bed, Lizzie— I promise. I will simply send for the dressmaker and tell her what your plan is for your costume. I have been an *extraordinarily* good customer and I am certain she will come to us."

She eyed the red cotton lying on the bedcover as she called for Beavers to bring her travel desk so that she could write a note to the dressmaker. "A *wonderful* color, naturally, but the cloth is far too coarse. I shall send a sample of it to Fräulein Schlosser, and she can bring some material that she thinks will serve. After all, a gypsy's skirts *must* move gracefully."

Lizzie started to observe that the gypsy girl's skirts moved like silk, even though they were made of cotton, but she caught herself in time. She could not let slip that

she had gone to see the gypsies in the company of Mr. Andronikos. She wanted to do nothing to overset the present
happy mood, for Lady Thalia appeared to be reviving
quickly now that she had a new project to think about.
By the time Fräulein Schlosser appeared, Beavers had
dressed her hair and given her a fresh cap and dressing
jacket. She was still pale, but she was once again animated.

Fräulein Schlosser, always appreciative of an excellent
customer, entered into the spirit of the thing immediately, and Lizzie's costume was soon planned—a peacock
glory of red, gold, and green. After the dressmaker had
left, they both heaved a sigh of relief, but Lady Thalia
was still studying her speculatively.

"And, after you arrive at the Riding School, do you
plan to take off your slippers and go barefoot?" she
asked. "No matter how cold it is?"

"Well, it would rather spoil the effect to be wearing slippers, don't you think? And I'm certain that I can whirl
about more safely on my bare feet than in satin slippers
with smooth leather soles. I should kill myself outright."

"Very possibly," Lady Thalia conceded. "However, if you
take to the dance floor in your bare feet, you shall very
probably be killed in a slower, more painful manner."

"That is true," agreed Lizzie. "We shall think about it. At
least we don't have to bother with masks. I should certainly
fall while turning if I couldn't see."

"Yes, and Matthew would not know at a glance that it
was you in the gypsy costume. My Cleopatra would be ru-
ined as well. Too often the effect of fancy dress is quite
destroyed by the addition of a mask."

The night of the fancy dress ball was clear but cold, and
Lizzie was deeply grateful that she was at least wearing
slippers in the coach instead of going barefoot. Her costume had arrived, looking as wildly exotic as Fräulein

Schlosser could manage to make it, and Lizzie had arrayed herself in it happily. She had brushed her dark hair until it shone and then floated loose over her shoulders, and arranged all of the gold jewelry, so much showier than anything she would ordinarily wear. She was even wearing a little rouge, and Lady Thalia, who was most definitely wearing paint, had outlined her eyes in black, as she had her own, using a brush and a dark paste that she had had Beavers concoct for her. Being Cleopatra, she had outlined her own eyes very heavily, and she wore a long wig, as brilliantly black as a raven's wing. Her white gown was narrow and thin to the point of indecency and she wore a handsome three-strand necklace made in the Egyptian fashion. On her feet were trim white sandals.

She and Lady Thalia both wore opera cloaks over their costumes and planned to cast them off at the last possible moment so that their outfits would have the strongest theatrical effect possible. They had agreed that when they came to the head of the wide staircase that descended to the ballroom floor, Lady Thalia would be announced first, and she would proceed halfway down before Lizzie was announced.

"After all, my dear, you can't expect me to try to enter after you give *your* performance," she had told Lizzie earlier.

"I would suggest that I wait until you are all the way to the bottom of the stairs. Then, should I fall, at least I shall not take you with me."

Lady Thalia looked thoughtful. "A very prudent suggestion," she agreed. "I have *no* wish to have a broken leg."

With this encouraging remark, Lizzie grew even more nervous. Mr. Andronikos was waiting for them, and he took Lady Thalia's cloak first and they watched as she was announced. Most of the names could not be heard

over the music and conversation, of course, but people
frequently turned to see who was entering and to inspect
their costumes. When Lady Thalia made her way lan-
gorously down the staircase, fanning herself with a large
palm leaf and looking regally over the people as though
they were indeed her subjects, a brief hush fell over
them and then there was a buzz of conversation and a
brief splattering of applause. Lady Thalia acknowledged
it with the very slightest inclination of her head.

Swallowing hard, Lizzie handed Mr. Andronikos her
cloak—and her slippers—and stepped to the head of the
stairway to listen for her name. The two gypsy fiddlers
stood close behind her.

"Please don't let me trip and fall," she was thinking
wildly, looking down at the sea of faces below. Unfortunately, Lady Thalia's impressive entrance had attracted
their attention and Lizzie was already being scrutinized.

"You look beautiful, Miss Lancaster," said Mr. Andronikos softly—but she could scarcely hear his words.

"Focus, Miss Lancaster, focus!"

She looked up sharply at the sound of Mr. Thoreau's
reassuringly crisp voice. He was smiling at her. "Focus
outward and you'll be quite all right. Don't think about
yourself. Think about the music."

Just then her name was announced and the gypsy fiddlers began to play, making their way gracefully down the
steps behind her. Anyone who had not been paying attention at that point immediately turned around to see
where the music was coming from. Even some of the
members of the orchestra seated at the end of the gallery
stopped playing to listen and watch.

Fortunately, however, Lizzie saw none of this. As the
music began, she did what Mr. Thoreau had told her to
do—she lost herself in it. She had always thought gypsy

music the most beguiling she had ever heard, and tonight—just for one night—she was a part of it. Remembering the movements of the gypsy girl, she had been practicing faithfully, and now she whirled down the steps, bending and turning in time to the music, a single rose in her hand. When she reached the foot of the stairway, she was greeted with a burst of applause, and someone called, "Throw the rose! Throw the rose!" And so she tossed it lightly into the crowd, and a handsome young man caught it with a crow of delight.

The gypsy fiddlers melted from the scene before she had even had the chance to realize that they were gone, and Lizzie found herself surrounded by admirers. She could not see Mr. Thoreau or Mr. Andronikos, but when the young man with her rose requested the next dance, she laughed and told him that she had best find her slippers first. Heeding Lady Thalia's warning, she had decided that barefoot dancing in the ballroom was both too cold and too dangerous among so many feet shod in leather. He escorted her to the top of the stairs once more, and there they located her cloak and slippers, still safely held by her friend. The young man retired to a discreet distance so that Lizzie could speak to the holder of the cloak and slippers privately.

"Thank you so much! You are the dearest of men!" she told Mr. Andonikos as he returned her slippers. Without thinking twice about it, she stood on tiptoe and kissed him on the cheek, and he smiled at her, his eyes glowing.

"For that, dear lady, I would swim oceans!"

"You will dance with me tonight, will you not?" she pleaded. "Promise that you will dance with me before you leave tonight—George." After his friendship and the success of the evening, it seemed inadequate to call him

Mr. Andronikos—besides, she thought, tonight she was a gypsy.

He suddenly grew serious and took her hand, raising it to his lips. "I promise that I will dance with you before I leave," he promised gravely. "Nothing could keep me from it, dear Lizzie."

"Well, this is quite delightful, Lizzie!" said Matthew, his tone indicating that it was anything but delightful. "First you make a spectacle of yourself, and then you come up here and fling yourself at this—this—" He paused, searching for words.

"Thank you, Matthew," she replied with composure. "I am glad that you enjoyed my entrance. I was a little fearful of falling on the steps, but Mr. Thoreau's advice got me through it, and—" Here she paused to glance at Mr. Andronikos and smile. "And George helped to see me through it all."

"That is exactly what I hear! Mr. Andronikos appears to have been very busy indeed!" retorted Matthew, giving his full attention to that gentleman. "I have heard from reliable sources, Andronikos, that you took Miss Lancaster away from the ball last night, and that you took her to a tavern unsuitable for ladies—or indeed for any person of reputation. In fact, you took her to a place where she could have found herself in a great deal of trouble!"

Mr. Andronikos shrugged. "You are making too much of a small matter, Mr. Webster. It was a necessary trip."

"Yes, indeed it was, Matthew," said Lizzie. "George was helping me because I begged him to do so, so pray don't be cross with him when you know that I am the one who has made you angry."

"Lizzie, would you please stop calling him by his Christian name as though he were your brother or—"

"Or my former fiancé?" she asked innocently. "George

has become my good friend, Matthew, so you may as well stop behaving in such an odiously toplofty manner. It really does not suit you."

She took George's arm and smiled at the young man waiting for her, who hurried over and took her other arm. Together they escorted her down to the dance floor, leaving Matthew to stew alone. In a moment she could see him pacing back and forth along the gallery, trying to walk off his anger.

Lizzie and the young man with the rose were midway through their dance when she saw a latecomer making an entrance. At first glance, she thought it was a young officer in the Hussars, apparently a member of Matthew's former regiment, when she suddenly had a clearer view. It was a lady—dressed impeccably in the Hussar jacket, cape, and breeches, her boots shining in the candlelight. She had removed her hat, and her fair curls fell loose. It was Miss Blackwell.

Lizzie glanced about quickly to see if she could see Matthew—and she did. He was standing frozen in the gallery, watching his fiancée descend the stairs, nattily attired in uniform. Dressing in breeches was a behavior confined to actresses, one considered far too fast for a lady. He looked stunned as he watched her, and for a moment Lizzie could almost feel sorry for him. But then she remembered his sharp criticism of her own behavior, and the unfavorable manner in which he had compared her to Miss Blackwell, and she hardened her heart. This was a lesson that Matthew very well deserved.

There was a light smattering of applause that died almost at birth, followed by a low murmur of comment, but Miss Blackwell continued her descent, unperturbed. Lizzie could see that Matthew was hurrying down to join her. That, she thought happily, would be a most interesting conversation to overhear. With that thought in mind, she excused herself from her partner, promising that she would be back in just a moment, and strolled in the direction of what was clearly an animated discussion. They were so entirely absorbed in each other—or at least Matthew was so entirely absorbed in what he was saying to Miss Blackwell—that she was able to come quite close before either of them noticed her. Matthew's face was flushed, and Miss Blackwell's rose-petal complexion was a little paler than usual.

"Well, if it isn't little Miss Lancaster, just passing us by chance!" she exclaimed as Lizzie neared. "Have you come to hear my scolding?"

Ignoring Matthew, she pulled the St. George medal from beneath her jacket so that it gleamed in the candlelight. "You see that my costume as a soldier is quite complete, ma'am. I even have my own talisman against danger." She left the medal dangling outside the jacket.

"That was unnecessary, Teresa," Matthew said in a low voice, then turned to Lizzie with misery in his eyes. "I am so very sorry, Lizzie. I intended to tell you about the medal, but I couldn't bring myself to do it."

"And why should it matter to me, Matthew?" Lizzie asked evenly. "I gave it to you for protection, and if you choose to give it to someone else, then that is your own affair."

Miss Blackwell smiled at her knowingly. "And I understand that you gave it to Matthew because you fancied yourself engaged to him, Miss Lancaster. Matthew told me all about it. What a pity you were so naïve."

"Stop that immediately, Teresa!" said Matthew furiously, and then turned to Lizzie. "That is not the way it was, so don't listen to her for a moment. I am so very sorry, Lizzie—if you would just let me explain."

"I believe that I understand well enough, Matthew—and again, I wish you happy. As I told you earlier, I think that you and Miss Blackwell will suit very well."

As she turned to walk away, Mr. Thoreau stood there waiting. Without a word, she took his arm and they left the dance floor, abandoning Lizzie's partner to his fate.

"What a fool I have been to think for a moment that he would return to being the Matthew I knew simply because I came here to find him! I have always fancied myself intelligent, but I see now that I lack all common sense and judgment! Miss Blackwell was quite correct when she said that I am naïve!"

"Most of us like to think that what we want is possible," replied Mr. Thoreau calmly. "But you have seen now, Miss Lancaster, what you have known all along—that we all change and that there is no going back. Even if he left Miss Blackwell, he would not be the same Matthew that you loved, any more than you would be the same Lizzie. It cannot be."

Lizzie realized with horror that great tears were sliding down her cheeks, and obediently followed Mr. Thoreau as he led her over to the privacy of a small grouping of orange trees and palms. He pulled out his handkerchief and patted her cheeks softly.

"Oh, pray don't do that, Mr. Thoreau. You will ruin your handkerchief! I am wearing paint, as you see, and it will make a tremendous mess." She caught herself mid-sob. "And I must look frightful with all of the paint running!"

"You could never look frightful to me, Miss Lancaster," he said, still patting her face dry. "I do have one criticism of you, however."

"What is it?" she demanded, hiccupping this time as she tried to hold back another sob.

"It does not seem quite fair to me that Andronikos, whom you have known for a much shorter period of time, now has the right to call you Lizzie, while I, whom you have known for ever so much longer—"

"Three weeks longer," she inserted.

"May only call you Miss Lancaster," he finished, ignoring her interruption.

"Please do call me Lizzie," she said, smiling in spite of herself. "And I shall call you Daniel."

"Agreed," he said, bowing. "And now, Lizzie, what would you like to do? Do you care to dance? To walk about for a little? To sit and talk?"

She managed a smile. "I should like to dance, of course. After all, Daniel, for tonight at least, I am a gypsy! I will not care a fig what anyone thinks of me!"

"Then dance we shall," he agreed, and they proceeded to do exactly that. Although it was not considered proper for a young lady to dance more than twice with the same partner, she and Mr. Thoreau broke that rule to the tune of several dances. Even when many others wished to dance with Lizzie, the pair smiled brightly at the interlopers and declared the next dance taken. Even Matthew—or perhaps, most especially Matthew—who appeared at last, was blithely refused.

"Please don't make a further spectacle of yourself because you are angry with me," he said to her in a low voice, ignoring Mr. Thoreau.

"Tonight, Matthew, I am—as you can clearly see—a gypsy! So I shall do just as I please!"

And Mr. Thoreau swept her away into the next waltz, leaving him standing forlornly beside a potted palm. Across the dance floor, they could see Miss Blackwell dancing with Mr. Mansfield. She too appeared to have danced the whole evening, but not at all with her fiancé.

They could see that Lady Thalia, at the moment, was happily engrossed in conversation with Talleyrand and his niece.

"I believe that you are universally admired, Lizzie," observed Mr. Thoreau, for she was the focus of many admiring—and some envious—glances.

"Not universal," she corrected him. Before her spirits began to sink at the thought of Matthew, however, and to show that she was able to focus outward as he had taught her, she smiled and added, "But very close to it, I believe. It must be immensely gratifying to possess a gypsy spirit all of the year."

Mr. Thoreau did not reply immediately because another gentleman arrived to request the pleasure of her company. At a glance from her, however, he once again declined to yield his place, and the newcomer, defeated, bowed and retired to seek another partner.

Indeed, Mr. Thoreau did not yield his place to another gentleman until Mr. Andronikos appeared beside them. "I have come to claim my dance, dear Lizzie," he said, bowing deeply. "That is, if Daniel will allow me to do so."

Lizzie made a deep curtsey and smiled at him. "I am glad that you remembered to see me before you leave, George," she said lightly. "I should not wish to be forgotten."

He exchanged a grave glance with Thoreau, before taking her hand and saying, still with an unaccustomed touch of gravity, "I shall never forget you, Miss Lizzie Lancaster."

Once the music began, he seemed much more himself, light in movement and manner. "Your evening has been a great success, Lizzie," he observed. "If you were to dance with all the men who wish to be your partner, you would still be dancing a sennight from now—and like the princesses in the old fairy tale, you would wear out countless pairs of slippers."

Lizzie laughed, thinking yet again what a pleasure it was to be with a man who enjoyed life so intensely. Daniel Thoreau took pleasure in life, too, but it was a steady, sensible pleasure. For him there were no peaks of joy or valleys of despair. For George Andronikos it was otherwise, although the peaks of joy appeared to predominate.

"You exaggerate again, but I thank you for the pretty sentiment. And I must thank you again, dear George, for helping me have this delightful evening. I should never have managed without you."

"But of course you would have managed, Lizzie—you will always manage. I merely happened to be the one at hand who could become a part of your plan." He smiled down into her eyes and lifted the hand he was holding to his lips. "Doing so has given me great joy."

"My brother is named George," she said suddenly. "I had not thought of it before, but in some ways you remind me of him."

"I am desolated, of course, to be compared to your brother—for how may I be your sweetheart if that is so?" he responded. "But I am honored as well, for you feel deep affection for him, do you not?"

"I do indeed," she answered, knowing that it was true, no matter how upset she had become with him for some of the things he had done. "He is always charming and always kind."

Mr. Andronikos inclined his head in a brief nod. "And I must be grateful, Lizzie, if you believe that I possess such qualities."

"You do, of course," she answered, "for you make it

always a pleasure to be with you and you have shown me great kindness. Unfortunately, however, George lacks something very important that you and Daniel both possess."

"And what might that be?" he inquired with interest.

"Focus," she said. "You serve a greater good than your own needs, and Daniel turns his attention outward to the world about him, as he has tried to teach me to do— but neither of you places your own personal interests before everything else."

"And your brother George, he does this?" asked Mr. Andronikos gravely. "He thinks first of himself?"

"Always," she sighed. "Or almost always, it seems. And I do not know how to help him change that. Indeed, I don't think he wishes to change!"

"Possibly not," he answered seriously, "but it may be that life will teach him otherwise."

Lizzie shook her head. "Perhaps it may happen, George, but I have little hope of it. When I have looked about me here in Vienna, I have observed that many people are just like my brother."

Mr. Andronikos nodded. "All too often that is true. But do you know what is amazing, dear Lizzie?"

She looked at him inquiringly, waiting for him to answer his own question.

"That sometimes, most surprisingly, they are not! Is it not amazing that there are indeed also many who place something or someone above their own personal good? We must find that encouraging, Lizzie."

She sighed. "Yes, I know that you are correct, but I confess that it is lowering when I reflect that I am not one of them. I certainly have no business criticizing my brother. After all, what have I been thinking of save my own pleasure?"

He shrugged lightly. "That is not necessarily such a bad thing. After all, it does no one any good to sit in sackcloth and ashes and moan of the end of the world. Even if you do no more than take pleasure in the day—and share that pleasure with others—is that not a gift to them?"

She thought about it a moment. "Well, I suppose that is true—if, that is, you do indeed *share* that pleasure with others. I'm not at all certain that I do so."

"But you do, Lizzie. You have shared it with me and with Daniel and Lady Thalia—and undoubtedly with others that you are not even aware of."

She looked doubtful, so he continued. "Think of it in this way, Lizzie. Have you not stopped to buy hot chestnuts and gotten a cheerful greeting from the man who handed them to you? Or passed a stranger on the street who smiled at you?"

"Well, naturally, I have but—"

"Then you have seen people who were sharing their pleasure in the day with others—just as you do without even realizing it. If the vendor had spoken to you rudely or if the stranger had frowned at you or looked weighed down with the troubles of the world, your response would not have been the same."

"No," she conceded, "but it seems a very small thing, nonetheless."

"Lizzie, life is composed of all those small things! It is not the momentous things that compose our lives—it is all the little ones!"

She was not completely convinced, but she smiled at him as the dance ended and they made their way back toward Mr. Thoreau. "You are always a pleasure, Mr. Andronikos—George, I mean. I always look forward to seeing you."

"And I to seeing you, dear lady," he said, kissing her hand once more, "but I fear that I shall not see you again, perhaps for a very long time."

"Why not?" she demanded, alarmed at his sudden return to gravity. "Are you leaving?"

He nodded, but before he could speak again, she said in a low voice, "Paris! You are going to Paris, are you not?"

Again he nodded. "But I shall always think of you, dear Lizzie, and thinking of you shall give me the greatest pleasure. Most of all, I shall think of you dancing down the steps tonight, with a gypsy in your soul."

She shook her head, suddenly completely deflated. "There is no gypsy, George. Just plain Lizzie Lancaster."

"Never plain!" he insisted. "If you cannot wear the colors of the gypsy every day, you can wear them in your soul. You have too much to give to allow yourself to become bleak in spirit."

"I shall remember," she said, trying to smile. "And I know that thinking of you shall always bring me joy."

"Dear Lizzie," he said softly, and bent and kissed her tenderly on the lips, ignoring the people around them. And then he turned and left, weaving his way through the crowd.

Mr. Thoreau took her arm and looked down at her.

"No more dancing, Daniel," she said. "Not tonight."

Seventeen

It was odd, Lady Thalia thought, that the absence of one flirtatious young man, no matter how charming, should have left such a void. Lizzie had seemed very low in the days following the departure of Mr. Andronikos for Paris. She said that he had business there—more of the business that he and Mr. Thoreau were involved in, no doubt. Some sort of import-export affairs, she suspected. Mr. Thoreau seemed to feel his loss as well. Of course, they had been friends since childhood, but she would have thought Mr. Thoreau would have been grateful to have an entire room to himself now instead of being obliged to share it with Mr. Andronikos. She sighed. Her health was much better now, but her own spirits were a little low as well. Soon she would be in no better a state than Lizzie.

Suddenly remembering what she had planned to do about Lizzie, she rang for Beavers to bring her traveling desk. A careful and tactful questioning of Lizzie had elicited more information about the Lancasters' situation—and about young George's gaming problem. She had pondered it all for a while, wondering just what she could do without appearing to help them, and she had finally struck upon a plan, one that she thought proudly that no one else would have been likely to think of. At first she could not see just how she could bring it about, but then she had thought of Timothy Holywell. He spent much of his time in London, he was clever and sophisticated and discreet—and he owed her a favor after not forewarning her of the travel conditions between Paris and Vienna.

She wrote a very long and carefully detailed letter to Timothy Holywell and sent it off immediately. If this did not work, she would think of something else.

Lizzie had been thinking about what Mr. Andronikos had said to her on their last evening together—and trying very hard not to think of his joining the French army and preparing seriously for battle. She had been doing her best to assume a cheerful façade, but she knew, both from the way Lady Thalia and Beavers watched her so carefully and from the greater frequency of Mr. Thoreau's calls, that she had convinced no one. She was indeed trying, but she could not feel her usual self. Everything, including herself, seemed dull.

Mr. Thoreau was present when a letter arrived, accompanied by an oversize bouquet of red and white roses, tied in broad blue ribbon.

He grinned at her. "Have you any doubt, Lizzie, just who has sent those to you?"

Lady Thalia had grown accustomed to the two calling one another by their Christian names, but she had begged them to be discreet and, when in public, to be more formal. As soon as she had once again recovered from hearing Mr. Thoreau say "Lizzie" so casually, she focused on what he had been saying and upon the bouquet itself.

"Why, Lizzie! That is *precisely* like the one you received

in Paris!" she exclaimed. "How lovely they are! Beavers, do put them in water immediately!"

Beavers bore them away, and Mr. Thoreau watched Lizzie with amusement. She was staring at the letter in her lap as though it might snap at her.

"What is it, Lizzie?" he inquired. "Are you afraid of what your captain of the Dragoons might have to say?"

"No. No, of course not," she replied, giving herself a little shake and taking the letter in her hand. She broke the blue seal and read swiftly.

"He is here, of course. We knew that must be so from the roses—but he says that he hopes that we will be attending the Carrousel tonight. He will be riding in it."

Thoreau gave a low whistle. "It seems that your captain must be quite an important fellow, Lizzie."

"He must indeed!" exclaimed Lady Thalia. "Why, there are only twenty-four riders in the entire Carrousel!"

"And they all must be from noble families and must have proven their courage in battle," added Thoreau.

Preparations for the Carrousel had been going on for weeks, and it was to be presented in the best medieval tournament fashion possible. It was to be held in the Hofburg's Spanish Riding School, and the event was the focus of great anticipation.

"And what else does your captain say, Lizzie?" Mr. Thoreau inquired.

"He writes that he has come to take the place of his cousin, who broke his leg during a hunt and so is unable to participate. And he also writes that each of the 'knights' who rides in the Carrousel has his own chosen lady among the audience, and that he would like for me to be his."

Mr. Thoreau raised his eyebrows and even Lady Thalia

looked taken aback. "This is more serious than we had thought, Lizzie. What will you say to him?"

To their surprise, Lizzie laughed and shook her head. "He tells me that I am not to feel that I have committed myself in any way should I choose to accept, and he reminds me that he knows no other lady here so, if I refuse, he will have none."

"I think that is *not* the case, Lizzie, no matter what he says. I *personally* know of dozens of women who would kill to be chosen," said Lady Thalia. "I myself would not mind it at all."

"I don't imagine it could do any harm, and it would seem ungracious to refuse," said Lizzie slowly.

"I would say that he has made it impossible for you to refuse without feeling that way," observed Mr. Thoreau a little dryly, and Lizzie looked at him in surprise. "Just consider, Lizzie. How did he find where you are staying? He went to great lengths to find you."

"And just in time, too," added Lady Thalia approvingly. "It's very clever of him to have discovered your direction."

"And so what answer will you send him?" asked Mr. Thoreau, watching her face.

"I believe I shall accept," she said. "It seems so unkind not to do so. He writes that his man is waiting for my answer, and that if I accept, he would like for me to send a scarf so that he may wear it tonight."

She rose and walked toward the door. "If you will excuse me, I must go and write him an answer immediately—and find a scarf that I may send."

Lady Thalia and Mr. Thoreau looked at one another for a moment.

"Well, it is all very flattering," she said.

"Yes, Captain LaSalle was most attentive to her in Paris."

"But you do not see any real harm in it, do you, Mr. Thoreau?"

He shrugged. "I daresay there is no danger of her losing her heart to him in the course of the evening."

Lady Thalia laughed. "Of course there is not! Are *you* planning to attend?"

He shook his head and grinned. "There is not a ticket available in Vienna, so I shall stay at home and think long thoughts."

"Nonsense! You *must* come with us. Lord Danvers now has the influenza that plagued me, and we would be delighted if you would take his place tonight. You simply must *not* miss what they are saying will be the spectacle of the century. And afterward there is to be a supper and a grand ball."

To her pleasure, he accepted and arrived to escort them that evening with his usual promptness. As they entered and took their places, he glanced at Lady Thalia and nodded. "You were correct, ma'am. Before the Carrousel even begins, it is already the spectacle of the century."

And so it was. All of the members of royalty—the emperors, kings, queens, princes, princesses, grand dukes, and grand duchesses—were seated on a raised dais, and their collective splendor alone would have set the evening off from all others. The diplomats were seated on one side of the galleries and the nobility on the other. The white elegance of the Riding School itself, with its forty-six Corinthian columns and magnificent coffered ceiling, made a memorable backdrop for the pageantry of the proceedings.

Lizzie watched it all, concentrating intently because she had felt herself growing more and more distant from everything that was taking place. She had written to Captain LaSalle and sent him a green scarf, she had eaten dinner and dressed carefully for the Carrousel and the subsequent ball, but she had done everything in what seemed to her a dreamlike state. So now she attempted to force herself to focus.

After the paladins entered the arena, attired in costumes from the fifteen hundreds, their horses handsomely caparisoned, they arranged themselves for the first exercise. For this, they tilted their lances at rings hung from ropes around the arena, attempting of course to put the lance through each of the rings. It all looked like something from a painting or a storybook, and many had been consulted as the Carrousel was planned.

As she watched the riders move through the sets of exercises—charging wooden heads mounted on posts and cutting them off with a single blow, slashing apples in half with their sabers, charging one another in an attempt to unseat the opponent—everything seemed to blur into one vivid whirlpool of movement. She could hear the military music playing, but it seemed to her that it grew more and more distant.

As the Carrousel drew to a close, she heard Mr. Thoreau say, "Lizzie, are you quite all right?"

"Of course I am," she had replied. "Just overcome by all of this."

He and Lady Thalia had contented themselves with her answer. Together, they had risen and walked down a corridor decked with flowers and orange trees to the hall where supper was to be served. As she walked, it seemed to Lizzie that the velvet gown that she was wearing had grown heavier and heavier. To her relief, they were finally seated, and minstrels moved among them, playing ballads from the days of knights and ladies.

"Lizzie, I saw you at the Carrousel, but I did not have the opportunity to come and talk to you. I have wanted to see you for days, but I didn't have the courage to face you."

She heard her name and looked up to see Matthew standing there—or at least wavering there. How suitable, she thought to herself, that the minstrel nearest them should begin the strains of "Greensleeves."

"Lizzie? Did you hear me? I should like very much to talk with you if you would just come and walk with me for minute or two."

"Yes, I heard you, Matthew," she said slowly. "I was just listening to the song."

"To the song?" he said blankly, and then he listened for a moment and flushed. "Yes, I hear it, too. Come walk with me and we will talk after the song finishes."

At that moment, there was a new arrival, and the impressive figure of Captain LaSalle bore down upon them.

"Mademoiselle Lancaster," he said reverently, going down on one knee beside her chair and taking her hand, "I am eternally grateful for your kindness in sending me your scarf to wear. It brought me good fortune." He kissed her hand and then held it to his heart. "You have honored me greatly, mademoiselle."

"Not at all, captain," she returned gently. "I am the one who is honored." It was curious, she thought. She could hear herself speaking, but she seemed quite far away from it all. And it felt as though she was speaking very slowly, but everyone appeared to understand her.

She turned toward Matthew. "Captain LaSalle, I should like to present Mr. Matthew Webster. Matthew, this is Captain François LaSalle."

LaSalle rose and the two men bowed stiffly to one another. Then LaSalle turned back to her and bowed. "Miss Lancaster, I cannot stay just now, but I wished to request the first dance with you—and, if you will allow it, the rest of the dances as well."

Lizzie smiled. She knew that because she felt her cheeks lift slightly. "Of course, Captain." She had meant to add that they would see about the other dances after the first was over, but she could see that she had not, because he kissed her hand, said something to her that she did not quite take in, bowed to the others, turned, and walked away.

"Lizzie!" she heard Matthew gasp in protest. "Please don't do this again!"

"Oh, Matthew!" she said slowly, as though she had quite forgotten him. "Your walk."

She rose from her chair and took a step toward him but, as she did so, it seemed to her that he—and the rest of the world around her—suddenly receded from her at a shocking rate, and she felt herself falling.

Eighteen

Over the next weeks, Lizzie lay, as they say, "at death's door," and even after the doctor had determined to his own satisfaction that the worst was behind her, he shook his head when Lady Thalia demanded absolute assurance that there would be no relapse. Influenza had brought death to more than one in Vienna during these winter months. Helpless, Lady Thalia and Beavers took turns at her bedside, and Mr. Thoreau and Matthew called daily to ask about her progress, as did Captain LaSalle until his leave was over and his presence required once more in Paris.

"I pray for her good health, madame. Please tell her so when she is herself again."

"I will indeed, sir," Lady Thalia assured him. He had been a faithful caller, begging her to give him something to do that might help Lizzie. There was, of course, very little that anyone could do except pray, as Captain LaSalle had said. He also continued to deliver fresh roses each time the last bouquet had begun to fade. Upon taking his leave of Lady Thalia, he had assured her that they would still be delivered regularly, even in his absence.

As for Lizzie, she lived for weeks in a strange sort of half-world, inhabited by real people and dreams, merging together in fantasies that were sometimes pleasing, sometimes frightening—but always fantastic. In one, she married Captain LaSalle, and at their wedding, everyone threw violets at them as they left the church. As he helped her into their carriage to leave, she looked back at the crowd and into the unsmiling eyes of Napoleon Bonaparte, a violet in his lapel. In another, she was home at the Lodge, watching out the window for Matthew. Suddenly she noticed her hand, which looked odd. Looking in the glass at her dressing table, she saw that her dark hair was grey and her face lined with wrinkles. In still another, she married Daniel Thoreau and traveled around the world with him, giving money to groups that were planning revolutions. As the kaleidoscope shifted, she was a gypsy, dancing in the streets, and Teresa Blackwell, her hand securely on Matthew's arm, tossed her a coin. Then she was at the Carrousel once more, and instead of the wooden head on a post, George Andronikos stood there in the middle of the arena, and the paladin was bearing down upon him with a sword.

She had opened her eyes many times during her illness, but those caring for her had been able to tell that she was not herself, for the people she saw and spoke to were not present in the room with them. There were periods when she appeared to be resting normally, and they would grow hopeful, but then the troubled times would return. So it was a very happy moment when she finally opened her eyes late one January afteroon, saw Lady Thalia sitting there with her book, and said quite distinctly, "May I have a cup of tea, please?"

Lady Thalia looked at her, shut her book, leaned closer to her, and said, "Lizzie? Is that truly *you*?"

Lizzie looked at her helplessly. Lady Thalia was looking at her so intently that she feared something was wrong. "Yes," she said, wondering who else she might be. "Are you quite well, Lady Thalia?"

To her shock, she saw that tears were running down her friend's cheeks, but she was smiling.

"Yes, I am doing *wonderfully* well now that you have come back to us, Lizzie!" Losing all semblance of dignity, she ignored the bell cord and ran to the door calling, "Beavers! Henry! *Someone!* Lizzie has requested some tea!"

When Beavers hurried in with a tray for her, they helped Lizzie to sit up in bed. It was surprising, she thought, that she could not do that herself. Then Beavers brushed her hair and sponged her face and neck before setting the tray on her lap.

She discovered that she needed help even to lift the cup to her lips, and she looked at Lady Thalia in puzzlement. "I must have been sick," she said. "I thought that I had just had a nightmare."

"And so you did," replied Lady Thalia. "A *very* long one. But we are delighted that it is over, Lizzie dear."

"So it *was* a nightmare?" asked Lizzie. "How long did I sleep?"

"It was a nightmare caused by sickness, Lizzie. You have been sick for a very long time."

Lizzie's eyes had alighted on the vase of roses near her bed, and she smiled. "Not really so very long then. The roses are still fresh."

Lady Thalia and Beavers looked at one another. "That isn't the *same* bouquet of roses, dear."

"Captain LaSalle brought another? That was very kind of him." She thought for a minute, trying to remember. "I was going to dance with him."

Lady Thalia leaned toward her encouragingly. "Yes, yes, you were, but you got sick before you could do so."

Lizzie's brow creased as she tried to bring back that evening. "I remember bits of the Carrousel," she said. "And how very heavy my gown was, and how far away everyone seemed." She paused a moment, thinking. "Matthew! I was going to talk with Matthew!"

Lady Thalia nodded. "That is when you collapsed, Lizzie. Matthew carried you to the carriage, and he helped me to get you home while Mr. Thoreau went for a doctor."

Lizzie lay back on the pillows, turning her head from side to side as she tried to remember more. Beside Lady Thalia was a small table with a pitcher of water, a glass, Lizzie's medicine—and her gold music box.

"Why is my music box there?" she asked. She usually kept it on her dressing table. Even with all the heartache over Matthew, she had not been able to make herself put it away.

"Because that was the *one* thing that seemed to calm you, my dear, when you were at your worst. Beavers or I would open it and you would grow still and listen to it."

Lizzie felt a tear rolling down her cheek. "'Greensleeves,'" she said. "The minstrel was playing it and Matthew was going to listen to it with me before we talked."

Lady Thalia nodded.

Lizzie lay quiet for a few minutes, still puzzling things out. Suddenly she asked, "Have you been with me all the time I have been sick?"

Lady Thalia nodded again. "Beavers and I have taken turns. One of us slept while the other watched."

"But how dreadful I feel for what I have done to you, Lady Thalia! You came to Vienna to see everything that was happening and I have made you miss some of the events you were so looking forward to and live in a sickroom instead!"

Lady Thalia shooed away the comment with a wave of her hand. "Nonsense! This was *much* more important than any party or ball could be—and, of course, Catholic homes do not have dances during Advent, so things grew much tamer then."

Lizzie stared at her. "Is it already Advent?" she asked. "That was several days away when I took ill."

Lady Thalia looked slightly uncomfortable, but then she leaned close to Lizzie and took her hand. "You have been sick quite a *long* time, my dear. Advent is over."

"Advent is over?" she asked, astonished. "And Christmas?"

"Over," replied Lady Thalia. "As is New Year's." She smiled. "Twelfth Night has only just gone, though."

Lizzie went to sleep almost immediately, but they were relieved to see that it was now a peaceful sleep. Henry had hurried around for the doctor when she had first awakened, and he arrived after she had fallen asleep. He examined her quickly, then turned to Lady Thalia with a look of satisfaction.

"She has no temperature, her pulse is steady, and she appears to be breathing easily. If what you say about her rational behavior is true, then I believe we may safely say that Miss Lancaster is on the road to recovery."

He went on to caution them that it would be a long recovery, and that she should by no means rush it. Lady Thalia, looking down at her, could only agree. Lizzie was still deathly pale, and she was so thin that she looked as if she could be broken like a twig. Together with Beavers, she planned a nourishing diet for the invalid, one that would help her to build her strength. They agreed to abandon barley water for a nourishing tea caudle, and Beavers, who had strong Scottish ties, firmly advocated the introduction of porridge onto the menu. Now, too, they would be able to gradually abandon the broths they had been spooning into her mouth each day, and work her gently toward more substantial fare.

For the next fortnight, Lizzie did little but sleep, but it was a restful, healing sleep. During the brief periods when she was awake, she ate and asked an occasional question, often drifting off to sleep in the middle of both. Once she awoke to see Daniel Thoreau seated beside her, but she decided that must have been a dream, for when she looked again, he had gone.

"*Was* Daniel here to see me?" she asked the next day. "I rather thought he was, but then I thought I might have been dreaming."

"He was *most* definitely here, my dear. Of course, he has been here to call *every* day since you took ill—and he has been *wonderful* about getting the doctor and the medicines and being here as moral support. Yesterday he asked to see for himself how you are doing."

"You must thank him for me, Lady Thalia."

"You will be able to thank him yourself this afternoon if you feel well enough for a real caller."

Lizzie shook her head. "Perhaps tomorrow," she said. "I must have a bath and wash my hair—although I know I shall probably drown if Beavers doesn't help me. Doing just that will take all my energy. Tomorrow I shall feel more like receiving a caller."

Lady Thalia smiled. "Now I know that you *are* truly getting better, Lizzie. Worrying about your appearance is a *very* good sign, indeed."

"Have I had any other callers while I was ill?" Lizzie asked hesitantly.

"More than I could *possibly* count," Lady Thalia assured her. "*Droves* of young men that you have danced with at the balls have come, most of them with nosegays.

If you walk into the drawing room, you will see that we look like a greenhouse. The doctor said not to put them in here, but I *insisted* that the captain's roses be where you could see them. He has sent them every week."

"How lovely of him," murmured Lizzie, but without noticeable enthusiasm.

"And you have had *letters*, of course. Beavers has put them all away for you to read when you feel like doing so." Lady Thalia hesitated a moment, then continued. "And, Lizzie, I did *not* tell your family how serious your illness was when I wrote to them. I had to let them know that you were ill, of course, because they would be expecting your letters. But if I had told them how *very* ill you were, they would have attempted that dreadful trip, worrying about you all the way, and probably have become ill themselves."

Lizzie did not reply, and she finally said anxiously, "I *do* hope that you think I did the proper thing, Lizzie."

Lizzie seemed to come back to life with that, and she patted Lady Thalia's hand. "Naturally I think you did the proper thing. You have taken excellent care of me, for which I am *most* grateful, and I can only be sorry that I have created such a problem for you."

Lady Thalia again protested that she had been no problem, but after they had both been silent for several minutes, Lizzie said, "Did anyone else come?"

Lady Thalia nodded. "Matthew came every day. He waited to see me each time so that he could hear the latest report, and he begged me to let him come in to see you."

"And did you allow it?"

"No. I did not think he had that right—and he is, of course, still engaged to Miss Blackwell."

"I understand, Lady Thalia," she said softly. "Indeed,

you do not have to worry about me. I shall be quite all right without Matthew."

"Of *course* you will!" she responded encouragingly. "And you have Mr. Thoreau coming to call. *That* will give you something pleasant to look forward to."

Lizzie smiled. "You seem to have become quite fond of that gentleman while I was ill."

"You have *no* notion what a support he has been, Lizzie," she replied earnestly. "I *gladly* take back every criticism I ever made of him. He has been a *rock*!"

Amazed by Lady Thalia's glowing opinion of Mr. Thoreau, she confided it to that gentleman when he came to call the next day. "You have made quite an impression," she concluded with amusement.

"Lady Thalia has been beside herself ever since you collapsed, Lizzie," he replied. "Not only was she worried about you as a friend, but she felt the entire responsibility for your well-being. She was terrified that she would have to go home and tell your parents that you had been lost while in her care."

All sign of amusement disappeared from Lizzie's face. "The poor lady. I knew it had been difficult—and very taxing physically, of course—but I had not thought about that aspect of it."

"Well, happily for all concerned, she will not have to face that particular horror," he said cheerfully. "We must be grateful for that."

"Well, *I* most certainly am," she responded. She held up a letter, one from a stack on her bedcovers. "This is from George," she said.

"Your brother?" he asked.

She shook her head. "George Andronikos. He wanted to wish me well. He had heard—from you—about my collapsing."

Mr. Thoreau nodded. "I wrote to him immediately. I knew that he would be most concerned about your welfare."

"Do you know what he is doing?" she asked.

"Naturally. He is becoming a Hussar, like your captain."

"He is not *my* captain, as you very well know, sir! Stay with the subject, please. Do you know of any of George's *other* activities?"

Mr. Thoreau shrugged. "He doubtless attends the theater and has an extremely active social life." He grinned at her. "I do hope that you didn't think of settling down with George. It would never answer, you know. He is too much a will-o'-the-wisp."

Lizzie smiled in spite of herself at the thought of anyone settling down for long with George Andronikos. She opened the letter and showed him the paper upon which it had been written.

"Look at it, Daniel. The whole of the sheet is edged with a wreath of violets."

"I see that it is," he replied, scarcely glancing at it.

"And so he is working for Napoleon?" she asked.

Again he shrugged. "I do not answer for George," he said. "His affairs are his own."

"Very well. Do *you* support Napoleon, Daniel?"

"You already know my thoughts about him, Lizzie," he responded. "I believe that you can answer that for yourself."

"But I have heard that when the British burned Washington, there was a great outcry of support from the French. I thought perhaps you might have changed your mind."

"No, Lizzie. I still favor democracy and a constitution— which is precisely the reason that I would never support Napoleon."

They sat in silence for a moment, and then he said, "You were still ill when I had my good news, Lizzie."

"Indeed? What news would that be, sir?"

"Our countries are no longer at war. Arrangements for a peace were finally agreed upon at Ghent just before Christmas."

"At Ghent?" she said, looking at him closely. "Does that possibly explain your journeys there?"

"You have far too suspicious a nature, Lizzie Lancaster. It is not becoming," he chided her gently. "You should be celebrating the peace with me, not prying into my affairs."

She smiled, knowing that he was completely unruffled. "I am very glad to hear of it, Daniel. Will you be going home soon?"

"Are you trying to rush me away?" he inquired, his brows raised.

"No, of course not. We should be delighted to have you stay—particularly now that you have become Lady Thalia's great favorite."

"You manners are sometimes quite appalling, Lizzie. I believe that I must speak to Lady Thalia about them," he observed, smiling. "There is other news, too. Castlereagh is returning to England and Wellington is coming here very soon to take his place."

"Is he indeed? It is comforting to know that the Iron Duke will be so close, although I felt far more secure before George informed me that there is not any longer much of an army for him to command."

"Well, if we are fortunate, he will have no need of it," replied Mr. Thoreau. "He will be keeping your friend Matthew very busy, I am sure."

At the mention of Matthew, Lizzie sank back among her pillows, and he watched her, troubled. "Is there something wrong, Lizzie?"

"It is Matthew. Lady Thalia said that he came every day to see me, just as you did while I was ill. He wants to talk to me."

"And do you want to talk to him?"

"No. Not I don't really wish to see him at all—but I feel as though I should, as though *he* needs to talk to me."

"Then you must do whatever you think would be best."

She nodded. "I suppose I shall see him tomorrow. Will you come and see me afterward?"

"Naturally I will. Let me know what time I should arrive and assuredly I shall be here."

She put out her hand to him. "What a great comfort you are, Daniel. I don't know what Lady Thalia or I would have done without you."

"You would have managed very nicely," he replied, smiling. "Both of you are more than capable of taking care of any difficult situation in which you find yourselves."

She heard the echo of George's words to her in what he said, and she wondered if what they said was true. She was quite certain that Lady Thalia could manage anything, but far less certain about herself.

She looked at him and smiled. "But we are both very glad that we have had you to rely upon, Daniel."

When she met with Matthew the next day, she felt as awkward as she might when meeting with someone she scarcely knew. Conversation was stilted, and he kept casting sidelong glances at her, as though to assess the damage the illness had done.

"I am mending, Matthew!" she said impatiently. "And I do not plan to turn up my toes, so you needn't keep watching me as though you fear it will happen at any moment."

"Don't be angry with me, Lizzie. I am only concerned about your welfare."

"And you have inquired into my welfare, and I have answered you. I am grateful for your concern. What else do we have to say to each other?"

Matthew cleared his throat. "I need to tell you about the St. George medal, Lizzie."

She shook her head violently. "You do *not*! I have told you that I had no desire to know the details of the story."

"I didn't just *give* it to Teresa, Lizzie. I wore it every day and she thought it was a pretty thing, so she took it—just as a child would—without realizing what it means to me."

"Miss Blackwell appeared to be quite well informed about me and about how you came to have the medal, Matthew. Are you sure she took it in all innocence?" Lizzie knew the answer to this herself, but she was quite certain that Matthew was too besotted to admit the truth to himself.

He shook his head eagerly. "Of course I am. She is not vindictive, even if she is at times—a little unthinking. She did not intend to hurt your feelings when she told you that you had been naïve."

"Well, that is good to know, Matthew, for otherwise I might have misinterpreted her motive. I might have believed her to have a streak of malice in her nature."

"Malice?" he said, trying to sound affronted. He stared at her a moment, then shook his head. "It's no good, Lizzie. Everything you're saying is true, but I'm quite trapped. I proposed to Teresa, she accepted, and I cannot break our engagement. I shall have to see it through."

Lizzie could see the misery in his eyes.

"Lizzie?" he said in a voice so low she could scarcely hear him. "If I were no longer engaged to Teresa, would you consider marrying me?"

She stared at him coldly. "No, Matthew. I'm afraid that you've shown me that you're not to be depended upon. I would not marry such a man as that."

He stood, bowed to her, and went silently from the room. She should have felt wonderful, having humbled him and heard from his own lips that he regretted his decision and would marry her if he could. She had planned to make him a very uncomfortable young man, and she had succeeded beyond her wildest dreams.

Strangely, however, all that she could feel was a great sadness that seemed to engulf her. Not even Daniel's visit immediately afterward could cheer her. She told him precisely what had happened, reproaching Matthew for his infidelity and herself for her cruelty in telling him the truth.

"And so, Lizzie, you would not wish to marry him, even if he were free?" asked Mr. Thoreau, watching her expression carefully.

She moved restlessly on the pillows. "How could I, Daniel? He betrayed my trust. There is no gaining that back again."

"No, that is true, of course. But remember what we talked about once before. You can never go back again to what has been. He will never be the same Matthew nor you the same Lizzie. Your decision would have to be made upon who you both are now."

"Well, there is no point in even thinking about it since he is still engaged and he will not betray *that* trust, at any rate! I suppose that I should have had a formal engagement and a ring to bind him before he left for the Peninsula. Then things might be otherwise now."

She gave a brief, unamused chuckle. "Miss Blackwell was quite in the right of it, however much I may dislike her. She said that I was naïve, and I most certainly was!"

"It is true that you will never be so innocent again," he agreed. "But would you wish to be so?"

Startled, she looked at him for a moment, then sighed and shook her head. "I don't know, Daniel. Just now I truly don't know."

Nineteen

The arrival in Vienna of the Duke of Wellington created a new wave of receptions and balls and breakfasts, but that all meant little enough to Lizzie, who was still too weak to participate in any of them. She insisted, however, that Lady Thalia go out once more, for Beavers and Henry were always there to care for her needs.

"I shall feel less guilty if you are out and enjoying yourself once more," she told Lady Thalia firmly. "And that will undoubtedly speed my recovery."

Thus encouraged, Lady Thalia once more plunged into the social whirl of Vienna, bringing home delectable tidbits of gossip and news with which to regale the invalid. Daniel Thoreau, still a daily caller—the only one she allowed at this point—brought her more solid political observations, to which she listened attentively.

"The Duke is an interesting man," he told Lizzie. "I believe he encourages the social activity to keep the meddlers busy. Vienna abounds in troublemakers, gossips, and spies, so anything that will keep them busy is desirable." The Congress, an unheard of experiment among the countries involved, had moved slowly and weightily and had, Metternich told Wellington upon his arrival, accomplished nothing.

"While you were still ill, Lizzie, a secret treaty was

signed between England, Austria, and France in order to secure themselves against the perceived threats of Prussia and Tsar Alexander's Russia. Since it was secret, it took a full twenty-four hours before it was known all over Vienna, rather than becoming immediate food for conversation and speculation the moment it was signed."

"Does Wellington agree with it?" she asked. "After all these years of war, it seems odd to be in an alliance *with* France instead of against her."

"That is the work of Talleyrand, of course, who could convince anyone that a raven and a nightingale are precisely the same bird. But Wellington does apparently agree. He is not a slippery customer like Talleyrand and Metternich, but he does appear to have the same sort of cosmopolitan view of things."

"What do you mean?" Lizzie asked.

"He believes that there must be a balance of power so that we may have a stable Europe, so they must be certain that legitimate sovereigns rule within all the countries concerned, and that no one power—or group of powers—gains too much control. Wellington is like Castlereagh—he sees that England has an interest in keeping the Continent stable and out of war. Too many of your countrymen, including those in Parliament, do not see the importance of concerning themselves abroad when they have pressing problems at home. Mine, of course, are no better," he added.

Lizzie thought about what he had said. "And if they are seeking stability at all costs, Daniel, that means that George—and others like him—will be crushed if they try to upset matters."

He nodded gravely. "Yes. For the sake of peace, such uprisings would be quelled as quickly and ruthlessly as possible."

Lizzie rose and walked to the window, looking down at the snow-covered streets. "I dreamed of him when I was ill. I saw a soldier bearing down upon him to kill him."

"In a war, that of course can happen, Lizzie. I cannot tell you that it would not. However," he said, deliberately lightening his tone, "you must remember George. If anyone can survive, he is the one. And who among us can be certain of just how things will develop?"

That night, Lady Thalia decided to stay at home and recruit her strength, for she had been out each day and evening during the past fortnight.

"I am *exhausted*, Lizzie, and I have neglected you *most* shamefully! I know you must be bored to distraction, sitting at home all day."

Lizzie laughed. "No, I have not been bored, ma'am, nor do I wish you to feel that you must sit at home with me. I have read and thought about any number of things, I have discussed the world with Daniel, and both he and Lord Danvers have very kindly kept me supplied with newspapers and books."

She did not add that she had found a curious contentment in the past two weeks. Nothing was expected of her, for she was to be resting, and there was none of the busyness of a household that there would have been at home at the Lodge. She missed all that—and she knew that homesickness could fall upon her at any moment—but her days were reassuringly quiet and regular, insulated from all the bustle of the outside world. She found that she had much to think about, but at times her mind would simply drift and she would think of nothing at all. It was all very peaceful.

"You seem to have grown quite serious once more, Lizzie—rather like you were when you were a very young girl." Lady Thalia had been thinking of the change in her, wondering if it was the lingering effects of the illness, or something deeper.

"Yes, I have thought about that, too," Lizzie confessed. "I think perhaps I was far wiser then—although very naïve about the ways of the world, of course."

She thought again of Miss Blackwell and frowned. "I was not meant to have a gypsy spirit. I knew that, of course, but it seemed that trying on a few personalities that were different from my own should do no harm."

"Nor *has* it," said Lady Thalia firmly. "You needed go get away from home and experience a little of the world. Then you may come closer to choosing what is right for you."

Lizzie nodded. "I think you are correct, Lady Thalia—and I shall be eternally in your debt for giving me the opportunity to do so. It is just that it has been harder than I had expected it to be."

Lady Thalia patted her hand. "Many things will be difficult, my dear—*but*, on the other hand, some will be surprisingly simple and joyful. You must simply accept them as they come and make the most of them."

"Like the oyster making a pearl of the bit of sand that is irritating it?" ventured Lizzie, smiling.

"*Exactly* so!" exclaimed Lady Thalia, relieved to have elicited at last a positive remark from her charge. "Oh, and I very nearly *forgot*, Lizzie. Henry brought up the mail and there is something here for you!"

She hurried back to the tray beside the entrance to the drawing room and picked up a letter addressed to Lizzie in an unmistakably masculine hand.

Lizzie opened it curiously, and glanced at the signature. "Why, it is from George!" she exclaimed.

"It does not look like his handwriting, though," said Lady Thalia, watching her.

"No no, not George Andronikos—my brother George!"

"Indeed!" she replied, and waited while the letter was read.

At last Lizzie dropped the letter into her lap, and stared at Lady Thalia. "He has restored my dowry!" she said in disbelief.

"But how *wonderful*, Lizzie! Is he *certain* of it? Does he tell you anything more?"

"He says that our father will be writing to me about it, but that he wanted to be the first to tell me since he knew that losing it was his fault."

"That was good of him," said Lady Thalia, still watching her closely.

Lizzie nodded. "But the most extraordinary thing about it is that he *won* the money!"

"Do you mean by *gambling*? I thought that was how he had gotten himself into trouble in the first place."

"Yes, of course it was! But he says he was determined to do something about the problems he had caused, so he used the diamond stickpin that our grandfather gave him, and managed to win back everything that he had lost during the past months! Is that not the most *extraordinary* news?"

"Most extraordinary," agreed Lady Thalia. "Does he say anything more?"

"But that is the most wonderful thing of all! He says that the gentleman who lost to him told him a terrible story about a young man he knew in his youth who had gambled away his family fortune, and had driven his father to taking his own life rather than facing ruin!"

"What a perfectly *dreadful* story!"

"Yes, of course it is—but it apparently made George see things in a different light. He hadn't thought about the possibility of such dire consequences for his own actions, and he swore to that gentleman and to our father that he would never gamble again. This time he has gone back to the Lodge of his own accord, and he is determined to learn how to take care of the property."

Lady Thalia leaned back in her chair and silently blessed Timothy Holywell. He had managed the affair even better than she had hoped. She had simply laid out the problem for him, and asked that he try to address it, using his own clever means.

"*Well,* my dear! This means that there will be *no* more talk of your becoming a governess nor of marrying the first gentleman who asks you! This is *splendid* news!"

"Yes, yes, it is," said Lizzie thoughtfully. It meant, too, that the family had no pressing need of the settlement that Matthew's father had arranged for once they were married. She had no immediate demands upon her now, and she need not feel that she had plunged the family into even more dire straits by failing to marry Matthew.

There was, she found, a great deal to think about.

Her recovery, as the doctor had predicted, was a long and very slow one. By the beginning of March, she was able to go for a short carriage ride on a fine day, and she had begun to gain back a little of the lost weight.

"You simply must *force* yourself to eat more, Lizzie!" Lady Thalia had insisted, viewing her with a critical eye as they were about to go out for a drive. Lizzie was wearing one of the gowns made by Fräulein Schlosser, but it looked as though it had been made for someone else. Although its line was simple and capable of covering a multitude of shortcomings, even the fitted bust and sleeves hung loose.

Lady Thalia turned to Beavers. "Order the most delectable things you can think of for dinner, Beavers—perhaps a thick soup and venison cutlets with cream sauce. And by all means, order dessert."

"*Apfelstrudel?*" inquired Lizzie, smiling.

"Most certainly *not!*" retorted Lady Thalia. "I am gaining all of the weight that you have lost, Lizzie. Very soon I shall have to go back to Fräulein Schlosser for larger gowns!"

Then she smiled. "Did I tell you, Lizzie, that Mr. Thoreau brought me an *apfelstrudel* while you were so ill?"

"I knew that he had done something to win you over, but I did not know that was how he managed it," conceded Lizzie, enjoying the dreamy expression on her friend's face. "He is a very resourceful man."

"Well, quite enough of *that,*" responded Lady Thalia, resuming her customary briskness. "Beavers, perhaps a torte—with as much whipped cream on it as possible."

Lizzie remained cocooned in her snug little world for a few more days, but when the change came, it arrived with a vengeance.

Lady Thalia had gone to a breakfast, but she came rushing back to the hotel almost immediately.

"Lizzie! Lizzie, you *cannot* imagine what has happened! Bonaparte has escaped from Elba!"

Lizzie stared at her, and Lady Thalia, her bonnet askew, nodded violently. "That was *precisely* my own reaction! I could not *believe* that such a thing could be true! But it is, Lizzie, it *is!* It will be war once more!"

Lizzie walked to the window and looked out. Although it could not be told from here, on her last rides to the Prater she had seen that early spring was upon them once more. It was time for the violets.

That day they waited impatiently for the arrival of Mr.

Thoreau so that they could catch up on the latest news. Lord Danvers was out, as was his wont, and undoubtedly would not return until late. When Henry announced Mr. Thoreau, the ladies pounced upon him at once.

"Do tell us, Mr. Thoreau, just what you have heard!" begged Lady Thalia, taking his arm and guiding him to a chair.

"Yes, Daniel! We are going wild here with only our own imaginations to fill in the spaces."

"It appears that Wellington and Metternich both received the news early this morning," he told them, speaking as calmly as he always did. "Wellington was supposed to hunt in the park at Schönbrunn this morning at seven, but when they brought his horse around for him, he sent it back. He had already heard. Metternich received the news while he was still in bed, and he bolted over to tell Talleyrand as soon as he was dressed."

"But where is Napoleon now?" Lizzie demanded.

Thoreau shrugged. "No one appears to know—although they all seem to agree that he would not go first to France. Some think he will land in Italy, where his brother-in-law is still King of Naples. He could find immediate support there."

"So no one really knows anything," remarked Lady Thalia unhappily. It seemed to her that knowing nothing was a great deal worse than knowing the truth of the matter, even if the truth was unpleasant.

Thoreau shook his head. "It will take time," he replied.

"There is one thing that we do know," said Lizzie, and the other two looked at her inquiringly. "We know that everything will change."

* * *

That, of course, was true, and the focus of everyone at the Congress of Vienna was now upon the renewed threat of Napoleon. Their quarrels were set aside so that they could organize themselves. Very soon, the members of the Congress drafted and signed a statement that declared that Napoleon was an outlaw, and would be treated as such.

News sifted into Vienna all the month of March. Contrary to what had been expected, Napoleon had indeed landed on the coast of Provence, accompanied, it was said, by a thousand men, forty horses, and two cannon. However, as he marched toward Paris, he was joined by deserting members of the French army and bands of peasants who cheered him on. Paris fell to him without a shot, the king, his court, the whole of the government and most of its supporters, having already fled. According to some of the stories, Napoleon was carried into the Tuileries on the shoulders of the crowd.

"He is most certainly back," said Mr. Thoreau to Lizzie one afternoon late in March, "but I believe he made a serious tactical error by not waiting until the Congress was over."

She looked at him, waiting.

"It would have taken far longer for those who oppose him to organize themselves and come to an agreement about how the problem should be addressed. As it is, they will be ready to face him very soon."

Lizzie discovered just how rapidly things were moving when Matthew came to call upon her. It was the first time that she had seen him since their discussion of the St. George medal, and she was troubled to see that he looked tired and strained.

"It is good to see you looking so much better, Lizzie," he said warmly.

"There is no need to tell me what is not true," she replied. "I have a glass and I know that I still look like a walking skeleton, Matthew."

He shook his head. "You look quite wonderful. I was frightened by your appearance when I saw you last."

"Scarcely a gallant thing to say, Matthew," she pointed out. "I believe I like it better when you are flattering me."

"Please let us not cross swords today, Lizzie," he said, sitting down and drawing his chair close to her. "I have come to say good-bye."

Lizzie found that it was difficult to swallow. "Good-bye? I take it that the Duke is leaving."

He nodded. "We will go to Belgium. Do you know if you plan to stay in Vienna?"

She shook her head. "I don't know what Lady Thalia's plans are," she answered. "But the doctor has said that I must not travel for another month, and Lady Thalia has said that when we do leave, we shall have to make the journey in easy stages. I'm afraid that I've become a dreadful burden to her."

"I don't think she regards you as a burden, Lizzie. She thinks very highly of you—as do all those who know you."

She turned her face away, not wishing to remember that time so long ago when he had said good-bye before going off to war.

He took her chin and turned her face gently back toward him. "Are you thinking of our good-bye in the garden, Lizzie?" he asked. She saw, with some astonishment, that his eyes were filled with a tenderness that she had not seen there in a very long time.

She nodded, afraid to speak and betray herself.

"So was I. We were little more than children then, you and I. When I think of it, it seems like another life."

"It was," she said briefly, looking away.

Once more he turned her face back toward him. "I came to thank you, Lizzie—not just to say good-bye."

She looked at him in surprise, and he nodded. "I wanted to thank you for loving me as you did—even though I didn't know the worth of it then." He patted his the front of his jacket. "I am wearing your St. George medal, Lizzie. I shall wear it until the day I die."

Not wanting to focus on his last words, particularly the mention of the day of his death, she said as lightly as she could manage, "And Miss Blackwell was willing to give it up?"

The creases around his mouth and eyes—creases that she had only just noticed—deepened and his eyes grew brighter. "She was not—shall we say—completely understanding about the matter, but I was able to convince her."

"I am glad you have it once more," she said. "It was meant for you."

"And it will protect me, as you had intended. I will, as I told you so long ago, put my faith in St. George—and in you."

He leaned toward her and kissed her long and tenderly, pulling her close to him. It seemed to her a very long time until he released her. "I shall always love you, Lizzie."

She looked up at him and patted his cheek gently. She knew that he was waiting for her to tell him that she loved him, too, but she could not bring herself to do so. After all, there was still Miss Blackwell.

Instead she said, "I wish that Mrs. Clary were here."

He nodded his head and forced a smile. "Yes indeed, and that Alice and Tussie were here to wave a great white sheet in farewell."

Kissing her once more, he rose and walked silently to the door, closing it gently behind him.

Lizzie was still sitting in the same position when Lady Thalia arrived two hours later.

"Are you ill, Lizzie?" she asked. "You look very pale and still."

Lizzie shook her head. "No, I am merely thinking of St. George and of steak and kidney pies—and of war."

Lady Thalia looked at her in genuine concern now. "I shall ring for a cup of tea, my dear. That will set you to rights."

Lizzie shook her head once more. "I do not think that can be done, Lady Thalia—not, at least, for a very long time."

That night when she went to bed, she set the music box beside her bed and listened again to its haunting melody. The world was shifting under her very feet, and she could not think of any place where she could go for refuge. As things stood at the moment, not even home seemed to offer what she needed. At home, there would be no Daniel Thoreau—and no Matthew.

And, after the war was over, there was no promise that Matthew would be one of those who was able to return home.

She listened to "Greensleeves" one more time, then closed the box firmly and tried to sleep. Her uneasy dreams shifted back and forth between the Christmas ball where Matthew had fallen in love with her, the garden where he had said good-bye, and the Carrousel with a paladin charging down upon a human figure rather than a wooden head—only this time it was Matthew rather than George Andronikos.

Twenty

By the end of May, Lady Thalia and Lizzie had arrived in Brussels. Lady Thalia would not allow them to leave until the doctor pronounced her charge unquestionably well enough to travel, and even then they went—as Lizzie had told Matthew they would—by very easy stages. Beavers and Henry accompanied them, of course, as did Lord Danvers. Once Mr. Thoreau was certain that Lord Danvers would be making the trip with them, he announced that he would go on ahead of them and make arrangements for their housing in Brussels.

"That is *more* than kind of you, Daniel," Lady Thalia informed him, for by then she too had come to use his Christian name.

"Are you going to Brussels to look after us or to be close to where all the activity is?" inquired Lizzie. Wellington was headquartered there, and Brussels was bustling with visitors and with the military.

He grinned at her. "Both, Lizzie. I could not possibly go home now—not until Boney is defeated once more."

"You seem very certain of that," she replied.

"One has only to read that Wellington is certain of it to have immediate confidence," he informed her, still grinning.

Lizzie looked more doubtful. "From the things Matthew

has told me about him, the world could be crumbling under his feet in the greatest earthquake of all time and he would calmly tell those about him that all would be well—it was only a tremor."

"Exactly," agreed Thoreau. "But the amazing thing about Wellington is that he keeps his word. Even though he is commanding this patchwork army of foreign troops and inexperienced British ones, I have every confidence that he will make it work."

When they finally arrived in Brussels and took up residence in the house that Thoreau had acquired for them, Lizzie felt that she had fallen into the midst of yet another social whirl. Although soldiers were everywhere to be seen, they were indeed *everywhere*. One saw them dancing, picnicking, going for long rides in the country, and generally enjoying themselves.

"*I* find it comforting," Lady Thalia announced when she mentioned it. "It makes me feel quite protected. And if worse *should* come to worst, we can take ship to England fairly quickly."

"Yes, we and a few thousand others with a similar desire to escape," said Lizzie dryly, conjuring a mental picture of what such a stampede would be like.

"You worry *far* too much, Lizzie," Lady Thalia informed her. "I had thought at first that you were *losing* some of that propensity while we were first in Vienna, but now I see that it is back again in full force."

"I believe it is called practicality," said Lizzie, but she softened her words with a smile. It was impossible ever to be truly cross with Lady Thalia.

"We are going to Lady Fulbright's ball tonight, my dear. Do you feel that you are up to attending? I shouldn't wish for you to exhaust yourself when you have not been accustomed to staying out late and dancing."

"I am looking forward to it," Lizzie assured her. "It will be very pleasant to see people dancing again, and I shall come home the instant that I feel tired."

The evening was, as she had hoped, a very pleasant one. Seeing the young girls in their summer gowns and the young officers in their finery made her feel nostalgic— quite as though she were fifty-nine rather than nineteen. She did not fill her dance card completely, leaving time to sit and rest. She was feeling worlds better than she had, but she had no intention of suffering a setback at this point.

Daniel Thoreau had joined her during one of these periods, and together they were enjoying the sight of a long-limbed member of the Foot Guard, looking rather like a particularly animated grasshopper, dancing with a very short, very round young lady. No words had passed between them. They merely watched and enjoyed— knowing that the other was thinking much the same thing.

"Well, how very cozy you two are!" exclaimed a voice sweet as syrup. "I have been hoping that I would en- counter you again, Mr. Thoreau."

Miss Blackwell was standing next to him, looking, Lizzie thought, quite ravishing in yet another of her di- aphanous gowns. She was suddenly aware that she herself was still quite thin.

"*Do* dance with me, Mr. Thoreau. You promised me in Paris that you would tell me about America—and possi- bly counsel me about my duties," she added coyly, giving him one of the sidelong glances that now irritated Lizzie almost more than anything she could ever have imag- ined. The omnipresent fan came into play, too, as she tapped Mr. Thoreau on the arm and leaned ever closer to him.

"I cannot imagine for a moment, Miss Blackwell, that your dance card is not full," he replied, smiling at her.

"Of course it is, Mr. Thoreau—but I would not let that stop me for a moment if you will but dance with me now." She held out her hand to him with an appealing little smile.

To Lizzie's dismay, he took her hand and stood up, turning back to grin at Lizzie. "I will return to you very soon, Miss Lancaster."

Miss Blackwell also looked at Lizzie—and smiled. Lizzie had not realized that so small a mouth could hold so many teeth.

She watched them dance for a while, then turned her attention to other couples, finding that the sight of Daniel dancing with Teresa Blackwell was most unpalatable. She glanced around the room to see if Matthew was also present, but she did not see him. Miss Blackwell was clearly on the loose. She discovered that she was suddenly exceedingly angry with Daniel Thoreau. She had thought him a sensible man, impervious to the obvious wiles of one such as Miss Blackwell. Watching him look down into her face and smile at her indicated otherwise, however.

Mr. Mansfield danced with Miss Blackwell next, and Thoreau rejoined Lizzie. "Well, I have come safely home, Lizzie," he announced cheerfully, "with only assorted small dents from the fan."

Heartened by his light dismissal of Miss Blackwell's tactics, Lizzie managed to smile at him. "I am glad to hear that you survived it, Daniel. I confess that I was surprised when you allowed her to coax you into dancing with her."

He shrugged. "It was not so very dreadful." He glanced over at her. "I see that *you* are not carrying a fan tonight, Lizzie."

"I have renounced them," she replied.

"A very good idea," he said, patting her hand. "Fans are not meant for everyone—and definitely not for you."

"I have no idea whether that is a compliment or an insult, Daniel."

"Ah, Lizzie—if you do not, I shall leave you to consider it carefully."

They were joined at that point by Lady Thalia and Lord Danvers, and the conversation became more general. Lizzie enjoyed the rest of the evening—until the very last moment when Miss Blackwell appeared once more, fan in hand.

"I shall look forward to our drive tomorrow, Mr. Thoreau," she said, smiling at him as though there was no one else present. "It was so gallant of you to offer to show me some of the sights of Brussels. Having arrived so recently, this is all quite new to me."

"I didn't know that you knew any of the sights of Brussels," said Lizzie grimly after Miss Blackwell had departed, trailing triumph in her wake.

"I shall find them," replied Mr. Thoreau blandly.

The next two weeks were a horror for Lizzie, for Daniel Thoreau was seen everywhere with Miss Blackwell. Matthew was away for most of that time, carrying messages for Lord Wellington, and he had no time to serve as her escort. Daniel Thoreau appeared to fit into that role very handily. Lady Thalia tried to calm Lizzie, but she was not to be comforted.

"It is quite hard enough that she snapped up Matthew,"

she exclaimed to her friend, who was listening sympathetically, "but I can almost understand that because he had the excuse of his youth and inexperience. He had never fallen into the hands of someone like Miss Blackwell. But for Daniel to do so! I had thought better of him."

Lady Thalia, who was equally mystified, did her best to comfort her. "A man, when all is said and done, Lizzie, is *only* a man," she said. "One simply cannot expect of a man what one can expect of a woman. No doubt Daniel cannot help himself and is suffering from an infatuation. It will pass."

"I hope that it does for his sake," Lizzie responded bitterly, "but it does not matter to me. I do not feel that we can ever be friends again in the same manner that we were."

Sighing, Lady Thalia did her best to keep their schedule busy so that Lizzie would have less time to fret over Daniel Thoreau. Whenever possible, she tried to avoid places where she might expect to see them, but that was difficult. They were seen everywhere together, and the gossip had begun. She could find it in her heart to pity Matthew, who was being served very poorly by his fiancée. She wondered if he already knew of the problem, or if one of his friends should tell him.

Lady Thalia was not forced to wonder for very long. Matthew, who had not come to call upon them since their arrival in Brussels, appeared at her door very early one morning. She was up and dressed only because she had expected to go riding with Lord Danvers, and she looked at him with astonishment when Henry showed him in.

"Matthew! Is there something wrong that you have called so early? Is there news about Bonaparte? Should we pack to leave?"

He smiled at her, looking happier she thought, than he had since he was a boy at home. "I am not here about Bonaparte, Lady Thalia. I am here to see Lizzie, if you please."

"Well, I daresay she *might* have awakened by now, but I'm not certain, Matthew. This is very early."

"Which chamber is hers?" he demanded.

"The first one at the top of the stairs," she replied. "Why do you ask?"

She was, however, speaking to an empty room. Matthew had sprung out the door and was at the top of the stairs before Lady Thalia could take in the fact that he was gone.

He stopped at the door, opened it a crack, and peeked in. Lizzie was sitting at her dressing table, brushing her hair. He walked silently over to her and bent so that he could look at her in the mirror.

Lizzie, having heard nothing, almost fell off the bench, and then she rapped his hand with her brush when he tried to catch her.

"Matthew! What do you think you're doing? You have no business to be here!"

"I know that, Lizzie. Come dance with me!" he exclaimed, opening the music box so that the melody would begin.

"Dance with you? Have you quite lost your mind?" she demanded.

"No! I have found it!" he answered, sweeping her up from the bench and into the dance. "I have loved you all my life, Lizzie Lancaster—though I didn't know it until I thought it was too late to ever be able to do anything about it."

"And what do you think you're going to do about it now?" she demanded, clutching her dressing gown as they danced.

"I am going to marry you and take you home," he replied, folding her into his arms and kissing her firmly.

By this time, Lady Thalia had made it to the top of the stairs, and she stood in the doorway watching with unabashed interest.

"But what about Miss Blackwell?" she asked, once she could speak again.

"She has cried off, Lizzie—and I am a free man once again—free to ask you to marry me. Tell me that you will!"

"But what of the war, Matthew? What of Bonaparte?"

"When that is over, Lizzie, we will go home—to stay. I have seen quite enough of the world. It will last me the rest of my days, so long as you are there with me."

It suddenly occurred to him that she had not yet answered him. He held her at arm's length and looked down at her gravely. "But I know that you have had a good many love affairs in this past year, Lizzie. Perhaps you have decided that one of them suits you better. I could not blame you if you had."

She looked at him for a very long moment, then walked back into his arms. "I have had only one love affair in my life, Matthew Webster. It has taken you long enough to come back to me."

Another interested spectator joined Lady Thalia in the doorway.

"Why, Daniel!" she exclaimed. "It is the most *delightful* thing imaginable! Lizzie and Matthew are to be *married*!

"Yes," he responded calmly, "I thought that they would be. I was rather hoping that they would marry soon, so that I am able to attend."

"Are you leaving, Daniel?" asked Lizzie, who had heard the last part of the conversation.

He nodded. "Very soon." He turned to Matthew. "I see that I am to wish you very happy—and I do, sir."

Matthew shook his hand vigorously. "And I must thank you again, Thoreau, for setting me free. I did not think it would ever happen."

Thoreau bowed. "It was my pleasure. Having realized by now, however, that I am not going to propose marriage— hence my unseemly haste to leave Brussels—I believe that Miss Blackwell has fixed her sights upon the hapless Mansfield. I believe the odds are against him."

Lizzie looked from one to the other. "Do you mean that you managed this between you?" she demanded.

Thoreau grinned and nodded. "It was obvious that you were both going to pine away, and that someone had to take a hand. I have always enjoyed a calculated risk."

Lizzie smiled and kissed his cheek. "You are a most amazing man, Daniel Thoreau! If I were not marrying Matthew, I would most certainly marry you!"

"I am overcome," he replied, bowing low. "Come with me, Lady Thalia," he said, turning to that lady. "We have wedding arrangements to make."

Lizzie looked up at Matthew as he pulled her close to him once more. "I am glad to be home again," she said quietly—and knew that it was true.

Epilogue

Lizzie and Matthew were married on the eve of the Battle of Waterloo, with only their closest friends at hand. Before the evening was over, news of Napoleon's approach sent the troops scrambling to their positions. During the days of the battle, those left behind waited for news, taking to the streets to give water and food and aid to soldiers who made their way back into Brussels.

The news finally came of the victory of the Allies, but Matthew had not returned. Uncertain where he might find him, for Matthew had ridden with messages from Wellington to his commanders across all the battle lines, Daniel Thoreau acquired a carriage and set out to look. Lizzie waited nervously, hoping for the best, and finally he pulled up in front of Lady Thalia's house, dust-covered and weary—but triumphant. In the carriage he had not one but two wounded men—Matthew and George Andronikos.

With the help of Lord Danvers, they got both of them inside and into beds with clean linen sheets. Carefully, the blood and grime and gunpowder were cleaned away, as they waited for a doctor to come.

"Thank you, Daniel," she said, gripping his hand tightly. "If you had not found him, he might have died before someone could help him."

"But he has not, Lizzie," he said. "He and George will be well and whole again in only a few weeks." He paused a moment, trying to decide whether or not to tell her, but he decided that the truth was best.

"I saw your captain, too, Lizzie."

"Captain LaSalle? Was he injured, too?"

He nodded. "I'm afraid that there was nothing that could be done for him, however. He was all but gone when I saw him."

Tears slipped down her cheeks. "But how dreadful, Daniel! How terrible a thing war is!"

"He recognized me when I bent over him—and he asked about you, Lizzie—the lovely Mademoiselle Lancaster."

The tears would not stop now, and it was long before they would. By morning, however, when Matthew was awake, she had done with them and managed to show him a smiling face.

"It is over, Matthew," she said, bending over him to kiss him and smooth his hair. "And we are going home."

"You said it best, Lizzie," he replied smiling up at her and putting his good arm around her. "We are already home. We are together."

ABOUT THE AUTHOR

Mona Gedney lives with her family in Indiana and is the author of thirteen Zebra Regency romances and is working on her next, to be published in August 2004. Mona loves to hear from readers and you may write to her c/o Zebra Books. Please include a self-addressed stamped envelope if you wish a response.

More Regency Romance
From Zebra

BOOK YOUR PLACE ON OUR WEBSITE AND MAKE THE READING CONNECTION!

We've created a customized website just for our very special readers, where you can get the inside scoop on everything that's going on with Zebra, Pinnacle and Kensington books.

When you come online, you'll have the exciting opportunity to:

• View covers of upcoming books

• Read sample chapters

• Learn about our future publishing schedule (listed by publication month *and author*)

• Find out when your favorite authors will be visiting a city near you

• Search for and order backlist books from our online catalog

• Check out author bios and background information

• Send e-mail to your favorite authors

• Meet the Kensington staff online

• Join us in weekly chats with authors, readers and other guests

• Get writing guidelines

• AND MUCH MORE!

Visit our website at
http://www.kensingtonbooks.com